"That young limb of Satan with her wild French blood"

MY LADY DESTINY

Lord Claude Destermere is dying, his daughter and only heir banished from birth to an urchin's life in England. The Lord's loyal secretary, Stephen Godwin, rescues the fifteen-year-old from her dreary existence and watches the new Lady Destiny become the toast of the English aristocracy. But the brilliant and fiery Destiny will need all her spirit to conquer the evil forces around her.

MY LADY DESTINY

Denise Robins

 AVON
PUBLISHERS OF BARD, CAMELOT AND DISCUS BOOKS

AVON BOOKS
A division of
The Hearst Corporation
959 Eighth Avenue
New York, New York 10019

First Avon Printing, September, 1978

AVON TRADEMARK REG. U.S. PAT. OFF. AND IN
OTHER COUNTRIES, MARCA REGISTRADA, HECHO EN
U.S.A.

Printed in the U.S.A.

MY LADY
DESTINY

PART ONE

1

Lord Destermere lay dying.

His wife Mahla, her brother Humbert, and a white-caped nun sat on either side of the big canopied bed, watching and waiting for the end.

It was in the year 1708 on the second day of February.

Dawn was breaking. Birds in the thickly-wooded grounds of the *Château des Cygnes*—one of the loveliest buildings on Lac Leman—had begun to wake. The plaintive intermittent piping was the only sound to break the intense silence. Lord Destermere hardly breathed. Now and again the nun leaned over him and put a mirror against his lips to see if it became moist.

Each time the religious woman made this gesture Lady Destermere put a hand to her throat and clutched the thick rope of jet beads which were wound around her long throat. Her eyes dilated. She drew closer to her brother. His handsome, florid face wore a faint derisive smile. Then as the nun drew back, whispering that "milord still drew breath," her ladyship relaxed. Her gaze met that of her brother with what could only be termed a slightly sinister look. Certainly it brooked neither pleasure nor relief.

A thin elderly man clad in black and wearing a bob-wig and Steinkirk which showed white around his lean neck was standing by one of the tall windows which opened out onto a veranda. He had been there for some time, his hands behind his back. Now he drew aside the heavy velvet curtains. At once the melancholy flickering candles burning in tall candelabra on the mantelpiece paled before the sudden light of morning as it filled the lofty chamber.

In the pearl-grey light of morning everything seemed to assume a different aspect. The features of the dying man in his white frilled bedgown became sharper. The magnificent red hair which Lady Destermere wore tied back with a girlish bow—black like her beads—seemed to coil and glow with the voluptuous colour and movement of serpents. The square face of the massive Baron Faramund, her brother, appeared dissipated and brooding. He wore a purple robe which gave him something of a look of a dissolute emperor; he had those heavily-lidded eyes and curled lips. His scant fair curls and the very blueness of his eyes were, however, essentially Germanic. He had been born and bred in Hanover.

Only the face of the nun remained serene and pure, unaffrighted, unchanged by the searching light of the day. Her lips moved in prayer. A rosary slipped through her ivory fingers.

Lady Destermere watched this rosary as though fascinated for a while, then rose and yawned, stretching her arms above her head. The Baron looked at his sister through half-shut eyes. He was quite attached to her. They had had the same father, and in general the same interests. They were both greedy for money and for power. Mahla was in her late twenties—he, nearing thirty-five. She was ageing, he thought this morning, with a cruelty that was part of his character. Nevertheless he admitted she still had strong sensual appeal and an almost unspoiled beauty, (if anything so fiercely feline could be so called by that name). She had been wasted, he thought, on Claud Destermere. After ten years of marriage, Claud had given her nothing but his name and the choice between this dreary *Château* in Switzerland which bored her to tears, or life in England at Destermere House in Richmondwyke, which was the family seat. That she found gloomy. For a time they lived in Paris. But Destermere's health had been poor for a long time now and his medical advisers had sent him here to Geneva to breathe the pure air which blew down from the mountain peaks.

The old fool had been dying on his feet almost since the day he married Mahla, Humbert reflected, with a savage discontent which he knew his sister shared. It would be intolerable if Claud did not succumb this very dawn to the ravages of the wasting disease which had been consuming him. They had waited long enough.

Once he was gone, Mahla would have control of the Destermere fortune. That was what she had bargained for when she first left Hanover to marry the Earl.

The soberly-attired gentleman who had just drawn the curtains was his lordship's Swiss notary, Monsieur Bertian. He had come from Geneva with a document which his lordship had signed last night. Milord had made a great effort to hold the quill, supported on one side by his secretary, Stephen Godwin, and on the other by Monsieur Bertian.

The contents of that document were as yet unknown to anyone in the *Château* save Mr. Godwin and the Swiss.

Baron Faramund gazed thoughtfully at his sister. He was amused by her appearance. She wore a white velvet mantua edged with black fur. With those jet beads, she already presented a spectacle of mourning. Quite charming and sad. What an actress she was, he thought. At will she could bring tears to glisten upon those fabulous lashes of hers.

Humbert was wholly German. But she, his half-sister, had been born of a mother who was an English Jewess. The little Mahalah, whose Hebrew name had been shortened to *Mahla* as she grew older, had learned to speak the English tongue at an early age. After ten years as Lady Destermere, she retained only the slightest trace of German accent, which most men found fascinating. Destermere had found it very fascinating indeed when he first met her at the *schloss* owned by her uncle, a certain German landowner of repute in whose mountain retreat some of the finest wild boar hunting was to be found. When Lord Destermere was in his twenties and still vital, he had been a remarkably fine sportsman. At the ball which followed a big day's hunting, Destermere met and fell violently in love with his host's captivating niece. He decided once again to risk a marriage.

Destermere was a charming but rather weak man who in middle age believed in virtue and deplored his own youthful departure from it. As he grew older he became religious and continually repented the sins of the past. He was a man of curiously naïve, trusting character. Until evil was spread before him, undisguised, he seldom recognized it. The red-headed Mahla, with her strong sensual appeal, easily blinded him to the fact that she was as corrupt as she was beautiful. It had made Humbert laugh to see the virginal crown of lilies set upon his half-sister's brow on the day of her bridal. He knew that she had lost her virginity before she was fourteen years of age. (Her singing-master had seduced her.)

The Faramund family were at that time involved in wars, heavy taxation and a variety of financial losses which had made it essential that the young Baroness should marry a wealthy man. Hence her acceptance of Claud Destermere. He bored her and she had never been faithful to him. Humbert knew that, also.

But she seemed to have maintained her sway over this kindly simple husband of hers. He could not bear her out of his sight. She had powers of persuasion and an aptitude for lies and intrigue which at times startled even her depraved brother.

The Baron, personally, had never been popular with Claud Destermere. He was received here only out of deference to Mahla, who was much attached to her brother. But now the end of Destermere and his disapproval is in sight, reflected the Baron. *The tomb* for him. The great riches of the House of Destermere for Mahla. Her unopposed authority over those full coffers.

Humbert waited impatiently for his brother-in-law to draw his last breath.

The notary pulled the curtains still further apart. Now all of them in the bedchamber turned to the majestic sight that met the gaze. A matutinal mist shrouded the peaks of the mountains facing them— heights still clad in winter's white. Snow had fallen over the grounds last night. As though in sympathy, Nature had spread her own shroud for the English nobleman whose end was approaching. But to the east in the sky there appeared suddenly a chink of miraculous blue which was reflected in the deep waters of the lake. Geneva was calm at this early hour. The city was barely stirring. It was only in the *Château des Cygnes* that there was movement. Lights burned in all the upper windows.

Earl Destermere opened his eyes. They had become almost colourless as is the case with the dying. His body was wasted to a skeletal thinness. They had not bothered to shave him. A stubble of gold beard showed on his chin. He had the look of a suffering Christ. Indeed, he called voicelessly on that sacred Name, beseeching pardon for his sins. His mind travelled back a long way to one particular episode in his past which now seemed to him of paramount importance. He had done a great wrong. He wanted to live until he had put it right. He muttered a name.

"Stephen. . . ."

At once the nun took his wrist and pressed her finger against the pulse. She was of German-Swiss extraction. She whispered in German to her ladyship.

"It is a miracle . . . milord is a little stronger. . . ."

Mahla's lashes drooped to hide the impatience and

11

disappointment in eyes that were as purple and flagrant as bright pansies. She bent over her husband.

"Is it not I whom you wish to call upon, my dearest?" she murmured, and pressed a lace-edged handkerchief against her lips.

The dying man looked at her. Even now that he was finished with the lusts of the flesh, the peace of his passing was disturbed by the sight of his young wife's flame-red hair, and the thick creamy skin of her matchless bosom.

"Mahla," he whispered.

She bent and kissed his emaciated hands.

"What can I do for you, beloved?"

He drew a deep sigh which seemed to come from the very depths of his heart. Her luxuriant hair was so close that he could inhale its musky fragrance. How madly he had loved this girl! He had always wondered why she should have devoted her youth and burning beauty to him, who at forty had become old and tired. He had wondered, also, why none of his family in England— distant relatives, who used to visit the Destermere House (for Claud was the head of the family)—had liked her. One of his aunts had hinted that he was a fool to trust the German Jewess. In consequence he had closed the door of the house to this particular lady. She was now dead. All his kinsmen were dead. Before his illness had brought him to bed he used to go to England. But of late he and the Countess had resided entirely in Geneva.

The Earl nursed another secret sorrow on account of the fact that Stephen Godwin, who was his protégé as well as his secretary, never really made friends with the Countess.

Nobody could ever complain of Stephen's manners towards Mahla. They were impeccable. He was courteous but cold. Once, Destermere had taxed him with this coldness and asked why he did not show more warmth and admiration for Lady Destermere. In the old days when they used to entertain lavishly, she used to be surrounded by fervent admirers. But Stephen avoided her.

When Destermere touched on this subject, the young man appeared so embarrassed that Destermere tried to ignore it and believe that the boy meant no offence to her ladyship. He was reticent by nature—with an austerity which even the fascinating Countess could not break down.

Destermere, personally, loved Stephen. The boy had been almost as dear as a son to him during the last six years; since he had first come to live with the Earl he had proved himself both efficient and loyal.

"Now that I am dying, I have no qualms about placing my business affairs in Stephen's hands," reflected the dying man.

But the ghost of that old sin committed in his youth haunted the death-chamber this dawn. It seemed to lay an icy hand on Destermere's failing heart.

"What can I do for you, beloved?" repeated Lady Destermere.

"I want to speak . . . to Stephen . . . and to Monsieur Bertian . . . alone. . . ," he gasped.

Mahla flicked her lashes at her brother, shrugged and moved with him out of the room.

"What has he in mind that he should be so secretive and banish you?" growled the Baron.

She shrugged again.

"Nothing. He hesitates to bore me with business matters. He has always been so—treating me like a child who must be protected from worries and troubles." Mahla whispered back, and her lips curved into an ironic smile.

That smile faded when in the lofty, marble-floored corridor she met the familiar figure of the English secretary hurrying towards his master's room. They came face to face. Lady Destermere barred Stephen's way. He was a tall youth but not much taller than her

13

ladyship, who was of exceptional height for a woman. She looked at him with those lustrous pansy-purple eyes which held more than an ordinary invitation. The Baron moved on, shrugging his shoulders, knowing well the passion which his sister had lately developed for her husband's secretary. Mahla had ever been one to desire the unattainable. She would not rest, thought Humbert, until she had made Stephen Godwin her slave. (Wasting her time, in Humbert's opinion.)

After tomorrow, once she held the reins of office, she could undoubtedly fling Stephen Godwin out. She would have no further use for him, and Humbert himself would see that the Englishman departed at speed. He thoroughly disliked him. The boy on occasions had shown a contempt for him which had fired the Baron's blood. There had been an incident only a week ago when Stephen had surprised the Baron in the library whilst attempting to molest a young, struggling Swiss maid. A fragile child whose big eyes had momentarily attracted the sensual German. Stephen demanded that he should release the girl instantly. After she had rushed away, trembling and in tears, blessing Monsieur Godwin for her deliverance, the Baron had stormed at him. What right had he to interfere?

Stephen replied:

"The right of any decent gentleman, Baron, to protect the virginity of a mere child. Little Marie-Thérèse is scarce thirteen and must be allowed to perform her duties in this house without fear of your unwelcome attentions."

At that, Humbert cooled and laughed in a sneering way. Looking Stephen up and down, he said:

"How come you know so much about Marie-Thérèse's virginity? Could it be that you have already tested it, Mr. Godwin?"

Stephen had turned white, made as though to answer, then swung round and walked out of the room.

The following day the Baron had tried to find Marie-

Thérèse and was told that the child had been sent home. An older coarser woman had been engaged in her place. He realized that he had the secretary to thank for this and cursed him for a pie-faced Puritan. But on telling his story to Mahla, Humbert was advised to say no more. Mahla did not want there to be trouble while Claud lived. *She* would deal with Stephen, she told the Baron, when the time was ripe. So the Baron took himself off on horseback to a nearby village to find a pretty peasant girl to take the place of Marie-Thérèse.

Now, outside the Earl's bedchamber, Lady Destermere tried to wheedle Stephen.

"You look fatigued. You were up all night with my lord, were you not?"

"I was, but I am not tired. I am only too happy to serve his lordship while I can," said Stephen quietly.

And he looked away from Lady Destermere scowling. Those huge lascivious eyes of hers made him uncomfortable. He had never been able to understand how a man like Destermere could be so blind to his wife's true nature.

Stephen found the red-haired, handsome Countess utterly unworthy of her gentle husband's kindness, and all the gifts that he lavished on her. Stephen knew too much about her lack of morals, and the atrocious way in which she managed to deceive her husband. There was a vein of stupidity in Destermere which young Stephen was forced to acknowledge. But the Earl was lovable and generous and Stephen respected him greatly and regarded him as a friend and benefactor. It had horrified him when Lady Destermere first began to display her passion for him. Some men in his position might have been flattered, but to Stephen, Lady Destermere's interest in him was an abominable thing. Until a month ago the knowledge that this was the woman who would inherit all that the Earl had to leave, that the great noble house of Destermere would pass into her hands, worried the boy exceedingly.

There was no one of the blood left to succeed the Earl. His only nephew, would would have inherited the estate, had died in a hunting accident two years ago.

Stephen had confided his fears in the Swiss notary when Bertian came upon the scene. Bertian, elderly and astute, had talked some sense into the Earl and finally persuaded him to sign a new final testament which would not give his widow so much power nor allow the estates to fall into her profligate brother's hands.

Then a month ago, Destermere had confided the story of his youth both in Bertian and Stephen. Since then Stephen had been to Paris on an exciting secret mission—and made various inquiries on behalf of the dying Earl.

Once armed with the fruits of this inquiry, Stephen was much relieved and could look with more confidence to the future.

He could look at the Countess this morning with less apprehension, too, knowing that a disagreeable shock awaited her and her brother.

"If your ladyship would kindly allow me to pass," he murmured coldly but politely.

Mahla glanced around the corridor. It was in semi-darkness. The Baron had disappeared into his own bedchamber. She sighed and lifted her arms to the secretary's shoulders. He shrank back but for a moment she pressed her sinuous body against his and looked with undisguised longing at his pale boyish face. The finely-cut lips . . . the wide eyes, grey and brilliant . . . the proud short nose . . . attracted her vastly. Stephen Godwin was not of aristocratic lineage but he looked noble, she thought, and Claud had told her that he was of decent birth. He did not wear a wig this morning. His own hair, dark brown, was tied back with a black bow. His coat and breeches were of clerical grey, relieved by the white of his Steinkirk.

His persistent coldness maddened the woman. There was something almost monkish about Stephen. He was

16

clever and, in her opinion, much too studious. He seemed never to be interested in recreation of a frivolous kind. Claud, himself, had told Mahla that the young secretary had never yet been in love.

To be twenty-four and not to have had a woman in his life seemed incredible to Mahla. In her home in Hanover, the young gentlemen of the house slept with the maids, if with none other; and diced and danced and enjoyed every form of vicious amusement.

She was all the more determined to be the first with Stephen. It would amuse her. Often she lay awake at night thinking of him—longing to bring a different expression into those light grey eyes which she found as icy as the waters of the lake. There was passion in him—she was sure of it. She knew men. This one had a warmth, a depth, still to be plumbed. He smiled rarely, but when that smile broke through it had an odd charm and radiance. And that he could feel deeply, she was aware, because of his whole-hearted devotion to his master.

"Stephen, my love," she whispered, and brushed a red coil of her perfumed hair across his lips. "When you have finished with your boring affairs, pray come to my room. My maid has orders to receive you. Knock twice. I shall be waiting."

Stephen recoiled. All his Puritan blood rose and flamed against this wanton witch of a woman.

"How can you speak so when your husband lies dying, milady?" he said indignantly.

She stepped back, fingering her jet beads, laughing up at him.

"You are foolish, Stephen. You miss much. You should really enter a monastery and be done with the world."

"I am not a Roman and I have no wish to become a monk," he said. "But when I finally choose to lie with a woman it shall be with my wedded wife."

Then he passed on and into the Earl's chamber,

17

leaving the Countess standing there, angry, but not too despairing. She knew Stephen, she thought. He was a man, and if he was no monk, she was positive that she would win in the end.

2

STEPHEN GODWIN STOOD beside the big bed gazing in grief upon his benefactor.

The colourless eyes opened and returned Stephen's gaze with recognition. The bloodless lips whispered:

"My boy. . . ."

That was enough to make Stephen's heart swell. He had been born with a sense of pride and individualism which had never found expression until he came in contact with Earl Destermere. In this bitter hour of impending loss, he remembered his first meeting with his benefactor, seven years ago when he was still in his teens, completing his studies at St. Paul's School. It was a school patronized by the noble Earl from Richmond-wyke.

At that time, young Stephen had just been orphaned and impoverished after the sweating sickness wiped out his entire family. His father had been a schoolmaster, his mother of gentle birth, and once he had had three adorable sisters and a happy carefree home. Then everything seemed to come to a full stop in his life.

He had been about to say good-bye to St. Paul's and take a tiresome job in the City as a clerk when Destermere came across him. Stephen had heard what he had said to the headmaster.

"I am impressed by the reports of this boy's talented work and read with pleasure one or two of his essays.

He has a frank countenance and a curiously noble air. It would be a tragedy to hide such a light behind the bushel of poverty."

Destermere, then paid himself for the completion of Stephen's studies, and after a year took him into his house to work in a secretarial capacity. He also encouraged him to begin writing a book of essays on the Marlborough campaign in which the boy was interested. From that time onward Stephen found Destermere a lenient employer and he learned to forget the loss of his own adored family in the service of a man whose weakness he accepted and whose generosity and kindliness he revered.

Stephen guessed now what the Earl wished to say to him. He must help the noble man who was gasping for strength to do what should be done before he died.

"Stephen ... go to England ... find ... *my daughter*. . . ."

"I will find her, sir," said Stephen in a low earnest voice. "I have today received a letter from Bath which will lead me to her."

"Take her ... to Destermere House ... I wish her to live there. . . ." whispered the Earl.

"Monsieur Bertian and I will do all that you have asked," said Stephen gently pressing his master's hand. "Be at peace, my lord. . . ."

"Bertian ... can hand things over to ... my notary in London, Godfrey Finch. You know his whereabouts. He served my father before me and is old but reliable. Approach also my friends and bankers—Sir Edgar Landseer, and Mr. George Featherly. The addresses are in my deed box. You have the keys, Stephen."

"It shall be done, my lord," said Stephen.

Now suddenly the Earl muttered:

"Wine. . . ."

The nun came forward and lifted a goblet to the Earl's lips. Afterwards, he signed a new document placed before him by M. Bertian. He seemed to gain strength and for a moment talked more easily although great gasps of breath between the words shook his wasted frame.

He recalled the past and his misspent youth. And of the time sixteen years later when he had felt a longing to beget an heir. His first wife had died in child-birth. He had been unlucky. And he had hoped when he brought Mahalah, the seductive and handsome young German girl to his bed, that she would give him that longed-for child, but it had never come, and in his generosity he had not blamed her.

He began to mumble many names and places and episodes which Stephen and the Swiss notary were able to piece together only because of what they had recently learned. To Stephen with his touch of austerity and his idealism, the story of the Earl's early love affair and the fruits of it was a sorry one. But when he considered it he said to himself, simply:

"Who knows what a man will do in the turbulence of his hot youth? Who am I to judge?"

But Destermere judged himself without mercy.

It had all happened as far back as seventeen years ago before Queen Anne came to the throne when the former Earl of Destermere and Claud's mother—at that time one of the most famous hostesses in London—had been alive. Claud, then at the age of twenty-two, had the cream of society at his feet, for he was a handsome, winning youth—a fine swordsman and rider to hounds and one who never lacked for amorous adventure. Women fell for him like ninepins.

His parents were urging him to take a wife, and they had settled upon Lady Grizel Colhoun, the daughter of a distinguished minister in the Court of William and Mary. The perfect wife for young Claud.

The gay youth—at that time bearing the family name of Lord Claud Frane—wished to please his parents but dreaded losing his freedom. He travelled with his mother and sisters to Bath where Lady Destermere who was not well, had been advised to drink the waters. Bored with life there after London, young Lord Frane entered into what he had intended should be only an amorous adventure, with the daughter of a tavern-keeper on the outskirts of the town. By name, Amabel. She was of exceptional beauty, and at the time little more than fifteen. She had a freshness and virginal charm which enraptured Claud. It was not so easy in those days to meet with the flower of innocence, and Amabel, though of lowly birth, had been strictly brought up.

Claud entered into a clandestine affair which threatened to become serious, and actually installed the young girl in a shooting lodge on the fringe of the forest where he and his young friends hunted stag.

He fell passionately in love with Amabel who was as graceful as the fawns in the forest, and had the same liquid golden eyes full of trust and sweetness.

She, on her part, worshipped the tall laughing handsome young nobleman and gave herself to him willingly. At first her father was infuriated and demanded that Claud should make amends. There might have been trouble for Claud except that Amabel's father was at the time floundering in monetary difficulties and had a weakness of character and an avarice which allowed him to barter his child's honour for gold. Claud paid him off and saw to it that their tavern flourished in future. After that there was no further trouble. The mother only made one or two attempts to see her daughter, then the poor woman died of an internal complaint and from then onward Amabel's father took to heavy drinking and evinced little interest in Amabel's fate.

It was, of course, Amabel who paid the price for that autumn interlude in her life. She lived there, in the little lodge, beautifully gowned to please her lover, and obsessed with her passion for him; happy to be kept in seclusion away from the rest of the world; waiting only for him to return from the chase to her arms.

For Claud it was an exquisite experience. He had never before known the passionate love of a really good woman, and there was nothing of the hard courtesan about Amabel. He realized later that it was he who was guilty and wholly responsible for this child who had sinned by delivering herself up to him.

Then came the time for the Destermeres to return to Richmondwyke. By now, Amabel was heavy with child. The dying Earl allowed himself today to remember and speak of these things with deepest shame. How patient Amabel had been, how trusting still, even while her young beautiful figure thickened and she feared for the future of the infant because she wore no ring upon her finger.

Suddenly Claud had decided that he would marry Amabel and legitimize his child. He found a priest and went through a ceremony of marriage with the girl. He confessed everything to his parents. His mother wept and implored him to pay Amabel off, as he had paid her father. The old Earl stormed. Never should a Destermere marry a common innkeeper's daughter. The child that was born should never inherit Destermere. He must annul this marriage.

For a grim never-to-be-forgotten week, the storm raged between young Lord Frane and his parents and Amabel did not see her husband. She wept in bitter loneliness believing herself already abandoned.

Gradually the old Earl who was a tempestuous gentleman of iron-will and unshakable principles, wore his young son down. Claud began to believe that he could not keep Amabel as his lawful wife and must wriggle out of it and announce his betrothal to the Lady Grizel Colhoun whom they wished him to marry.

While he was floundering, sweating, wishing on one hand to placate his parents, reluctant on the other to commit what was virtually a crime against an innocent girl and her unborn child, fate stepped in on the side of the old Earl.

Claud was stricken down without warning by a fever which left him delirious and too weak to move for many days. Like this he was delivered wholly into the hands of his mother who saw to it that he had no communication with his lowly-born wife. Afterwards, when he was well again, Claud was told that Amabel had departed and that he would never see her again. He rushed madly to the lodge only to find it deserted and shuttered. No one, not even his dearest friend, could tell him what had happened to her. Her own father did not know. But the old Earl intimated that he, personally, had seen to it that the young girl was removed to the care of a family in Paris. He had taken good care to spirit the unfortunate mother-to-be as far away from her husband as possible.

At first Claud had raged and wept and demanded the address in order that he might follow Amabel. Then the Earl produced a letter informing him that the girl had died in child-birth.

"And the infant?" Claud had asked, his head bowed in deepest shame and in an agony of sincere grief for his beautiful Amabel whom he had, he reflected, virtually murdered.

"Has been adopted. Mr. Finch has seen to that. . . . You will never find it."

When Claud approached him asking for the address in Paris so that he could see the child, he was refused it. Neither did he know whether it had been male or female. After a while Claud gave up all efforts to trace this infant.

So ended the shameful episode. In later years he felt that heaven had punished him, for his wife, Lady Grizel who was married to him with great pomp and ceremony, herself died in child-birth and their heir with her.

Claud shrank from marrying again, believing that a doom hung over him.

Years dimmed the memory of the golden-eyed Amabel but there were times when Claud Destermere woke to the memory of his unknown child—who still existed perhaps somewhere in Paris. Then, as though to shut out the memory he made his third marriage.

And not long after that the wasting disease had attacked Claud and he had also known that he would never father an heir.

A few weeks ago he had made up his mind to try and trace the fruit of his youthful sin—his child who must now, he reckoned, be at least sixteen.

"Find him or her," he bade Stephen, "be it son or daughter, in whatever circumstances it is found, let it be groomed and educated to take its rightful place. If it be a boy, you, Stephen, can well constitute yourself his tutor. If a girl, my wife will, I am sure, care for her and be tolerant of my sin."

When Stephen suggested that Destermere should tell his wife the truth at once, he had said:

"Not yet. Wait until you have made the necessary enquiries. The child may be dead—if so, useless to distress Mahla unnecessarily."

So Stephen, armed with only a few facts, set forth on his delicate mission. He had with him but one really important paper. A letter which the old Earl had failed to destroy and which Claud had found among his papers many years ago. It was from a certain Madame Rochet in Paris, acknowledging a certain payment of money. And although no mention was made of the nature of this gift, Claud was sure that it had something to do with Amabel.

It took Stephen several days to find Henriette Rochet whose husband owned a bakery not far from the Madeleine. At first she was inclined to be uncooperative, then the sight of a gold piece loosened her tongue. It was all a long time ago and she was now an old woman but she remembered very well, she said, the day when a young veiled lady in an advanced state of pregnancy was brought to lodge with her. During the winter of 1692—a hard winter in Paris. She also remembered only too well the birth of a child.

"A son?" Stephen had asked eagerly.

But to his disappointment, Madame Rochet shook her head.

"A daughter, and the English lady ... *pauvre enfant* ... expired. Of a broken heart as much as of an infection," the old French woman sighed.

Stephen had felt then a taste of that same shame that had stirred his master's blood from time to time. It was unbearable to think of Amabel's final agony.

"Well, where is this daughter to be found?" asked Stephen.

Ah! Mme Rochet was less inclined to say until another gold piece fired her imagination. Stephen, ferreting out the truth, could see that Madame had gone on receiving money from an unknown titled gentleman for some time, but had not spent it very honestly on the little girl for whom it was intended. Fearing that unpleasant facts were about to be disclosed, Madame whined that times had been bad; the bakery went *phut* and the little Destiny as well as all the other children, had been one too many to feed and clothe.

"Destiny!" Stephen repeated.

The Frenchwoman explained. As Amabel lay dying, Madame had bent over her, held the infant out and asked what name she wished for its baptism. The poor girl, only half comprehending, had whispered:

"Farewell. *This is my destiny.*"

"So, Monsieur," said Madame, "we christened the child *Destiny*. It is the English name for Fate, is it not?"

"Yes," Stephen replied, frowning. "It is the English name for Fate."

He had shivered in the Rochets' unattractive and somewhat musty-smelling bakery. It seemed to him a terrible fate, indeed, that here in this sordid place, the child whose rightful name was Lady Destiny Frane, had first drawn breath. She, the daughter and sole heiress to the Destermere fortune and estates.

Stephen learned now that when the little girl was four, she had attracted the attention of an English clergyman and his wife who had recently lost their own small daughter of the same age, and were on holiday in Paris. They had seen Destiny standing on the street corner outside the bakery and talked to her. They were at once in love with her and anxious to adopt the child.

"She was a great beauty like her mother. A devil, too, whom one could scold and never control. *Zut alors!* I was glad to be rid of her!" grumbled Madame Rochet.

Without protest she had willingly handed the child over to the English couple.

Stephen armed with this knowledge returned to Geneva. The Earl, much excited, sent a letter by special courier to this clergyman—the Reverend William Paull, who resided in Bristol. It was lucky that the Rochets had kept the reverend gentleman's address, meaning, of course, to tap him for money from time to time, although Madame Rochet had admitted that she had not heard one word from Mr. Paull for over ten years now.

Then came an answer from Bristol. Claud's daughter was not at the vicarage nor had she been with the Paulls since she was five years old. In a long letter of apology and explanation, the parson who had originally adopted the little Destiny, explained that his wife who was a sickly woman, had never been able to manage the child. She had proved difficult and excitable and not what they had hoped for. So once more the unfortunate Destiny had been passed on into the hands of a brother curate with a small living in Bath. A certain Sextus Barley. It had all worked out very strangely. For this man after hearing the story of the adoption of the little child who could speak more French than English, and who was so wild and unmanageable, discovered that she was the granddaughter of a blood relation of his own wife, Alice. A second cousin in fact of the tavern-keeper in Bath who had fathered Amabel. A strange involved history. But thus Amabel's child had passed into the care of her own relatives on the maternal side. It was the Barleys who had brought Destiny up with their own children. The Reverend Paull sent Stephen the address.

This was the final news that Stephen imparted this morning to his master.

"The Lady Destiny is living under the name of Destiny Barley at an address in Kestering, which is the adjoining village to Bath," he said.

This news seemed to impart a new strength to the Earl, for his breathing became more normal and he astonished the nursing sister by his sudden ability to speak and take part in the affairs of the world he was about to leave. She had sent for his physicians, but wondered if indeed the death would take place as imminently as they anticipated.

"My daughter," the dying man uttered the words as though they were sacred, "Lady Destiny Frane. Oh, Stephen, Stephen, it is destiny indeed. Go get her ... bring her here ... and pray that I may live to look upon her face at least once before I die."

Now Monsieur Bertian who had been listening to the exchange of words between the dying man and his secretary, leaned over the bed.

"I beg you my lord, to impart this news without further delay to the Countess. It will come as a shock and she should now be told."

"Yes, now that I know that it is all *fait accompli* and that I have a daughter to inherit my estates, I will confess all to my wife," nodded Claud.

Bertian and Stephen exchanged glances. Bertian handed Stephen the document which to his relief, the Earl had just signed and which they had witnessed. This gave his widow the right to enjoy his estates and houses, and certain monies to be paid to her regularly from the estates, while she lived. But the estate in its entirety would be finally inherited by the Lady Destiny Frane, and any such heirs as she might produce from her own marriage.

M. Bertian said:

"Until she does marry I would suggest, my lord, that you leave your legal advisors as joint guardians with her ladyship. Afterwards, your daughter's husband will of course have the right to control and advise her."

"And Stephen must also be in authority," nodded the Earl, as the nun moistened his cracked lips. "I wish also to appoint him as joint guardian with my wife. I have great faith in him. But my beautiful Mahla knows nothing of dry legal matters."

Stephen blushed, violently.

"No, sir, I beg of you—" he began to protest, unwilling to accept the responsibility.

But Claud Destermere shook his head and smiled. The old charming smile that had once beguiled so many.

"Nay—you are like my son. Destiny shall become your sister and you shall keep a watchful eye on her."

Stephen bowed his head. Perhaps, he thought, the Earl's strong hatred of his brother-in-law, the Baron, was behind his desire to include an outsider in the guardianship. But whatever it was, Stephen knew that if he was to take any real interest in Destermere's daughter, he must be glad that the wicked Lady Destermere would not have sole authority. There was nothing further Stephen could do to protect the future Lady Frane. He could hardly tell the dying man openly that his wife was corrupt and utterly untrustworthy.

"Go to Bath . . ." said Destermere. "Go quickly, Stephen, and let me look upon my child."

But even now Stephen hesitated.

"Forgive me, sir . . . my very dear lord . . . but would it not be prudent for you to summon her ladyship now and tell her of this project, before I depart."

"Agreed," seconded Bertian heartily.

So the nursing sister was sent to fetch her ladyship.

Mahla came into the bedchamber, having changed her white gown for a black velvet robe in which she looked more than ever beautiful—and strangely evil, Stephen thought with disgust, as he met her meaning glance. He watched her throw herself on her knees beside the bed, and bring the easy tears to her eyes. He heard her beguiling voice:

"What can I do for you, my beloved husband?"

Destermere turned his suffering Christ-like face towards her.

"Be good ... to my daughter ... I beg of you, my Mahla."

My lady sprang to her feet, her face crimsoning, her great eyes dilating.

"*Daughter*—what does he mean?" she demanded of Stephen.

"There is much to be explained," said Stephen awkwardly.

"He has no daughter!" cried Mahla on a shrill note.

Stephen glanced in an agonized way at the Swiss notary, hoping for the older man's support. Monsieur Bertian gave it. Speaking in his careful clipped English and as briefly as possible, he unfolded the whole sorry story to the astonished Countess.

When he had finished she burst out:

"The marriage cannot have been legal. The child is a bastard."

"No, my lady. I have seen the certificate. She is the legitimate daughter of the Earl," said Stephen quietly.

She swung round on him.

"You lie. There can be no such person. I am my husband's sole heiress."

"You were—but you are no longer, milady," said Stephen, taking some pleasure in angering the woman whom he found repulsive. "The Lady Destiny Frane lives, and will reside in future at Destermere House by

29

request of her father, where you will help to bring her to womanhood and entertain for her until her marriage. She is barely sixteen years of age."

"And when she marries?" asked Mahla hoarsely.

"Her fortune will pass into the control of her husband."

Mahla looked as though she were about to die of shock, Stephen thought. He stared at her fascinated. She changed colour from red to white and white to red again. She swayed where she stood, clutching at a jewel which she wore hanging from a gold chain about her long throat. A weak cry came from the man in the bed.

"Mahla . . . my wife . . . forgive me that I have not told you this before."

Then she turned on him like a snake and struck.

"You abominable man. You traitor. You have grossly betrayed my trust. I hate you. I will never—"

She stopped, panting. She had been about to say that she would never accept the care of his wretched daughter but she had seen a warning look in the eyes of both the men—the Swiss and the English secretary—who were gravely watching her. Mad with fury though she was, Mahla could see in a flash that if she did not accept this unwelcome bequest she might lose everything. There was still time for Claud to turn against her and cast her out without a penny.

She made an effort to control herself, sank beside the bed, and began to sob bitterly.

"No—no—I did not mean that I hate you. I spoke in blind passion. Oh, Claud, Claud, I will do whatever you want. . . ."

But now the Earl, seized with a trembling that shook his wasted frame, shuddered away from her. He had seen her for the first time as she was . . . a vixen . . . avaricious, savage with disappointment because he had produced an heiress. He ignored her tears and protests. He called in a high quavering voice upon Stephen.

"Yes, my dear lord," the young secretary sprang to

his side, took the extended fingers, and pressed them between his warm strong hands.

"Destiny . . . my daughter," the Earl gasped, "never . . . leave her. . . ."

They were the last words ever to be spoken by the Earl of Destermere. His great longing to look upon the face of his daughter was not to be realized. The shock of discovering the hatred and greed on the face of the wife he had loved and trusted had been too much for him.

He expired, still holding on to Stephen's hand, as though transfixed.

For a moment everyone stood speechless. Then the nun crossed the dead man's arms on his bosom and laid a crucifix upon them.

Lady Destermere rose to her feet. She was as white now as the snows out there on the mountain tops. Only her hair and her lips were crimson. And in her heart there welled a savage hatred of the dead man—a frustration which knew no bounds. She walked swiftly out of the room.

Stephen, the tears rolling unashamedly down his cheeks as he looked upon the body of his revered master, turned to the Swiss notary.

"It is ended," he said.

"As all human life must end," sighed the Swiss, crossing himself.

"He was a good man," choked Stephen. "What sins he committed in his youth, he repented."

"But he has left behind him a great folly in the person of that vile woman who bears his name," muttered M. Bertian. "Did you see how she showed her teeth when she heard that there was a daughter to inherit?"

Stephen nodded, shivering at the memory of Mahla's face.

"Alas, the unhappy Earl realized at last and too late the nature of the woman he married."

"That was why he bade you never abandon his daughter."

"It is a great responsibility," muttered Stephen.

"Nevertheless you are of strong disposition and have great courage, my friend, and will do your duty," said the Swiss with a kindly smile at the young secretary.

Stephen put a hand to his eyes.

"I feel that this place is cursed. I must lose no time now in arranging for my lady to close down the *Château* and go at once to England and open up Destermere House to receive Lady Destiny."

"Who knows what you will find when you see this girl?"

"Who knows?" echoed Stephen with a heavy sigh.

But he was not at the moment so much concerned with what he would find in the person of Destiny Frane as the trouble which he would have in dealing with Mahla and her evil brother. Thanks be to God, he thought, that the documents which the Earl had signed this very day, would limit her ladyship's control. And once in Richmondwyke in accordance with her father's wishes, Lady Destiny would be ushered into society and find a good English husband. At court there must be many friends who had once known and respected the Destermeres in the past. There would also be Mr. Finch who had always advised the family in legal matters. He and the bankers would give Stephen some support in his duties.

But the thought of those duties weighed heavily on Stephen. He was an unhappy man as he walked with Bertian from the death-chamber, leaving the nun to draw the curtains again, light the corpse-candles and call for women to help her lay out her dead.

Pausing a moment outside the door of the Baron's suite of rooms, Stephen heard high voices . . . gutteral German from the Baron . . . furious sobbing from Mahla. He passed on, his head bowed, his brows knit, wondering what lay before him.

3

IN HER BOUDOIR Lady Destermere alternately raved and sobbed at her brother.

"It is an outrage—to have this chit of a girl put in my place. If Claud were not lying dead I should go now and plunge a dagger into his cowardly heart."

Humbert sat by the wood fire which had been lit in my lady's chamber, and gnawed at his finger nails. The news had been a shock to him too. He was deeply in debt. He had run through his own fortune. He had nothing much left but a few derelict acres in the Hanovarian mountains and a rat-ridden *schloss* tumbling to pieces with damp and decay. For a long time he had anticipated, pleasurably, sharing in his sister's fortune once the Earl succumbed to the disease which had cut his life short at so young an age. Now—this! Humbert said nothing for a while but nodded in sympathy while Mahla tore at her hair. In a passionate fury she began to break all the delicate porcelain figures which stood upon the high mantelshelf. It seemed to soothe her to carry out such senseless destruction. Every time she smashed a valuable Sèvres or Meissen ornament down into the grate and shattered it, she laughed hysterically, until finally her brother held up a protesting hand.

"Pray control yourself, *meine liebste Schwester*. Do not allow the servants or that whey-faced secretary to hear you. Unpalatable though it may be, you will have to toe the line, or we shall, indeed, be ruined."

Panting, Mahla flung herself on to her chaise-longue. She put two clenched hands up to her forehead.

"Oh, the monster, the base deceiver, the villain!" she hissed through clenched teeth.

Humbert shrugged his shoulders. He was incensed against his late brother-in-law, and as sorry for his sister as for himself. But man-like, his emotions were less near the surface, and although a sensualist he was cold and scheming. In his brain now there were thoughts like a nest of vipers, cunningly twisting and turning, seeking a way out of this calamity.

"Tell me more about Claud's daughter—Lady Destiny. A strange name," he murmured thoughtfully.

Mahla wept.

"I know nothing more than I have already told you. M. Bertian and Stephen Godwin have papers in their possession to prove her legitimate claim to the title and the property. Oh, who would have dreamed that Destermere with his recent talk of heaven and hell and repentance for his sins, should have been capable of such a deed, and drag it into the open as he lay dying just in order to spite me."

The Baron gave a short laugh. Beside him on the table stood a jug of spiced ale which he particularly liked at this hour of the morning and a breakfast of meat and pies which he had just finished when his sister sent for him. One of the servants had carried the tray through to this scented ornate boudoir which was furnished in the style which Mahla liked best, full of Byzantine splendour. Humbert drank a deep draught of the ale, smacked his lips and said:

"My dear, the young girl who claims to be Destermere's daughter was scarcely conceived sixteen years ago in order to spite *you!*" And he laughed. When Humbert laughed, it was a sound full of evil though his blue heavily lidded eyes looked quite amiable, and he was a handsome enough figure in his chocolate-brown satin dressing robe. He nearly always wore a wig. He added: "Stop snivelling, my pet, and let us consider the situation."

Mahla sat up, her long thin fingers digging into the sides of the couch. She was magnificent in her rage and despair but she looked with sudden hope at her brother whom she knew to be a man of no morals and of an unscrupulous disposition which lent her certain support when she needed it.

"Can we not poison this girl?" she muttered.

"Pray do not be ridiculous. Do you wish to die by hanging?"

Mahla shrieked and shuddered.

He went on:

"Then let us consider our facts more rationally. Now listen...."

He began to talk to her in a soothing voice and in their native tongue. Words came easily to Humbert Faramund. He liked talking and he wrote poetry. He considered himself to be a man of taste and elegance, and when he wished to be charming, he had a decided way with the ladies. He had always found it effective. This seemingly kind and charming manner was like the sugar-coating of a bitter pill which many a woman had swallowed, and gone choking to her moral death, realizing too late the manner of man who had administered it. Perhaps the only person in the world of whom Humbert was truly fond was his beautiful exotic half-sister. Now, piece by piece, he extracted from her all the information that she could give him.

She knew little save that Stephen intended to go immediately after the funeral to England, to find Claud's daughter and take her to Destermere House at Richmondwyke. He and that notary, she said, for the moment had control of the exchequer.

"And I remain guardian only in name," said Mahla trembling with rage. "I am to introduce her to the Court and make a marriage for her, after which everything will be transferred to her husband. Oh, my dastardly brute of a husband!"

"Pray do not begin again," broke in her brother with a plaintive drawl. "Permit me to think, my love."

"Think what?"

"This husband...this man who is to marry the

Lady Destiny and control the Destermere fortune . . . he will be a lucky fellow," said the Baron softly.

"Who knows until we have seen what the girl is like—she may be cross-eyed and knock-kneed," said Mahla savagely.

The Baron laughed. He sipped his ale.

"But with so much money! . . . There are beautiful dresses to conceal the bow legs and one need not look into the crossed eyes. . . ." Again Humbert uttered his low evil laugh.

Lady Destermere rose. She had calmed down. A new look of interest sprang into her enormous eyes. She drew nearer to her brother.

"What have you in mind, Humbert?"

He patted one of her hands and smiled up at her.

"I am handsome, am I not, my dearest? I still look young, when I am in a good mood, despite my thirty-five years. I would not be too repulsive to a young girl, would I?"

Mahla caught her breath.

"Humbert! You mean. . . ."

"Yes," he nodded, "I mean that I am by way of being only an uncle by marriage to the Lady Destiny; but no more than that. No blood relation. Neither law nor church could forbid the marriage if I chose to invite my Lady Destiny to become the Baroness Faramund."

Lady Destermere uttered a cry of mingled terror and delight.

"Humbert—you genius! What cunning! What brilliance of mind! Such an idea never for an instant struck me."

The Baron rose and smoothed the ermine collar of his chocolate-coloured robe. He glanced in a mirror at his tall figure and leonine head and thought he looked very handsome indeed. He spread out his hands, moving the fingers one by one.

"You used to tell me in Hanover that nobody played a spinet so sweetly as I. I can produce the most delicious melodies and even sign them for my Lady Destiny. I can write her subtle and delicate poems. I can play not only upon the spinet but upon her heart strings, and thus weave a net for her—a silken net, my dearest Mahla, into which the golden bird will fall. I will not work too fast; but slowly, slowly, until I have broken through the barrier of her maiden modesty and won her absolute confidence. *Zut!* I am beginning to find pleasure in the prospect. It will be such a golden bird indeed that I am netting. And you shall benefit thereby, belovèd sister; for your husband's daughter shall become your sister-in-law. It will be an amusing, novel situation. It'll also mean a complete defeat for the monstrous husband who attempted to deprive you of your rightful inheritance."

Lady Destermere's mind whirled. She stared, brilliant-eyed, at her brother. How wonderful indeed, and how clever! What an artful ingenious plan! She had thought that all was lost, but now it would seem that despite her late husband's dying wishes, through Humbert she would prosper yet.

This child who had been adopted by foster parents ... country parsons ... she could be little more than an uneducated brat. She would be easily managed.

Mahla flung her arms around her brother's neck.

"You are splendid, my dearest brother!" she exclaimed.

"But you must also play your part," he warned her. "There is this young man, Stephen, whom you find so attractive (although God knows why), he must be managed with subtlety, or he might smell a rat and attempt to thwart us. I intend to marry Destermere's heiress."

"What do you suggest I do?"

Humbert shut one eye and looked at Mahla reflectively?"

"You are still enamoured of this idiotic secretary?" Mahla scowled.

"Believe me, my dear Humbert, he is no idiot. Claud

used to say that Stephen has exceptional brain and ability."

Humbert shrugged.

"In my opinion he is fit only to enter a monastery and remain there."

"I do not know what you have in mind regarding Stephen," said Mahla softly, warningly, "but I do not wish him harmed."

Humbert yawned.

"As you wish, dearest sister. Take the boy to bed and teach him all that you know. I really do not mind except that I shall brook no interference from him now that I have made up my mind to marry Destermere's daughter."

"I will manage Stephen. You can leave him to me. But are you not taking things too much for granted? Suppose this young girl has a mind of her own and does not fancy you, my dear brother."

Humbert smiled and pressed the tips of his fingers together like a self-satisfied Ecclesiastic.

"She will like me. She will accept my proposal when I make it, but as I have said—it must be a slow subtle process. Then before Master Stephen and his allies realize it, I shall have wedded and bedded the girl."

"You may not like her."

"I shall like her," nodded the Baron, speaking in a silky voice.

"What a man you are!" exclaimed Mahla with admiration.

"And now," he said, "you must play your part. You must seem to be in complete agreement with your dearest secretary, close down the *Château des Cygnes* and make your way to England where I shall eventually join you. I shall not accompany you or seem to be hand in glove with you. But I shall arrive at Destermere House, in due course. Let us say soon after the charming Lady Destiny arrives there. Then Uncle Humbert will make the acquaintance of his new niece."

Mahla listened thoughtfully to her brother's devilish laughter. Her mind was busy working like his, now darting this way and that, deciding what course to take, and how best to blind Stephen to the facts.

Later that morning she sent for the secretary.

He found her dressed from head to foot in black with black lace twined around her red head and long pale throat. Jewess though she was, she had put a gold necklet bearing a heavy cross, about her throat. Her face was very pale, and there were smudges under her eyes as though she had been weeping. She looked the personification of Christian sorrow—most becoming in her widowhood.

"This is a terrible day for us, dear Stephen," she said in a faint sorrowful voice.

Stephen, himself, in mourning clothes with only a white Steinkirk at his neck to relieve it, and wearing a neat bog-wig, gazed at his late master's widow suspiciously. He had no reason to trust Lady Destermere and he loathed her for the anguish she had brought upon the Earl in his dying moments.

"I have much to do, my lady," he said, "if I can be of no great use to you, pray allow me to attend to my papers."

"Not just yet," she said plaintively, "surely you will stay awhile to comfort me."

"Are you in need of comfort, madam?"

She forced a glistening tear which trembled on her fabulous lashes.

"Alas, you do me injustice if you think I am not torn with grief for the loss of my belovèd husband."

Stephen made no comment, but put his tongue in his cheek. She saw this and knew that he was not taken in by her. Her fingers tore nervously at her lace-edged handkerchief. She did not know in this moment whether she shared Humbert's contempt for what he called Stephen's monkish nature, or desired him. Desire

39

triumphed. She glided nearer him and putting out a hand, laid it on his shoulder.

"Stephen, you are all that I have left for comfort. I need you. I need your strength and counsel. Claud loved and trusted you. Will you not encourage me to do likewise?"

"I would wish you to trust me, milady."

"But not to love you?"

His eyelids drooped. His lips felt dry. Her hot demanding beauty had scant effect upon him, and his nostrils wrinkled, disgusted by the warmth of her room and the heavy perfume that emanated from her and the cloying scent of pastilles which she always kept burning on her hearth.

Stephen craved for fresh air—the cold pure air that blew from the mountains. He felt that milady's exotic boudoir was no place for him.

He had just knelt beside the bier of his benefactor and beloved master, the late Earl Destermere who lay now on a catafalque in an anti-chamber.

Two nuns were there to keep watch. Tomorrow, the funeral. Next day, the long journey to England with the embalmed body in order that it should be placed in the family vault of the Destermeres at Richmondwyke.

Stephen raised his eyes and looked at Mahla. The passion in those great pansy-purple eyes of hers made him strangely nervous.

"If you will excuse me, my lady—" he began.

She smiled, but took his arm and drew him gently but firmly to her chaise-longue.

"Nay—no hurry, dear Stephen. If you cannot love me, at least respect my wishes and talk to me awhile."

Thus she forced him to remain at her side. He mopped at his forehead. It would be difficult, he thought, to respect the wishes of this woman whose iniquities were so well known to him. Stephen and M. Bertian had agreed that an exceedingly difficult and

delicate position faced him. For this young girl whom
he was to find and install as the mistress of Destermere
House would have an unscrupulous stepmother to influence and control her. He, Stephen, and the legal
controllers could watch over her and add their counsel.
But Stephen regarded the future with dread. He had
asked himself many times during the last few hours . . .
what manner of girl would be find in Lady Destiny
Frane? At sixteen she would be a budding woman.
What a comical and stupid name—Destiny Barley—it
made him shudder. The sooner she was called by her
rightful family name of Frane, the better.

Nevertheless a certain fierce loyalty to the memory
of the departed Earl forbade him to suffer a moral col-
lapse and allow Mahla to evade the carrying out of her
husband's wishes.

"I have been left a strange legacy, Stephen," he heard
Lady Destermere say in a dreamy voice. "A young stepdaughter. It will be odd, will it not, Stephen, for me to
have an ignorant child in my care, and try to launch
her upon an astonished London?"

He glanced at her ladyship uneasily. She seemed very
affable of a sudden; resigned to her new position. Yet
so short a time ago he had seen her at the Earl's death-
bed, raving like a fish-wife in fury and thwarted greed.
He did not trust her.

She spoke amiably now of Destermere's daughter and
of his, Stephen's forthcoming journey to find the girl.

"You are planning, of course, to accompany my belovèd husband's body to Richmondwyke and then seek
out the heiress?"

"That is my intention, milady," nodded Stephen.

Mahla sighed. She spoke softly. She looked soft and
yielding. But her brain was ice-cold and she watched
the young man like an eagle measuring the worth of its
prey. He was different from any man she had ever met;
in some ways less handsome or gay or attractive. Yet

41

positively he fascinated her. There was something as fine and remote about Stephen as those mountain peaks which she hated, yet watched, as though mesmerized by their very inaccessibility.

One day, she told herself, he would reject her once too often and she would use more violent methods to conquer him. Her longing for him was becoming an obsession. Today, however, she remembered her brother's caution, and that other game which she must now start to play in league with Humbert. Her dear brother had promised her that not only should she regain all that she had lost in the way of money and influence, but that she should have this boy in her power. But for the moment she must watch and wait. It would not do to be too impatient. It would be more cunning to try first to make a friend of Stephen. So she simulated a vast interest in her stepdaughter and spoke to the secretary of the future with an interest that astonished Stephen.

"I have not always done the right thing with Claud but to show my remorse I shall become a real mother to the little Lady Destiny," Mahla said smoothly, watching Stephen through her lashes.

Deceived now despite all his watchfulness, Stephen relaxed. It would make things much easier if he could count on Lady Destermere's support.

"She will I am sure, be in need of your ladyship's wisdom and guidance," he said tactfully.

"She shall have it. You and I shall work together for her good," said Mahla in a sweet voice.

"I thank you. My own lot will not be easy as you may imagine, bearing in mind the responsibilities that have been put upon me."

"Let me share them, dear Stephen," said Lady Destermere in the same sugared voice. "To be sure my poor dead husband's child will not have had much of a start in life. I must vow to give her one now and to find her a suitable husband."

She uttered the last words in a matter-of-fact voice. Stephen gained confidence—and spoke to her with more friendliness.

"My late master would be much heartened to hear you speak like this, my lady."

Mahla touched her eyes with her handkerchief. She gave a faint sob.

Stephen, who neither understood women nor cared much for them, was impressed and began to wonder if he had done Mahla an injustice.

"My condolences, my lady," he muttered awkwardly.

"I have great need of your sympathy and friendship. Pray give it to me dear, dear Stephen."

His face coloured. Coughing, he rose to his feet.

"I am here to command, my lady. I am but his lordship's secretary."

"More than that," murmured Mahla. "The son he had always hoped for. The brother and guardian of the daughter he has so suddenly sprung upon us, and—my right hand."

Again Stephen felt awkward and sweated. But he also felt that the atmosphere between himself and the Countess had suddenly improved. It was a relief, and when Mahla held out one of her long white hands of which she was rightly vain, he bent over it and touched it with his lips.

"I am your ladyship's servant."

She stiffened and held her breath. She had to control the desire to draw Stephen into her arms and crush that pale proud young face to her burning cheek. *One day,* she thought, *one day you will do more than be my servant. You will be my slave.*

She let him go, and sat back against her cushions, panting, eyes glittering, chewing at her handkerchief. But she was content that she had made a satisfactory start and laid the first stones upon which Humbert could build his schemes.

4

THE DAY ON WHICH Stephen Godwin arrived at the parsonage on the outskirts of Bath to which he had been directed, seeking for a girl called Destiny Barley—was the coldest of the year. So cold that the pond on which the hamlet had been built, was frozen and the puddles on the mud-caked lanes milky-blue with ice.

Stephen had had to walk the last few yards of his journey, picking his way so as not to soil his polished boots and glad of the heavy cloak which he wore, and of the warmth of his cocked hat and gauntlets. He was followed by one of the postilions.

He seldom remembered a colder day in late February. As he passed through the hamlet which was composed of a handful of straggling cottages, he had seen few people out of doors save a blacksmith raising sparks at his anvil, and a few citizens hurrying in and out of their dwellings. Faugh! what a climate, reflected Stephen, who had grown accustomed to the sunshine, even in winter, that used to gild the mountain peaks and the glorious lakes of Switzerland.

This lane was too narrow and the ruts of the lane too deep for the horses which had pulled his travelling coach from Richmondwyke. He had left it there by the village Cross and sent the coachmen into the one and only coffee house, for nourishment. Despite the magnificence of the big black Britzska which came from the Destermere stables in Richmondwyke—and it had a richly padded interior with the latest glass panels to shield passengers from draughts—it had been a dreadful journey. A journey of one hundred and six miles. Snow between Devizes and Bath had melted and caused the Britzska to stick in the mire. The constant fear of highwaymen during the last lap of that lonely drive across the desolate Wiltshire Downs, assailed the coachmen, although they were well armed.

Stephen, personally, was no coward but the drive had taken three days because of poor weather and now, fatigued and apprehensive, he found nothing to cheer him in the sight of the house wherein he expected to find Destermere's daughter.

It was a derelict parsonage, he had been told by the innkeeper up the road—no longer occupied by the clergy. It appeared that even Mr. Barley's friend, William Paull, who had first given Stephen the address, was unaware of the fact that the Rev. Sextus Barley himself, had died a month ago. According to the innkeeper, there had been no Mrs. Barley for the last four years. She had died when her last baby was born. The adopted daughter had since then looked after her so-called father, managed his house and—so Stephen heard to his dismay—a bevy of little Barleys.

"Alas, Destiny has a good heart but a wild nature," the innkeeper described the girl. "She nursed Mrs. Barley in her last illness, and cooked for Sextus Barley till he died. But when our good citizens deemed it right her little brothers and sisters should be taken to the Poor House, she fought like a tiger to stave off the day."

Stephen's heart had sunk, as the innkeeper, chuckling and speaking of Destiny with a certain amount of admiration, described how a certain Miss Abercorn who visited the needy and was a respectable churchgoer and friend of the late Mrs. Barley, had gone down to the old parsonage to fetch the children and take them to the Institution in Bath.

A regular battle it had been, he said. Young Destiny had barred the door and even heaved furniture up against the lower windows, and screamed out at Miss Abercorn that she would die rather than let the bairns be taken to a public institution.

The children were terrified and begged to be allowed to go on living with their "sister." When Miss Abercorn had asked how Destiny intended to support such a family, Destiny had screamed back that she was young and strong and knew how to spin and would weave cloth, and sell it. Also that she could grow vegetables, had a store of potatoes enough for the rest of the winter, a goat to give milk, and a few straggling hens to lay eggs.

"Good heavens," Stephen had replied. "And what happened then?"

Miss Abercorn brought a gentleman to help her get the children. They tried to force the door but short of smashing it or setting fire to the whole place, like burning out a lot of rats, they could do little. So they had given up. Greatly incensed, Miss Abercorn had withdrawn from the fray, saying that the day would come when that young limb of Satan, Destiny, with her wild French blood, would eat her own words. Starvation would bring them in time.

"That was only a week ago, since then none of us have set eyes on the family," said the innkeeper.

"Great heavens! "Stephen repeated, and hurried with alarm towards the deserted old house. He could see now that it was falling to pieces, for a bit of the roof had already caved in. Paper was stuck against some of the broken panes.

True, there were vegetables planted at the back of the building, and one portion of land dug ready for sowing, but the rest of the garden was a wilderness with brambles thick, and weeds profuse. An air of misery— of incredible poverty—hung over the whole place. Complete silence reigned as Stephen neared the front door, but he fancied he saw bright eyes peering at him; small faces pressed against one of the lower windows. No smoke rose from the chimney. They must be without a fire, Stephen thought with horror, with the temperature rapidly falling below twenty degrees. The only sound was the bleating of the goat tethered by a chain pulling at some coarse roots—a skinny animal, despite its full udders.

Here lived the Lady Destiny Frane, daughter and heiress of the sixth Earl of Destermere.

When Stephen thought of his late master and of the opulent luxury of Destermere House which he had left three days ago, he shuddered. This was worse than he had expected. He felt weak at the thought of the task that lay before him. He almost wished that he had brought Lady Destermere with him. Indeed, Mahla had changed much and very pleasantly, since they all left Geneva.

After the Earl had been laid to rest she had arrived at Destermere, opened it up with great gusto and, to Stephen's delight, stayed in residence alone. She had permitted the Baron to return to Hanover. Whatever happened, Stephen could never like or trust Humbert Faramund. But Mahla seemed full of good resolutions. She had begun at once to redecorate and prepare a wing of the house for Destiny Frane. She expressed herself quite excited at the idea of receiving her stepdaughter. They would be great friends, she told the secretary. Whatever Mahla had done in her lifetime to grieve the Earl, she would make up for it by giving her full attention to his daughter.

Stephen was no fool, but Mahla expressed so much willingness to play this part that even he had been deceived.

Now he told the postilion to wait for him at a distance, lifted the silver-headed cane which he carried and beat it on the door.

"Are you there? Let me in, someone," he called authoritatively.

No answer. The wind blew against Stephen's face cutting like a knife. The morning was dark, with snow-clouds billowing from the North. The goat regarded the handsomely clad stranger with its light strange eyes and wagged its beard in a sagacious manner while it continued its mournful chewing.

"Let me in!" repeated Stephen and rapped the door again. Now he fancied he heard muffled voices and scuffling, then the sound of a child crying. An adult voice called out:

"Be quiet, Matthew Barley. Stop snivelling or. . . ." The rest of the sentence was lost upon Stephen who never learnt what was about to be done to the said Matthew but he guessed that the voice belonged to the young girl who was in charge of the children.

He shivered and drew his high fur collar closer about his neck. It gave him a peculiar sensation to realize that he had just heard the voice of Claud Destermere's own daughter. Soon he heard it again:

"Whoever it is, tapping at my door, can go away. It will not be opened to you."

Stephen narrowed his gaze and reflected. It was not an uneducated voice; for so much he was thankful. In fact it had a very pleasant sound. But the innkeeper had spoken of her "wild blood." If there was wildness in her, Stephen thought cynically, it was inherited from the Destermeres. The same fever, perhaps, that had burned in the veins of her father when he was a youth.

Now Stephen shouted:

"I order you to let me in. My name is Stephen Godwin. I come from London to bring you news of the greatest importance. News of your father—*your own father*. Do you hear me? Do I speak to one who bears the name of Destiny?"

Silence again. The wailing of the younger child had ceased. Suddenly an upper window was thrown open. It crashed back in the wind against a tangle of creeper. A girl's face and the upper half of her form appeared in view. She leaned down.

"News of my father. My *own* father!"

"Yes," he said looking up at her.

"Then you have not come to force my brothers and sisters into a Poor House?"

"No."

"Do you swear it?"

"I swear it," said Stephen impatiently. "Pray come downstairs, my Lady Destiny, and allow me to come in and speak to you for I find this cold wind bitter and I have travelled over one hundred miles to reach you."

The girl stared down at him with mingled doubt and wonder. Certainly she could see that he was a stranger to these parts and very handsomely if soberly attired, and what he said had struck her like a lightning flash. She had never since she could remember had a father— and certainly not a mother. Who was this distinguished person who spoke to her of a *father,* and addressed her as *my lady?*

With lingering doubts, she called down again:

"I warn you, sir, that if you lay a finger on one of my brothers or sisters, and attempt to force them out of this house, I shall shoot you; for I have a pistol and can use it."

Now Stephen found it suddenly funny to be threatened with shooting by a chit of a girl barricaded in a house that looked rat-infested and about to fall down. He burst out laughing.

"I have no wish to die, I do assure you, my lady. Pray admit me and I shall not betray your trust," he said.

The girl looked utterly confused. He tried but could not see her plainly. As protection against the cold she wore a woollen hood half across her face, and a scarf wrapped about her throat. Then she asked:

"Why do you address me as 'my lady'? Are you escaped from a mad-house, sir?"

No, but I come to one, he thought wryly. He shouted back: "For the love of God cease this chilly exchange of words and let me in."

The face and figure withdrew. The window was shut.

A moment later Stephen heard bolts being drawn, and the door squeaking and groaning on its hinges was opened. He signalled to the postilion to wait for him, then he stared with great eagerness at the girl who had unlocked the door. The other children, wherever they were, had been apparently left upstairs.

Stephen entered the hall. The door swung behind him. He unbuttoned his cape but thought that it was almost as chilly in this unheated house as outside in the raw morning. Now the girl removed her hood and scarf. That he was face to face with Destermere's daughter he could not for an instant doubt, she was his image.

Tall for her age, he thought, as she must be in her fifteenth or sixteenth year. Painfully thin, with Claud Destermere's wide-set eyes, green with golden flecks, and heavy black lashes. The same short, proud nose and wide good-humoured mouth. Only the colour of the hair was different—Stephen imagined she had inherited that from her mother. It was as black as the wing of the raven. He noted how the locks were tied back with an old leather thong, not even a ribbon. He was shocked by the girl's whole appearance. The young face was drawn and old; the pale pure skin stretched tightly across the fine bones; the eyes far too big and hollow. She looked starved, he thought.

She wore a long brown dress of rough home-spun which hung loosely on that too-slender frame. With his passion for detail, Stephen even noted her hands. Dear heaven, how like *they* were to the Earl's in shape. Fine-fingered, aristocratic, with almond-shaped nails and narrow wrists. But they were chapped and red, and she looked, he thought, sadly in need of a wash. Oh, the poor child, the poor, *poor child*! That Lady Frane should have come down to this! Little wonder the conscience of the Earl had smote him at the end. For this was the fate to which he had consigned his own flesh and blood—even if he had not meant it to be so. She looked no more than a pathetic, rather sullen peasant-girl, thought Stephen, and she snarled at him like a young animal.

"I have let you in but I shall not hesitate to push you out if you are on the side of those who try to take my brothers and sisters away from here."

"You are not over hospitable, my lady," he said drily. "Is there no room in which we can foregather and converse?"

She shrugged her shoulders, gave him a suspicious look but finally led the way into a downstairs room which was tolerably clean. But the walls dripped with water and the wind howled down the chimney into an empty grate. There were rags for curtains and no furniture save a worm-eaten table and a few chairs. The girl looked around with a faint ironic smile.

"You see all I have, sir. I have sold everything of value in order to buy bread for my little family, and I can offer you no refreshment save half a tankard of goat's milk which I can ill spare."

Aghast, Stephen stared at this curious girl.

"And how long did you intend to remain thus—shut away from the world, in such desperate need?"

"Until I have finished my spinning. Then I can market my stuffs and shall have money to buy food."

"And your age is——?"

"Sixteen come Michaelmas," she said in a low voice. Then she stuck out her lower lip and snapped: "Why do you persist in addressing me as 'my lady'?"

"Because, my dear," said Stephen, "you are an Earl's daughter and not as you may imagine, any relative of the late Reverend Sextus Barley, neither were you related to the French family who originally nurtured you in Paris. You know nothing of your parentage, I presume?"

She scowled.

"Nothing. Save that I have no parents alive, nor any rights of my own," and her thin face coloured painfully. Stephen could see that she was not lacking in pride.

51

"But here in this house I am mother to the four little ones whom death robbed of their mother's care."

"How many little ones did you say?"

"Four!" she repeated.

"Four!" echoed Stephen in turn, and sat down suddenly on one of the chairs. He took a small silver box from his pocket and applied a little snuff, delicately, to his nostrils.

The house, he thought, smelled fusty with damp and rotting wood. A large spider crawled suddenly across the ceiling. It dropped down on its line of web. There was a sudden scuffling and squeaking in a corner of the room, which suggested mice. Stephen wrinkled his nose.

"Four children, and *you* left alone to support them— and only fifteen years old. It is indeed terrible."

"Terrible only because we are not left in peace and they hate us and wish to separate us," said the girl in a passionate voice.

"Who hates you?"

"Everyone in the village because I will not do as they say."

"But my dear child, all they want, so I have heard, is to remove you to a proper dwelling and to give food and shelter to these four mites whom you are harbouring."

"They would be taken to a Poor House for unwanted infants. Maybe you do not know what torments and hardships and misery await such children," exclaimed Destiny, and both her cheeks burned scarlet. "They are innocent and I am their sole protector, for their mother died after giving birth to little Matt four years ago. I had to do everything for Mr. Barley and for the family. Cooking, scrubbing, sewing. But I did not mind. The children are not my flesh and blood but they are all I have ever known or loved. I know that I have been rebellious for it is my nature. . . ." And now she looked down sullenly, twisting a fold of her dress between her reddened fingers. "Something comes over me at times so I cannot feel meek and willing to mouth long prayers as Mr. Barley wished; and sometimes I longed to go dancing with the other girls in the village. But I did my best to be good and now when I am left alone with this family I will not watch it torn apart and my children sent to unimagined suffering. They love me as much as I love them. I will die—or kill—before I relinquish them to that old toad, Miss Abercorn."

Stephen was shocked—quite unused to such fierce menacing words from a gentlewoman. Difficult to reconcile himself to the fact that the Lady Destiny Frane and this young savage could be one and the same.

She was crazily obsessed with these wretched little Barleys. How was he going to deal with her? He had to make a snap decision. He marched to the front door, opened it and beckoned one of the waiting postilions. He whispered a few words to the man who nodded and began to run down the narrow road with alacrity as though glad to move his limbs on this icy day.

When Stephen returned to the girl inside the parsonage, she had called the children down and gathered them around her. Stephen blinked at them. He was embarrassed by small children, never having had anything to do with them. They were clinging to Destiny. She had her arms like two protective wings around the starvelings. Stephen wondered how she could love them so well. They were not very clean. Their noses ran. One of them was snivelling. The younger of the two girls might have been pretty if she were clean, for she had bright gold curls. They each had frayed wool shawls pinned around them to protect them from the cold. They looked, he thought, like sorry little scarecrows. Destiny faced him with defiance on her face.

"If you have given orders that my children should be taken from me, I shall kill first them and then myself," she said in a fierce, trembling voice.

Stephen, shocked by her violence, rubbed the back of his head and scowled back at her.

"In truth!" he said testily. "You are being most awkward, my lady. Pray recall, too, that these are *not* your children. They have no claim upon you at all."

Now all four children stared at Stephen, then broke into wails.

"Do not let him take us, Dessie. Oh, Dessie, save us!"

"Hush, my darlings. You shall not be took from me," said the girl and pushed them all behind her, reminding Stephen comically, even in this crisis, of a mother-hen, clucking indignantly, marshalling her chicks to safety. He relaxed and gave a sudden laugh.

"I find you ridiculous, child," he said.

Her great eyes flamed at him. She said through her teeth:

"Find me what you wish, but touch one of these little ones and I shall keep my word. It shall be their corpses you take and not themselves, alive."

Stephen groaned.

"Great heavens, I beseech you to calm yourself. I have not given orders for your brood to be put into a home. I have merely ordered one of my men to bring food from the village for I am sure you are all hungry."

Silence. Matt, the youngest child, turned and sucking his thumb, gazed shyly at the stranger. The eldest girl, Jemima, whose face looked wizened and pathetically adult, also turned and stared at him, then at Destiny.

"Dessie, he said *food*. I am, indeed, monstrously hungry."

"Me, too!" said the second girl, Lucy.

"Me, too!" echoed little Luke.

Dear God, they are starving, I warrant, thought Stephen and spoke more gently to Destermere's daughter.

"You see. I am not going to harm you but feed your flock, so pray stop behaving as though I were your mortal enemy."

Destiny turned red, then white. Her lashes fluttered. The longest lashes he had ever seen, he thought, and truly she had courage. Fretted though he was by the difficulties of the task his late master had set him, he could not but admit that in this slim young girl—still so much of a child herself—there flamed a dauntless spirit. He added:

"Will you not trust me, my Lady Destiny?"

She seemed to crumple up and burst, suddenly into choking sobs. The children all joined her. There was another period of embarrassment for Stephen, during which he tried to comfort them all but failed; so finally he let them embrace each other and continue to weep. At last the girl clasped her poor chafed hands together and said:

"Upstairs, all of you. Jem, take the young ones and wash their faces and comb their hair. Stop crying now, all of you. Do you hear? Then come down to eat, since this gentleman has promised you a meal."

They stopped weeping, linked hands and were led by the eldest girl out of the room, like little marionettes jerked on a string, thought Stephen. Four of them! Why in heaven's name did the Barleys have to be so fecund? These poor parsons bred like rabbits, he thought disgustedly, and wondered how he was going to deal with the family. Get Destiny back to her father's home, he must, but take the four little Barleys he would not.

Destiny said:

"I shall be glad of food for my little ones if you have really sent for it and not for Miss Abercorn."

"I have not sent for Miss Abercorn," he said, trying to be patient.

"Thank you," she whispered.

He looked with pity at the sunken young face. Now he found the big swimming eyes breathtakingly beautiful.

"Will you not sit down for a moment and rest and listen to me?" he asked.

She seated herself on a chair and pushed the black

silky hair back from a forehead which was pure and white—sculptured like marble, thought Destermere's secretary.

"I am confused, sir," she said in a voice scarcely above a whisper as though all her passionate rage, her fierce protective spirit had fled, leaving her limp and hopeless. "I do not understand what your visit means."

"When you have had sustenance and a little wine, I will try to explain," he said, and began to walk up and down the cold empty room, his hands clasped behind him.

"Sustenance or not, I can still try to comprehend what you have to tell me," she said, her gaze following him with a growing curiosity.

He stopped in front of her.

"Then listen, my Lady Destiny," he said.

5

IN ALL THEIR LIVES the Barley children had never eaten such food and in all *her* life Destermere's daughter had not tasted a meal like this one which was spread on the table in the diningroom of the old crumbling parsonage.

Two of Stephen's servants had carried a hamper from the village inn. The children, now clean and decent, sat wide-eyed, astonished, as the men spread a long cloth on the table and piled the repast upon it. The best that the local innkeeper could muster at a moment's notice. Destiny had found crockery, knives and forks, and tankards of a kind to take the good red wine which was poured out and which Mr. Godwin insisted upon them all drinking.

There was cold beef and a fowl and a pile of sausages; sponge cakes and jellies, and cheese. Loaves of bread, and hunks of yellow farm-butter. A jug of milk for the little ones, and fruit. Stephen, aghast, watched the Barley family devour this food, wondering when their empty little bellies would rebel against such sudden over-feeding. Nevertheless, he was quite gratified by their screams of delight and constant chatter of appreciation. But soon all his concentration became centred upon Destiny. She ate as hungrily as the rest although trying not to show how desperately she needed the food. Gradually the colour stole back into her face and he even heard her laugh when the youngest child covered his face with jam whilst stuffing the sponge cake into his little mouth.

The laughter had a pretty sound, he thought, and she was being more friendly and helpful, but it was obvious that she could not yet fully credit the fact that her fortunes had so changed and that, suddenly, from being the adopted child of an impoverished parson— a child without a name of her own—she had become a wealthy, titled heiress.

She had listened to all he had told her, as though stunned. When he questioned her about herself she could remember little, it seemed, of her early life in Paris, although the French language came easily to her and sometimes even now she found herself using a French word of exclamation, echoes of that long ago. She could recall cuffs and blows from the baker's wife; a portion, too, of the journey she had taken in the first instance from Paris to England. Once there, she remembered being involved continually in battles with a woman who did not understand her and who tried to tame her and subdue her naturally high spirits. And finally her admission into the parsonage here and settling down to a life in this house where she became little more than a domestic drudge for the parson and his wife.

An unhappy and most unsuitable beginning for the

Earl of Destermere's daughter, Stephen considered, and small wonder that when told of the Earl, her father, she felt no natural affection or leaning towards him.

"I hate him for what he did to my poor mother!" had been her first hot, resentful cry.

When Stephen reminded her that the whole sorry episode had occurred when Lord Destermere was a young, reckless man, Destiny said she thought no better of him on that account, and, in truth, Stephen, himself, found it difficult to extol Claud Destermere's character or sing his praises for what he had done sixteen years ago. He could only tell Destiny that now all would be made up to her and she would come into her own.

But there was still this question of the Barley children. After the repast, while the two coachmen cleared the table, Stephen sat in a corner of the room, sipped his wine and wondered what best to do.

At the other end of the room with the children now fed, hiccuping and happy, Destiny sat wrapped in her own troubled thoughts.

Like the children, she had eaten too much and had a pain in her chest, but she felt very much better. This last week had been terrible, barricaded in the icy old house without food or fuel and wondering how long she could save the children.

Even now she was not quite sure that she could trust Mr. Godwin. Now and again she stole a look at him. Never in her life did she remember seeing so personable a young man and one so richly dressed.

The man under whose roof she had lived so long had always been shabby and ugly in her sight. A sanctimonious hypocrite, with little kindliness or understanding. In the original instance he had given a roof to Destiny because he saw in her an unpaid servant who could assist his sickly wife.

When the girl was not in the kitchen she was busy caring for one of the newly-arrived infants. She remembered little if anything of gaiety in her life. The Rever-

end Sextus put even his own small children to harsh
tasks of learning from the Scriptures—lessons for which
they were not mentally equipped. Destiny protected
them fiercely from his anger and more often than not
took all blame upon herself and was punished accord-
ingly. But at times she could no longer bear the parson's mean, cruel treatment of the little ones which ill-
matched his so-called Christian piety. Then she dared
to raise her voice in defence of the children, and Mr.
Barley had endeavoured to tame her spirit, but failed.
Destiny had courage and a vivid imagination. She used
to spin tales of fairy-like splendour and beauty for the
four children—culled from that bright groping mind of
hers. Then had come a day in Destiny's life about which
she had spoken nothing to Mr. Godwin. It was far too
horrifying and shamed her every time she remembered
it.

The Reverend Sextus Barley had returned from a
church service on an evening as chilly as this one. He
was not accustomed to wine, but on this occasion it
would seem he took refuge in strong drink in order to
warm his starved limbs. Destiny had come out of the
kitchen to find him standing in front of the meagre fire
in the drawing-room and was shocked to realize that he
was tipsy—as she had seen the rough men, returning
from the inn after a carousel on a Saturday night. She
shuddered whenever she remembered that tall, thin
frame in the black coat and breeches; the narrow, bitter, colourless face, the dirty wig awry. She had bobbed
to him, as usual, asking respectfully what he wished for
the evening meal. The children were in bed. As a rule
Sextus looked back at Destiny with eyes of cold dislike,
for she was the only human being who had dared to
oppose him or his wishes. But that night he gazed upon
the young girl differently—in a way she only half understood but which struck terror in her heart. Then he
had thundered at her:

"How dare you come into my presence wearing that gown?"

She had clutched a fold of the offending garment, well aware that it had belonged to that poor creature, the late Mrs. Barley. A shabby merino, too small for Destiny, drawn tightly across her young swelling breasts. She had stammered out her excuse; she had only been given one gown of her own in the last three years and she had outgrown it. Last night it had split beyond repairing 'so she had found this new one in the dead woman's wardrobe and put it on.

The Reverend Sextus listened to the explanation and began to mutter drunken extracts from the Scriptures decrying the vanity of people in this world and the child's need to prepare herself for the next.

"You are a common thief!" he had finally shouted at her. "Get upstairs and remove that gown which does not belong to you."

Trembling, she had stood and defied him.

"I have no other, sir. I cannot go about naked."

"Naked," he had repeated, "*naked.* . . ." Then, as though the word aroused some hideous latent yearning in him, he changed his tune. He lurched towards her, gripped her by the shoulders and brought his mean, spiteful face down to hers.

"*Why not naked?*" he had asked in a meaning, sibilant whisper, and his wine-laden breath fanned her cheek.

Terrified, she shrank from him. She knew nothing of sex save for the crude facts which nature occasionally forced upon her by her observation of animal life, or the kissing courting couples she saw in the village from time to time. She knew nothing of love, except what she had read in books. But there was one volume of medieval sonnets in this house, which she treasured. Long romantic and charming verses they were, and suggested delights which the young girl barely understood but which seemed to her more beautiful than anything in real life.

Now in the drunken parson's sudden assault upon her she recognized a terrible danger and could feel only the utmost repugnance towards the parson. As she had struggled in his lecherous embrace he had whispered:

"Truly you have become a woman, Dessie, and a comely one. I have been too long without a wife. You are no relative of mine. There is nothing to stop me from marrying you. How would you like to become Mrs. Barley, my love?"

She had screamed at him.

"I would loathe it just as I loathe you. Let me go!"

His tune had changed again and he struck at her knocking her down, and not before the poor merino gown had been torn from her shoulders, revealing their whiteness. Then he made another lustful grab at her. She had struck out at him in blind fear. It was then that he had staggered, clutching at his heart, and with a ghastly groan, fell in a black heap upon the floor.

She had run wildly out of the house into the cold night to the dwelling of the village physician who came and pronounced that the Reverend Sextus Barley was no more.

Destiny, now wearing another of Mrs. Barley's miserable gowns, bowed her head. The passing of this evil man meant for her a release. It was only after the funeral that she realized that Miss Abercorn meant to try and break up the family and take the children from her. Then she barred and bolted them and herself from the outside world. She dedicated herself to the care of the children. On them she lavished all the passionate warmth from the depths of her nature, which was intrinsically a generous one. In particular she adored little Matt. The poor child was mentally retarded, but because he clung to her and could speak only the name "Dessie", she lavished most of her devotion and pity on him.

She had begun now to feel she need not be afraid of Mr. Godwin. He treated her with a cold, formal courtesy which she had never received from any man before. But in spite of her wretched upbringing, she had a natural intelligence and grasp of matters. Suddenly she spoke to Stephen:

"Mr. Godwin, sir, you tell me that I am an heiress of some considerable wealth. Is that truly so?"

"It is," he said somewhat impatiently, "and I beg you now, my lady, to make preparations to leave this house, for the winter's day is all too short and it is time we started on our journey to Richmondwyke."

She ignored this.

"If I am so rich, can I not afford to educate my little brothers and sisters in the best possible manner?"

"Yes—since you persist in calling them your brothers and sisters, my lady."

"I do persist!" she said, tossing her head.

"Nevertheless it would not be right and proper for you to introduce them into Destermere House."

"Why not?"

Stephen licked his lips. When this chit of a girl defied him he was floored. It was most unnerving.

He muttered:

"Because the orders I received from my last master were to find you and to take you to your rightful home but not with a bevy of parson's children. It would cause a scandal in the district and much necessary gossip about your upbringing. The Countess proposes to tell all and sundry that you have lived abroad for the last few years."

"That would be a lie!" declared the awkward girl.

"You must leave your upbringing now to the Countess."

Sullen and frowning the girl said:

"If I am the daughter of an Earl and a lady in my own right, why can I not do as I please?"

Stephen coloured.

"Because you will be in the care of your guardians and remain so until you marry," he said.

"I shall never marry," she said.

He stared at her curiously.

"And why not?"

"That is my affair," she said, looking away from him, cheeks crimson. She was remembering Sextus Barley.

Once more Stephen lost patience.

"We will not waste time discussing that now. I beg you to accompany me into the coach."

"I will not go without the children," she said, stubbornly.

"There is no room for them in the coach. We will find them suitable lodgings."

"No, I will stay here with them until another coach is found to take them to Richmondwyke with me."

Stephen gulped. Of a truth, Lady Destiny Frane was no easy task to handle. He was forced to admire her, except that she made things so devilish difficult. Through the dirty window panes he could see fresh flakes of snow whirling from the sky. The weather was worsening. Something must be done to force the girl's hand, he thought in despair.

He said:

"Do not make things harder for me than they already are. I have my duty to perform concerning you, and you have yours. It is your duty to come with me now and take up your rightful position in your father's house. I promise you that at a later date something will be done about these children."

He saw her clench her hands.

He added:

"I give you my word as a man of honour that I will not let them be placed in any Institution nor shall Miss Abercorn be left to deal with them. If you will come with me now we will find a suitable place for them to stay until their future can be decided."

Destiny looked from side to side like a hunted creature. She began to moderate her manner and plead with him.

"Do not separate us, I beg of you, sir."

He felt a growing pity for her but sighed.

"I tell you they cannot come with us. It is impossible."

"And what if I refuse to go with you?" she asked, hysterically.

He bit his lip.

"Then, my lady, alas, I must still carry out my vow to your father and ask my coachmen to carry you forcibly to the coach and leave Miss Abercorn to deal with the children.

Destiny screamed.

"No, *no*!"

"Then pray act as I suggest," said Stephen, feeling most uncomfortable. Be damned, he thought, if the child did not make him feel a brute. "Money is no object. We shall pay somebody well—perhaps the innkeeper's wife—why should she not house and feed and care for the children until such time as they can rejoin you? She seemed a pleasant body."

He saw the light of hope spring into Destiny's wild eyes.

"Then they *will* be allowed to join me eventually?"

"No doubt," muttered Stephen.

He hoped devoutly that once the girl was installed in her new home and had taken her rightful place there, she would see the impossibility of including the four children in her household, and be content to have them adopted.

He went on talking to her persuasively. He would give money to the innkeeper and his wife and ensure that the little Barleys were well fed and looked after. She could send them gifts. But not, Stephen threatened, unless she would behave as he wanted now. His patience was almost at an end.

Destiny at last was forced to face up to the inevitability of leaving the children behind her. She could not let them starve in this icy house any longer; that she had to admit. Matt was coughing dreadfully and Lucy was not well. She knew and liked the couple who kept the inn. Mr. Jupp was a stout, jovial man and Mrs. Jupp equally kind and eminently respectable. There was always plenty of warmth and food at the inn and the Jupps had children of their own. Two giggling girls. Certainly it would not be an unattractive home. Many a time in the past Destiny had envied the young Jupps their doting parents and congenial life as compared to the wretched existence they all led in the Parsonage.

She could see that nothing she could say would change Mr. Godwin's mind. Finally she surrendered.

"Very well. I will take the children to the inn, and if Mr. and Mrs. Jupp will care for them, I will leave them there for the present. They must not stay here another night . . . in this bitter weather. . . ." her voice broke.

She put her arms out, calling the children to her, and they ran to her and began to wail again, forgetting their magnificent dinner, howling when they were told they must be parted from their dearest Dessie.

By the time Stephen had finished, he felt a criminal for not permitting Destiny to take the young Barleys with her. He could not bear all this weeping but he thought it best for her ladyship's sake that she should begin her new life unhampered by this little crowd of dependents.

Half an hour later the deed was done. The Jupps appeared a little put out at the idea of making such a large addition to their existing family but the sight of the gold pieces in the leather purse extended by Mr. Godwin appeased them; especially as they were promised more. The Jupps were also deeply impressed when told of the extraordinary fortune of the young girl.

"Oh, just imagine . . . your *ladyship*!" said Mrs. Jupp,

panting and dropping a curtsy to Destiny. "I congratulate you, my lady, I am sure."

Destiny found this both amazing and embarrassing, and protested when two of the maidservants in the inn followed suit and curtsied and tried to kiss her hand. She had eyes and ears only for her little ones who were standing with linked hands, watching her and crying. At length Stephen besought her to follow him out to the coach. She muttered:

"God bless you all, my little darlings. I will come back to fetch you soon. . . ."

Then she preceded Stephen through the door, out into the snow.

The wind was icy and the snow blinding. The beautiful horses drawing the Britzska coach stamped and snorted, anxious to be off.

Like one in a fevered dream, Destiny stepped into the padded interior of the coach and sank back in a corner. She was shivering violently despite the warmth of her woollen cape—another of the late Mrs. Barley's garments. Her mind was confused and her heart full of grief as Stephen seated himself opposite her and they moved away from the inn. Away to what? Destiny knew not. A life of riches, of luxury, such as she had never dreamed of, perhaps. But it was also the unknown. All that was familiar to her—those four poor little children whom she had so long protected and loved—she left reluctantly behind her.

6

WHEN DAYLIGHT BEGAN to fail, Stephen, staring under frowning brows out of the coach window, realized that he had been a trifle optimistic in presuming that they would reach Devizes before dark.

Turning, he glanced at the girl. She had slumped in the corner with her head against a cushion and was asleep. For a time she had sat opposite him silently weeping, greatly disturbing Stephen who at heart was a gentle and kindly man. He had induced her to drink some more wine. The unaccustomed liquor, a warming pan at her feet, and the jolting of the coach as the four splendid horses raced against time, had lulled her into oblivion.

Once when Stephen noted that the worsted cape had fallen away from her, he picked it up and wrapped it around her, and noted with some dismay how thin she was and how deadly pale. The thong tying her hair had broken loose from the long locks which fell in a heavy dark cloud down to her slender waist. Beauty was there, he thought, but hidden and repressed like the girl's own nature. She had had a shocking start to her life.

He had counted on staying tonight at Devizes. He would have been certain of good accommodation in the town. It had assumed some importance lately for business flourished there. In the factories the finest cloths today were being fabricated, and all round Devizes were tributary villages and hamlets where women and children busied themselves with spinning.

Stephen had meant to stay the night at the famous White Hart Inn. But they seemed nowhere near the outskirts of the town. He could see nothing now save hills and pasture land. Once he caught a glimpse of the River Avon winding through the valley. He heard the postilions cracking their whips and urging the animals on. But it was tough going. Even the well-made Britzska swayed and rocked and the snow had not ceased to fall since they left Bath.

Travelling in these days was no pleasure, Stephen thought with a sigh. He was thankful that his men were fully armed against the possible attack of highwaymen in such lonely country.

It would not do to be caught here in a snow-drift. Heavens, what a night!

He opened one of the doors and ordered a halt. Thomas, the head coachman, got off the box, came down and thrust in a red face wet with snow which he wiped away.

"Yes, sir?"

"Have you any idea how far off we are from the town?"

"Abel, who knows this road, sir, says it be too far to reach before total darkness, sir."

Stephen muttered under his breath. The girl in her sleep of exhaustion hardly moved or felt the icy draught which howled into the interior of the coach.

"Then do not risk attempting to reach Devizes," he said. "If you see a farm or cottage with light for beacon, pray stop."

"Yes, sir," said the man and disappeared, slamming the door. The coach rocked on. Stephen's attention was now concentrated on the stormy scene outside. One of the horses stumbled and fell on an icy patch. It took some time to get the animal up again and disentangle it from the traces. Stephen cursed softly under his breath, reproaching himself for this turn of events.

About ten minutes later, the coach jerked to a standstill. The men's voices were shouting above the wind and woke Destiny up.

She felt stiff and cold. Her lashes blinked. She sat up:

"Mercy on us, where am I?" she cried in a daze.

"We can drive no further," said Stephen abruptly. "Can you wrap yourself up, my lady, and step out into the night with me."

"Where are we?"

"Some distance from the town of Devizes."

She did not really know where that was. Most of her life had been spent in the parsonage. Now she looked out curiously and saw lights in the darkness; coachmen running with flambeaux which made the snow look pink, and shone through the whirling snowflakes. It was very cold. She refused Stephen's helping hand and sprang lightly, unaided, into the snow, thankful that she wore her strong, peasant's boots.

A few moments later she found herself in the kitchen of a small farmhouse which was built of stone, mean and ill-furnished. The farmer and his wife were a young couple—peasants of coarse mien. There was an infant sleeping in a wooden cradle by the fire and a mangy, ferocious-looking dog chained close beside it. The animal raised his shaggy head and growled as the strangers entered. The farmer, looking at Stephen's richly-clad figure, appeared impressed and a little scared. His wife stared at them and kept bowing and bobbing.

"We have little to offer, your highness," the farmer began in a flustered way. "We are only poor people. The sheep 'ave done bad this year. We 'ave lost many in the snow-drifts. My horse is sick. We 'ave only half a ham hanging and some bread and milk and—"

"Never mind, never mind," broke in Stephen impatiently. "You shall be compensated. What bedrooms have you?"

"Two, your highness."

"Stop calling me by that silly name. I am Mr. Godwin."

"We are honoured by your visit, my lord, sir, Mr. Godwin and my lady," stammered the farmer's wife, looking with passionate inquisitiveness at Destiny.

"Stop *bobbing,* woman!" exclaimed Stephen, who was feeling in none too good a temper.

Now Destiny turned on him.

"You frighten her. She is trying to please you."

Stephen stared at her, then began to chuckle. The determined spirit again—even now when she was in strangers' hands and away from her natural surroundings. It was easy to see that Destiny was accustomed to speak in defence of those whom she thought to be in need of it. He liked her for that. He addressed the farmer's wife more mildly:

"What beds have you, my good woman?"

"Two, sir, one which I share with my man and one in the other chamber," she said, "where my poor mother slept but she is dead this twelve month," and continued her curtsying.

The farm was isolated, summer or winter. This pair seldom saw visitors.

"Only two beds!" exclaimed Stephen, dismayed. "I have four men to accommodate."

"The stables are warm," put in the farmer, "and there is fresh hay. They can shelter there."

"And you and your wife, sir, can have our best tester bed," added the woman.

Stephen coloured. He glanced at Destiny and saw that she, too, had turned bright pink and was staring sullenly away from him.

"This is my Lady Destiny Frane, and she is not my wife," he said tartly.

The farmer and his wife glanced at each other. Stephen added quickly:

"I will sleep down here in a chair. Put my lady upstairs."

"You take the bed. I am used to hardship—" began Destiny.

"The bed is for you, my lady." broke in Stephen, with cold formality.

She stared at him. Her eyelids felt weighted. Her heart was sore and her mind full of the memory of the little ones.

She felt resentment against Stephen for forcing her to leave them. She was in no way impressed because he treated her as a fine lady. She was not particularly interested in her change of fortune. Because it was her nature to do so, she offered to help the farmer's wife who looked at her in horror and said that my lady must not move from her chair nor soil her hands. The girl therefore seated herself by the fire, braiding her long dark hair into two plaits and warming her fine, reddened fingers at the blaze. Stephen went out to see that his men were properly bedded down for the night and the horses watered and fed. After he had gone, the farmer's wife gave Destiny a sly look and said:

"What a fine handsome young man he is, my lady. Are you to be wed?"

"Certainly not," said Destiny indignantly.

The farmer being out of the kitchen, his wife dared to giggle and made a coarse reference to the joys of the marriage bed, and how wise my lady would be to indulge in them this very night, rather than sleep alone in the cold.

She was astonished when Destiny sprang to her feet, faced her with blazing eyes and bade her hold her tongue.

The woman saw that she had been indiscreet, apologized with abject servility and muttered that she had meant no harm.

But now this thought had been put in Destiny's mind, she kept remembering Mr. Barley's attack on her and wondered if all gentlemen were alike, she sat trembling and nervous for the rest of the evening, never once looking Stephen in the eyes. He did not know what ailed her but supposed that she was fretting for the children.

Finally, after a repast of thin onion soup, some of the ham and the last bottle of wine from the hamper that Stephen had brought with him, it was time to retire.

Stephen bowed to Destiny.

"Good night, my lady, and I trust you sleep well."

She looked at him, he thought, with hatred, and hastened out of the room.

Left alone, Stephen stretched his legs in front of the dying fire. Despite the discomfort of the chair, he nodded to sleep for he was singularly tired after the events of the day and the long hours of travel.

In the room up above, without undressing, without even washing—for no water, soap or towel were offered her—Destiny lay on a hard wooden bedstead and tried to sleep. But she lay awake long—listening to the howl of the wind and the spatter of the sleet which was now beating against the farmhouse windows. She was bitterly cold and miserably lonely. All her life she had slept with one or more of the children. She disliked the darkness and it became obvious to her that there were fleas in the bed which made her twist and turn and scratch. Finally, when she heard a scuffle and squeak, she thought she saw in a corner two bright eyes. A *rat*. That was the end for Destiny. She uttered a shriek and ran out on to the landing. The farmer and his wife, in a dead sleep, did not hear her, but Stephen was on his feet at once, and with a lighted candle stood at the foot of the wooden staircase and watched the young girl rush down. She looked thoroughly scared. Her hair was now loosened and in a dark mass tumbled over her shoulders. Her eyes were enormous.

"My lady—what ails you?"

She stumbled towards him, and for all her courage and independence, sobs began to choke her now. It was a tired, frightened child who joined Stephen in that kitchen.

"There were rats in my room, and . . . and fleas," she whimpered.

He smiled. He had loosened his collar and removed his wig. His brown hair was tousled. He looked less formal and more homely, so Destiny thought. Much as she resented him, she wanted his company, and the warmth of the kitchen. The dog had followed its owners up the rickety staircase. Destiny sat in the rocking-chair. She shivered violently.

"Let me stay down here with you, Mr. Godwin. . . ." she stammered.

"Of course, or I will go up and take your bed with the rats and the fleas if you wish," said Stephen, still smiling. She seemed such a *little* girl tonight and so defenceless and sad, of a sudden. He could hardly believe that she was Lady Destiny Frane. For the first time since their somewhat unfortunate meeting, he felt a kind of tenderness towards her.

"No—I will stay down here with you. We will talk together if you wish," he said.

She nodded and unclasped her hands. He went on:

"Would you not like to hear more about your father, my Lady Destiny?"

Now the tears dried on her cheeks and she looked up at him, her face wistful in the candlelight.

"How strange that title sounds!"

"Nevertheless it is yours."

"It has all happened so—so suddenly. I cannot believe it."

"You will believe it when you see your father's house."

"When shall we reach there?"

"If the weather gets no worse, the day after tomorrow. I aim to reach Reading by tomorrow night. And then Windsor. Richmondwyke is another twenty miles further."

"Why, after all these years am I to become what you say I am—the daughter and heiress of an Earl? What does it mean?"

He explained as far as he could, whitewashing his dead master's misdeeds in order to make the young girl think with respect of him. He ended:

"The sins of hot youth must be understood and forgiven, my lady. On his death-bed, the Earl had but one wish—to give you the name and estates to which you are entitled."

She nodded. She began to feel even a faint yearning for her father ... a sorrow that he had not lived long enough for her to know him.

"And my stepmother—does she truly want me? Is she kind?"

Stephen scowled and regarded the tip of his toes. He felt uncomfortable at the memory of the red-headed witch who awaited them.

"Lady Destermere is all agog to receive you and help you to fill the important position which you now hold," at length he said.

"What is she like?"

Stephen felt still more uncomfortable and mumbled that Destiny must wait and see. Now she was wide awake and filled with curiosity which brought a deluge of questions from her—all of which Stephen attempted to answer.

He soon realized that she knew absolutely nothing about life outside this miserable parsonage. She knew that Queen Anne sat upon the throne of England. She had seen the rich pass by in their coaches. She had taught herself a little from the limited library at her disposal. She knew something of the writers Addison, Steele and Swift. But of Court life she was woefully ignorant. Stephen found himself spending the small hours until the dawn broke giving her some insight into the life she would lead at Richmondwyke and English society.

Now Destiny listened with absorption, her hands clasped about her knees while Stephen described London, the fine ladies of high rank and their beaux. She heard for the first time of the entertainments at White's Chocolate House in London—and the Coffee House in St. James's. Stephen said that he would leave Lady Destermere to describe more fully the whirl of existence which Destiny must eventually lead when they went to London—dashing around in her carriage with her laced and powdered footmen, making her social visits. How she would hold her levées and drive on a Sunday in the Park. How in the evenings there was usually music and card-playing and even jaunts into the City for intimate little suppers at India House. She would have more beautiful clothes than she could ever wear. She would give dances and attend State Balls.

She broke in:

"But why—why must I spend so much money when there are all the starving people who need it?"

Stephen's grey eyes regarded the girl thoughtfully.

"That is a question which I cannot answer," he said, "even though I may agree with your outlook."

"I do not think I want to be rich."

"Neither can you wish to be poor, surely? What of the rats and the fleas?" he smiled.

"Can there not be some agreeable medium? Something for everybody?"

He stared at her again. What a quaint child. He could not but admire her. Hers was a humane, social outlook which he rarely if ever encountered in the world today.

Destiny sat brooding over the thought of the rich idle life which Stephen was trying to prepare her for. For her, the monotony of life in the parsonage had been enlivened only on occasions by a village fair. Pedlars' stalls, drinking booths, the sports of rough peasants which she had disliked. Once she had seen a man in the stocks, and once a miserable wretch being stoned on his way to the gallows. She had shrunk from such heartless cruelty. But luxury—gaiety and wealth as described by Stephen—were quite unknown to her.

"I do not feel capable of occupying such a position," she muttered.

"Naturally not at the moment. But you will soon acquire the necessary attributes that a great lady must have."

"Great lady, *me*!" Destiny gave a queer, hoarse little laugh, cupped her white young face between her hands and stared broodingly at the young man. After a moment she said:

"Will *you* have much to say in my future?"

"Your father appointed me joint guardian with your—your stepmother and the bankers," he said uneasily.

She made no answer to this but yawned and shook her head as thought stupefied.

Stephen rose.

"You are still sleepy, and in need of rest, my lady. Let me take you nearer to the fire—or what is left of it, and find a cushion for your back."

At once she shrank back from him. He read a fury and dread in her brilliant eyes which he could not understand. He took it for granted that she found him personally offensive. He drew back, annoyed.

"Very well. Pray stay where you are and do not let me inconvenience you," he said icily.

She did not answer but leaned her head back and shut her eyes. Later he glanced at her and presumed that she slept. He was not a little surprised and dismayed to see that tears were forcing themselves from under her lids and rolling down her sunken cheeks.

He had come here to find Destermere's daughter eagerly and with friendship in his heart and with the wish to serve her. He felt that he had failed. Obviously she neither trusted nor liked him. What would happen to her when she came under the domination of Destermere's widow? He felt apprehensive of the future.

A little later he dozed. He imagined that my lady had followed suit for there was silence except for the sound of her gentle, regular breathing.

Then she gave a shriek that brought him to his feet wide awake again, rubbing his eyes.

"Heavens! What ails you, my lady?"

Destiny was cowering in her rocking-chair, feet tucked under her and holding her gown away from the floor. It was daylight. The kitchen was full of that pallid blue luminosity of a winter's dawn. The fire was out and it was deathly cold. Overhead, boards were creaking. The farmer and his wife were awake. Stephen stared at Destiny.

"What is it?"

"I saw a rat," she faltered.

He relaxed and laughed.

"It is time that mangy cur came down again to protect you from the vermin, but of a truth, I regret that I ever had to bring you to this dwelling. The weather must be blamed and not my plan." The colour stole back into her face. She put her feet to the ground, but as she stood up, so numb was she with cold that she tottered. She was caught and steadied by the grave young man who had designated himself her guardian. She could feel the warmth of his hands against her icy fingers which he started in friendly way to chafe.

"Poor little thing, you are like a frozen bird," he muttered.

For an instant she half lay against him. She seemed to have no strength, no circulation. Timorously she looked up at his face. It was pale and with a stubble of beard showing in the pallid morning light; an aesthetic repressed young face, yet with considerable strength about lips and eyes. But she could not easily read his character, nor had the long hours journeying with him lightened her load of sorrow at being torn from her young charges. His stories of her new grandeur had not weaned her to accept her change of fortune happily. And suddenly the old terror of man seized her. Her eyes blazed. With some surprise, he decided they were like a panther's, with those golden flecks and unusually large black pupils. She struggled frantically to get away from him.

"Let me go!" she hissed between her teeth.

Utterly without comprehending, he did so. She staggered back to her chair, hid her face in her hands and began to cry.

Upon my soul, thought Stephen, I do not understand this strange, stormy, young creature. She has a violent side which alarms me.

But he was beginning to see that she was not only a

child in grotesque garments, unkempt, half-civilized. He had felt the female softness and grace of her when she first collapsed into his arms. Her bones had seemed small, even fragile. Yet she was strong and there was nothing of deliberate feminine seduction in her. But it was as though for one instant he had glimpsed a fire burning behind the screen—the fascination of her budding womanhood in the long lovely line of her throat and small curving breasts.

Ye gods, he thought, *what has my Lord Destermere bequeathed to my care in the form of this little savage? What will become of her?*

And immediately following that question, he wondered what battle royal would be joined within the next few days between this girl and the red-haired Countess. With all his soul, Stephen wished that any woman save Mahla were waiting at Destermere House to receive my Lady Destiny.

7

LYING AGAINST HER PILLOWS in a large four-poster bed in one of the big bedrooms at Destermere House, the widow of the late Earl sat reading a letter. It had just been brought to her by a small be-turbaned negro footboy named Ramilles, whom Lady Destermere had recently imported, a chubby dwarf with enormous popping eyes like a pug dog's. He fawned upon her and she spoiled him and found him amusing. But he was despised by the other men servants who had long been in the service of the Destermeres.

Ramilles was allowed to hold the candelabra while his mistress bathed, which was once a week; and to follow her around when she walked through the house or gardens—bearing on a velvet cushion a tiny Maltese terrier whom Mahla alternately kicked or caressed, much in the same way that she behaved to the little blackamoor himself.

She had just finished drinking her morning chocolate. Her personal maid was busy picking up the extraordinary confusion of clothes which had been left scattered all over the room by my lady. Silk petticoats, a pair of cherry-coloured stays, a duff-coloured gown of flowered damask, muslin headcloths, fringed gloves, feathers. My lady was crazy about clothes. She spent as much as she dared on them, well aware that her late husband's bankers and notaries were in the background to curb any mad extravagances.

For her, Countess of Destermere, *an allowance*. For the Lady Destiny Frane, anything that she wanted. Each time she dwelt on this thought, Mahla chewed her lips with fury.

She had already heard that name, "Lady Destiny," far too often. It was on everybody's lips. All London society knew now about this mysterious daughter who had arisen from an unknown past and was to take her place as Claud Destermere's daughter. Everybody knew that it was for Destiny that the doors of the great house would be opened in a few months' time when one of the biggest balls of the season was to be held to introduce the young heiress.

It was not an agreeable outlook for Lady Destermere. She could only be thankful that her late husband had expressed the wish that there should be no period of mourning for him. So, once his body was laid to rest, she could shed her black veils and her social life could proceed. After the years of enforced boredom and lack of amusement in Geneva, Mahla sought after what entertainment there was available in London and Richmondwyke during the month of March.

Already, the Duchess of Ancaster whose estates adjoined those of Destermere House, had called on Mahla and suggested that when she, the Duchess, took her own daughters to the Court of Queen Anne, the young Lady Destiny should join them.

Mahla had agreed. She was being careful to make herself affable in the district and to assume the dowager's mantle for the time being. But only for a time, she thought viciously as she finished reading her letter. Humbert would help her quickly to put an end to the farce. The Duchess spoke of Destiny's chances with the various eligible young men in London, mentioning the young Earl of this, and the Duke of that . . . but in Mahla's estimation there would be only one possible husband for Destiny. The Baron Faramund himself.

This letter, written by the Baron from the rooms which at the moment he was occupying in St. James's, did much to comfort Mahla, who had been in a bored and fractious state of mind ever since Stephen Godwin left for Bath. It was not only that Stephen had gone to fetch Lady Destiny Frane to her home but that he persisted in his refusal to become her consolation.

"He spurns my advances and spies on me but I am so heavily in debt that I dare not rouse too much antagonism either from him or Claud's bankers,"

so she had recently written to Humbert—

"but I hope you will come back to live here with us soon, for without you the place is like a morgue."

In reply, Humbert answered:

"Be just a little patient, my dearest Mahla, and I will be with you. You can safely leave both your stepdaughter and Herr Godwin to me. Meanwhile our schemes are materializing. The physicians have

*paid attention to my health and looks. I am sacri-
ficing the pleasures of eating and imbibing and
have become more youthful of figure; without my
paunch. I have ordered some handsome new garments. The latest thing in London, as worn by Sir
Roger de Coverley, are pearl-coloured stockings
with red shoes. Dressed and pomaded, I should be
able to dazzle the eyes of even a young maiden.
Meanwhile my agents have found me a charming
retreat less than a mile from Destermere House. It
was built by a certain French gentleman for his
maîtresse and is entirely panelled in satin with
gilded ceilings and the dainty furniture beloved by
Louis XIV. The maîtresse, incidentally, drowned
herself in the lake after a quarrel with her seigneur
but that for me does not detract from the delights
of the spot, and it should make an idyllic nest to
help lure the little bird we are hoping to trap. I
dared not get in touch with you when I first drove
from London to see the place which incidentally
bears the name of Little Lake House. It is built on
Great Lake estate belonging to your neighbour, the
Duke of Ancaster. It has been shut and tenantless
since the suicide.*

*"I shall send my most trusted servants down to
open it up and I will of course be calling myself by
another name (as we have agreed). I shall live as a
recluse. The district will see nothing of me. I shall
make myself a charming host to your stepdaughter—or should I say your future sister-in-law?
Upon which humorous note I take my farewell of
you . . . liebling Mahla."*

The note of humour was indeed struck and reduced
Mahla to laughter. That he should have rented Little
Lake House was a surprise and excitement. She knew
about the tragedy that had taken place there. Everybody did. Villagers shunned the lake. But, thought

Mahla, the small, elegant house would be an ideal hideout for her brother.

And what a deliciously bold yet excellent scheme. Humbert had hit upon it when the two last met in London to discuss his approach to Destiny. It was obvious to them both that she would never begin to regard a "step-uncle" in the light of a possible suitor. The true facts of the relationship must only be disclosed to her *after* she had married Humbert. In particular, Stephen must not know that Humbert was in pursuit. So Mahla's brother must cease to be the Baron Faramund and become a Russian Prince. Yes, as *Prince Alexis Malinkoff* he would be introduced to the girl. He would not be invited to Destermere House nor cross Stephen's path. Humbert and Mahla had already decided on the story they would tell Destiny. The Prince was "delicate" and unable to bear the rigours of the Russian climate. He had had an English mother. He could speak perfect English and had often travelled in Europe when the late lamented Princess was alive. He had come to live quietly in the delicious little country house with all its Parisian elegance, in a true English setting, until his full health returned.

Humbert played and sang divinely. As "Prince Alexis" he would play the spinet to the young girl, and woo her in the most romantic fashion. Old for her he might be, but he could still be fascinating when he wished, and to aid and abet this scheme he had given up his excessive eating and drinking in order to regain his figure.

It was all going to be very amusing, Mahla decided, and it would make up for the boredom of the life which she had to lead. She rose from her bed, tore her brother's letter into shreds and felt in a somewhat better temper, although she was annoyed because she dare not try out her new yellow satin in order to attract Stephen. She must still wear sober attire, fitting for a matron recently widowed, even if not complete mourning. So she chose a maroon silk damask, with a fur-trimmed mantua over it. Despite all the fires in the great house, Mahla always felt the cold and grumbled excessively at it.

She descended the stairs soon after midday, having given orders to the servants to be on the outlook for Mr. Godwin's coach and to line up in the hall when they arrived to receive her young ladyship.

There was much activity in the great kitchen at the east end of the house. Enormous joints, capons and ducklings were already on the spit.

Mahla had brought with her a French chef of the name of Renoir, who had cooked for his lordship in Geneva. A splendid cook but an ill-tempered man. He and Ramilles and Lucette, the Swiss maid whom Mahla had also imported from Geneva, were very unpopular with the regular staff.

There was the stout, active and efficient Mrs. Perkins who had been housekeeper here when Claud was a boy. Mahla was well aware that Mrs. Perkins disliked the "foreign invaders," as she called Mahla's servants. Neither had Mrs. Perkins a great respect for my lord's widow. But she was looking forward to the arrival of his lordship's own daughter.

Mahla would have liked to dispense with Mrs. Perkins's services, but when she had mentioned this to Stephen he had suggested that it would be against her own interests to dismiss the woman. Everybody in the district knew Mrs. Perkins and respected her. Certainly Mahla had to admit the woman managed the domestic staff most efficiently; so Mrs. Perkins remained.

Any woman but Mahla, whose taste lay in the bizarre and showy things of life, might have found Destermere House to her liking. On an equal with Ancaster Great Hall, the Destermere House was one of the most noble buildings in the county. It had been constructed in the reign of Henry VIII and had the appearance of a miniature castle, with two towers at each end and a charming court completely hidden from the outside world by massive stone walls. The house was built of those charming rosy Flemish bricks, with stone dressings and window frames, and long narrow windows—diamond-paned. The grounds consisted of forty acres of magnificent woodland, green pastures, and formal gardens fringed with yew hedge leading down to the river's edge.

The interior of the house was as magnificent as the outer structure. The chestnut avenue that led to the house was long and wide and of uncommon beauty.

But in spite of these marvels, Mahla found the place utterly boring. So long unlived in by the late Earl, it was inclined to be damp and dreary unless thousands of candles were set to burn in their sconces, and great logs heaped continually on the fires.

In summer it was pleasant to wander through the herb gardens or pick the roses, or sit in a pavilion by the water and watch the little craft go down the shining river between delicate alders and weeping willows. But in winter, when the grounds were buried under the snow and the winds howled through the great corridors of the house and draughts lifted the tapestries and the rugs, Mahla hated it. She hated it now even in this bright March weather.

She avoided the big dining-hall with the minstrel's gallery and the huge banqueting rooms full of shining oak, magnificent Dutch and Flemish paintings, and lavish display of silver and china ornaments; she kept as much as possible to her own boudoir where it was warm and exotically furnished.

She hated the fact that as Countess of Destermere she had many dull domestic duties to perform.

But it would not be for long, Mahla kept telling herself. No—not long once dear Humbert got to work.

Her present consolation lay in the flagrant fancy which she had taken to a new young groom whom she had noticed in the stables when she was mounted yesterday. An excessively handsome boy of nineteen, with the face of a Greek god, and red curls to match her own. Why not match them, she had asked herself lasciviously when he stood there holding her mare and she had read the undisguised admiration in his eyes? For she knew she cut a dashing picture in her chestnut-brown riding habit, with a tall beaver hat and floating veil on her head.

"Your servant, my lady," he had muttered, looking up at her with those adoring eyes which were a sop to her immense vanity, since Stephen Godwin's eyes continued to rest so coldly upon her.

For an hour or two, she reflected, the groom might be more than a servant to her—she might allow him to share her supper at midnight, when the rest of the house was abed. So she had touched his shoulder lightly with her crop, and ridden out of the courtyard smiling to herself.

She did not even know this boy's name, but asking the head stableman casually at a later hour, discovered that it was William. Common-place enough. But the youngster was of uncommon beauty. Mahla cast a thought in the said William's direction on this cold March morning.

She bade Ramilles set the little dog, whom she called Cou-Cou, down and go fetch some sweetmeats to feed him with. She must do something to pass the time until Mr. Addison, a London dressmaker, who was bringing some new gowns to show her, arrived.

Stephen should have been here yesterday, she thought crossly. No doubt the coach from Bath was held up because of this atrocious snow.

Now Mrs. Perkins, a plump little woman, respectably clad in black with muslin cap and voluminous apron, half walked, half ran towards her ladyship. She bobbed excitedly.

"My lady, *she is coming*!"

Lady Destermere stood up, her cheeks mantling.

"You mean—"

"Yes, it is my Lady Destiny . . . my dear master's own daughter," exclaimed the good woman, all of a quiver. "I will ring the bells, my lady, and have the servants gather together."

Mahla fixed an unfriendly gaze upon the old house-keeper.

"Tush, there is no need for too great an exhibition. It is not the Queen herself who arrives," she snapped.

"It is his late lordship's very own daughter!" repeated Mrs. Perkins stubbornly, and with a toss of her head, departed.

Mahla moved forward to the window and peered out, frowning.

She saw the Britzska drawn by the four finest horses from her late husband's stables come sweeping around the drive. They were pulled up in the courtyard with a flourish and a shouting.

First from the coach there emerged the familiar figure of Stephen. The sight of the slenderly-built boyish secretary made Mahla clench her long fingers. He had for so long been a challenge to her. And now what of the girl who—so unjustly in Mahla's opinion—had come to inherit Destermere House?

Humbert's future wife!

It was in that guise that Mahla looked on the girl who was being helped from the coach. At first she felt like laughing. She stared with scorn and astonishment at the ill-dressed child; at her flapping cape, her mean boots. What in heaven's name was this freak, my lady wondered? Where had Stephen found her? From what kind of home had she been torn?

Stephen advanced and formally introduced his young companion.

"The Lady Destiny Frane . . . the Countess of Destermere."

"Welcome to your house," said Mahla slowly, and with a honeyed sweetness which certainly did not deceive the young secretary who knew the widow far too well.

But to Destiny it seemed a pleasant enough welcome. She raised her eyes and looked up into a delicately-tinted face which she thought very handsome. The magnificence of Mahla's attire, of the huge pearls she wore, and the glittering rings on her fingers, over-awed the young girl, as did the breathtaking grandeur of this house. *Her* house, they called it.

"I bid you good-day, madam," Destiny faltered under her breath, and curtsied. But immediately Mahla took her hand, raised her and said:

"You must not curtsy to me, dear child. And you must call me 'Mahla', since we are neither of us of an age to allow a relationship of stepmother and daughter. But I am your late father's wife and shall be your true friend—shall I not, Mr. Godwin?" She turned and smiled at the secretary.

Stephen muttered, "Yes," and stood there scowling. He had not enjoyed the journey with Destiny. Now that they were back in Richmondwyke, he half-regretted not engaging some woman to buy more suitable clothes for the wretched young girl. He could see the look of sorrow on the face of Mrs. Perkins and the other servants as they saw Destiny. Maids, footmen, cooks, scullions— all lined up to welcome their young mistress.

Poor child, he thought. She looked utterly bewildered.

But he, too, added a greeting of genuine kindliness.

"Welcome to Destermere House, my Lady Destiny."

Now at close quarters, Mahla gazed with intense interest at her stepdaughter. Do away with those scarecrow clothes and deck the child out in fashionable finery and she would be quite an engaging morsel for Humbert. Mahla's quick feminine gaze noted every detail of the girl's flawless skin and enormous tawny eyes. And what night-black hair! Oh yes, she bore a strong resemblance to Claud, thought Mahla, and she had something more than he had ever possessed; a subtle quality, a smouldering fire *somewhere*.

The Countess took the girl's hands, drew her rapidly along the line of staring, inquisitive servants, then announced that she would take her upstairs to rest before the meal which was to be served at three o'clock. She bid Mrs. Perkins order two of the maids to carry up a tub of steaming water. Wrinkling her nose with disgust, Mahla had soon decided that the young girl was shockingly in need of soap and water, and must also have her hair well-washed.

The members of the staff dispersed, whispering and chattering. Mrs. Perkins remained with the secretary who had tossed his coat and hat to one of the men and was standing in front of the fire now, trying to smother his yawns. He felt as though he had not slept for days.

"Oh, sir," ventured Mrs. Perkins with a curtsy, "the pretty dear is the spit of his lordship—in truth she is!"

"She doth resemble him," nodded Stephen.

"You look a-weary, sir," went on the housekeeper, who, like all the servants, had a soft spot for their late master's gentle and loyal secretary.

He smiled, and told her that it was a weariness that would soon be dispelled by a couple of hours' rest.

"If you will forgive me asking, sir, it has been a-worrying me, sir, but who is to give the orders in the house now—her young ladyship, who is the heiress, or my lady the Countess, sir?"

Stephen frowned. He passed a hand over his forehead. He longed to divest himself of clothes and wig and be rid of the vermin which he was sure he had acquired in that dreadful farmhouse two nights ago. He said:

"We shall see how things proceed, Mrs. Perkins. It is a delicate situation. For the moment, Lady Destiny, having had little tuition, is not fitted for her position; you understand? She has been brought up in an impoverished parsonage. The Countess will therefore continue to run the establishment."

Mrs. Perkins looked disappointed. Stephen knew well that Mahla did not command much respect in her late husband's English domicile. His lips twitched at the memory of the look she had given him just now as she led Destiny away. Confound it, the woman had no decency. Claud Destermere was barely cold in his grave before she had started her amorous campaign against him, Stephen, again. He wondered what she was up to now—uneasy rather than pleased by the honeyed sweetness which she was showing the unfortunate young girl. At least he must be glad that that terrible brother of hers, the Baron Faramund, had faded out of the picture and was not here to influence Mahla to perform greater evils. For Humbert, in Stephen's opinion, was not only an evil man, but dangerous.

8

LATER THAT DAY—when the early darkness had fallen and thick curtains shut out the cold blue dusk of that winter's afternoon, Lady Destiny Frane came downstairs.

She had not appeared at the banquet that was prepared for her welcome. The rich meal had been served to the Countess and Mr. Godwin in the big dining-hall which was panelled in cedar wood and hung with gilt-framed paintings of the horses which had occupied much of the time and attention of Destiny's grandfather; the old Earl. He had, in fact, died of a hunting accident.

With a slightly amused smile curving her red lips,

Mahla informed Stephen that "the poor child was worn out, and after her ablutions had been put to bed and was not yet awake nor likely to be for some time. She was in a dead sleep."

"It is as well to let her rest," Stephen agreed.

Through her lashes Mahla looked at the secretary and said, still smiling:

"You have brought home a savage. What sort of people were these two who adopted Claud's child?"

"She is unfortunate. She grew up in a mean family," muttered Stephen. "But she has plenty of intelligence."

"Oh, yes," nodded Lady Destermere, "*and* spirit. She will not be too easy to handle. There will be plenty for me to do before I can launch her into society, my dear Stephen."

"She will soon learn."

"She is not without attraction," murmured her ladyship.

Stephen rose from the table and moved towards the door.

"I am not, as you know, partial to feminine charms," he said. "To me, Lady Destiny is still a child and the daughter of my late master to whom I swore loyalty and for whose sake I will do my best."

"Always so conscientious, dear Stephen," Mahla murmured. "Well—we must work together in this effort to teach Lady Destiny Frane some culture and poise and how to play her part in society. The sooner we find her a husband the better. No gentleman will seek her hand until she is educated."

"We must have a care, as to what type of gentleman we present to Lady Destiny," said Stephen, frowning. "It must be remembered that control of the vast fortune and the great houses she will inherit will be given into the hands of this man. So when she marries, it must be well, and one who can be trusted to care for her and guide her wisely."

Mahla sat silent, turning and turning her rings around

her long fingers. Suddenly she raised her eyes to Stephen. A low laugh escaped her.

"How solemnly you speak of this young girl's future, Mr. Secretary."

"I gave a solemn undertaking to her father, madam."

She thought of Humbert, so soon to establish himself in the little French house on the Ancasters' estate. She laughed again. Uneasily Stephen glanced at the Countess, then excused himself from her presence, saying that he had many papers to go through and was still engaged in making a catalogue of the late Lord Destermere's library, which had long wanted doing.

That same evening, when the servants lit all the candles and the house was glowing softly and the fires stoked up, Stephen came out of the library and saw Destiny coming down the stairs.

She walked alone, one hand on the balustrade and the other holding up a fold of her skirt showing the tip of a satin-clad shoe.

For a moment Stephen stared at the young, beautifully-gowned girl, without recognition. It was only on second glance that he realized that it was the miserable child he had driven from Bath to the house of her inheritance.

Great heavens! he thought. The change in her was fantastic enough to make any man draw breath. It was amazing what finery, and the expert hands of Lady Destermere's Swiss maid, had achieved.

Destiny wore what was obviously a gown borrowed from her stepmother. It was a little long for her and a little full, but the maid's clever hands had arranged it so that it fitted the young girl quite well. The petticoat—the latest fashion—was of heavy, ruby-coloured satin, drawn in at the tiny waist. Over it there was an open mantle of silver lace, fold upon fold of the glittering, transparent material. The neck was low, in the mode of the times, showing the white girlish shoulders, outlined by a trimming of lace. The black hair had been washed, perfumed and brushed until it shone with the satin of a raven's wing, and was piled high, then brought down into glossy curls on one side of her neck. As she approached Stephen, he saw that pink powder had been dusted on her high cheek bones, giving her a little colour. Her eyes were wonderful. He bowed.

"Good evening, my lady. I scarce recognize you," he said with a faint boyish smile which made him look winning and much less severe than the man with whom she had travelled.

"I . . . I do not feel myself in *this*. . . ." she said with an awkward laugh, and plucked at the satin of her dress. She went on to tell him that her dressing had taken nearly three hours and that she had been scrubbed until she begged for mercy, then submitted to lacing, and fussing and a-pulling at her hair.

"If this is what I must do each day, I will die of boredom!" she declared.

Now Stephen laughed outright.

"You will grow used to it, my lady, and the result is, if I may say so, most gratifying."

She had reached the foot of the stairs now. Turning, she looked up at all the tall portraits in their huge frames which were hung on the panelled walls and along the gallery.

"Are these all my relatives, Mr. Godwin, sir?"

"They are, my lady. All the Destermere family, of which you are the last."

She drew a long breath.

"I am living in a fantasy."

"It is, nevertheless, fact," he said quite kindly, and crooked his arm.

"Why do you do that?" she asked, eyeing the arm doubtfully.

"Pray place your hand upon this arm, my lady, and walk with me that I may conduct you to a chair."

It was her turn to laugh and he thought he had seldom seen a greater transformation than when this sad, half-starved child showed her white small teeth in laughter.

Destiny did not take his arm. She walked alone to the fire and stood staring into the flames. He guessed that she was thinking about the White Hart Inn in Bath and the children she had left behind. He was right. She was consumed with anxiety for them.

Food and wine and the long hours of sleep in a comfortable bed had restored much of her physical strength, and because she was only fifteen, her body was resilient and responded to the good treatment she had been offered; luxuries hitherto undreamed of. And what female would not have been thrilled by the beauty of the suite of rooms which she had been told were hers. The splendour of this satin and silver dress, for instance; the fine cambric underwear and silken stockings; the perfumes and the jewels. Yes, she had even been presented with a ruby necklace and bracelet which she had been told were only the least of the jewels now locked away and waiting for her. The fabulous collection once belonging to the late Countess of Destermere. When Claud married his present wife, Mahla had been given her choice of jewels but she did not care for rubies and she was not particularly worried now that she had to hand a few valuables over to the young girl. She would soon get them back, Mahla told herself.

When Destiny had first awakened, she had looked with utter fascination at her big gilded bed and satin bed-clothes, and the splendid candle-lit chamber in which she found herself. It was the biggest and best of the rooms in the west wing, entirely panelled in pearl-grey satin with rose-painted nymphs on the ceiling, and rose-and-gold brocade framing windows which looked upon the gardens and the river.

A huge fire, scented with aromatic herbs, burned in the hearth. Exquisite paintings by French masters, framed in rose-coloured velvet, hung on the walls.

She had been dazzled by it all. She kept reminding

herself that she was the daughter of an Earl. That all the servants in this house were hers. That the house itself was hers. That Mr. Godwin himself was *her* secretary.

The rest of the evening passed pleasantly enough. Lady Destermere was in an excellent mood and took the girl around the house. Dinner was served in the great dining-hall which fascinated Destiny. She looked with wonder at the wainscoting of rich oak panels—the carving of armorial bearings—the scrollwork over the doors of heraldic devices, the glorious Gobelin tapestries, the splendid curtains of rich purple velvet. Candles in silver sconces and huge candelabra, burned everywhere.

During the meal the table glittered with the heavy family silver, the fine glass and china of which the late Countess had been so fond. Destiny found the food far too rich for her. Course upon course. Soup, fish, capons, a joint of beef, and piles of pastries and luscious fruit from the greenhouses. In Destiny's opinion, all a sad waste and extravagance, when the world was so full of hungry, starving poor.

They retired after the meal to a small room which was panelled in flowered yellow satin and almost too hot, so big a fire burned in the grate. Here there was a spinet, a cabinet full of china birds, an escritoire, and gilded chairs with brocaded cushions. An elegant intimate little room which pleased Destiny more than the huge palatial ones in the house. It was in here, she was told by Stephen, that her grandmother used to spend most of her time.

Mahla talked unceasingly, till Destiny was in a daze. There must be dressmakers, to come and plan a wardrobe for the girl, she said. A dancing master to instruct her in the steps of the cotillion, and teach her deportment, of course the Court curtsy. A tutor to give her lessons in English grammar and improve her handwriting. She must also learn to play the spinet and to sing.

As for manners and customs, Mahla announced that *she* would be Destiny's instructress.

"Mercy on us, I will never learn all these things!" said Destiny, a trifle sullenly.

"Oh, yes, you shall. You shall in time be introduced to many pleasures, also. She shall go to London to see the Queen and attend the theatre and walk in the Park, shall she not, Stephen?" Mahla asked the secretary.

Stephen, who had been listening to the curriculum which the Countess had worked out for Destiny, was feeling himself a trifle dazed by it. He grunted a "yes." Then, finding the room too hot and perfumed for his taste, he got up and left the ladies alone. After he had gone, Mahla sat with her stepdaughter by the fire. She sent for Ramilles and little Cou-Cou. Destiny regarded the tiny Maltese terrier with a certain pleasure and then fell to thinking of the four children again and how amused they would have been at the tiny dog's antics. But she regarded the beturbaned, capering dwarf with horror, and after he had gone she declared that she did not like him.

"He has a wicked eye," she announced.

Lady Destermere smiled.

"And you have a discerning one, my dear, for you are quite right. Ramilles is a limb of Satan."

"Yet you take him with you everywhere," exclaimed the young girl, wide-eyed. "And you. . . ." she paused.

She had been about to say, "And you allow him to hold your candelabra and look upon you when you are naked in the bathtub."

For that is what she had been told by Lucette, and she had felt ashamed and scandalized. Lucette had laughed and said that fine ladies today did more than that, and hinted at a profligacy which Destiny did not begin to understand. Such things had never come her way. She had led an entirely sheltered life except for that one unfortunate incident with the parson ere he died. But she did not feel altogether happy or easy with her stepmother tonight on account of Ramilles, and of what Lucette had told her. There were moments when she felt like tearing off her satin dress, putting Mrs. Barley's rags on again and rushing out into the snow— even if it meant walking barefoot back to Bath and her four little lambs.

When her stepmother asked her if she had ever met any young gentlemen and considered the possibilities of marriage, she went scarlet and fumbled with her handkerchief. She did not meet her ladyship's gaze.

"Oh, no, no, never," was all she could say, as though she had just been asked if she had ever committed a mortal sin.

Lady Destermere looked at her scornfully.

"But you know, my dear, at fifteen you are of an age to consider such matters."

"They have never entered my head. I met no gentlemen at the parsonage."

"But have you never turned your thoughts to the delights of love?" asked Mahla in her most beguiling voice.

"No, never. I know nothing of such things. I love only my little sisters and brothers."

Lady Destermere laughed to herself. The "little savage" was as pure as the driven snow. Yes, quite evidently Humbert would have to put in some clever work. No girl, in Mahla's opinion, lived who could not be wooed and won.

Now, a trifle timidly, Destiny raised her eyes to her stepmother and said in a humble tone:

"Could it not be arranged for my adopted brothers and sisters to join me here if such a huge establishment is always to be my home?"

Mahla was about to say: "Certainly not." But some quick cunning told her to remain sympathetic even on this absurd matter.

"No doubt in time we can send for them, my dear."

"Oh, thank you, madam, my lady," stammered Destiny.

"Have I not asked you to call me by my Christian name, and you should look upon me as an older sister?"

Destiny thanked her and added:

"Mr. Godwin, he is my guardian, as well as you, is he not, Mahla?"

"Yes," said her ladyship, less amiably.

"Alas—he was without pity when I asked to be allowed to bring the children with me."

Mahla seized upon this, and played it to her advantage.

"You will get no pity from your late father's secretary, my child. He has none. He is as hard as nails."

"But that is shocking," exclaimed the girl.

"At times, venomously unkind," continued her ladyship, enjoying herself, for she thought that the less of friendship that existed between Stephen and Destiny, the better. "Pray place all your confidence in me and let me decide upon what is best for your happiness," she added.

"Thank you," said Destiny meekly and rose to her feet.

In the hall she met Stephen coming out of the library. Once more the young secretary was struck by the extraordinary beauty of Lady Destiny Frane. A dignity that could not be taught sat upon her like a crown. He bowed.

"You are retiring, my lady?"

"Yes," said Destiny in a very chilly manner, and decided that she would have as little to do with him as possible after what her stepmother had said.

"May I wish you a good night," said Stephen, with a faint attempt at friendliness.

She ignored his smile, deliberately turned her back upon him and walked up the stairs.

Stephen felt curiously upset by this. Why the snub?

What had he done? He shrugged his shoulders, and moved off to go to his own rooms. That night he could not sleep. In the small hours, wrapped in the fur-lined robe which he wore sometimes when he worked on his manuscripts late into the night, he took a candle and walked along the gallery.

Then he fancied he heard the opening and shutting of a door. He stood still a moment. Now, hearing footsteps, he hastily drew back behind a long curtain which fell across the archway through which one reached the rooms of Countess Destermere and the newly-arrived Lady Frane.

At length, to his extreme astonishment, Stephen saw a tall figure which at first he did not recognize; then it drew nearer. A young man came creeping along—unaware that he was being seen. He made his way down the staircase. Stephen, looking down on him, felt a thrill of dismay and disgust.

He knew the intruder now. William, the red-headed stable boy. Once or twice Stephen had spoken to him. A nice enough lad and, Stephen supposed, with his red curls and handsome eyes, he might well attract a female. But this was abominable! Stephen knew well enough where the boy had just been.

My Lady Destermere was up to her old tricks. The boy had been lured into nocturnal amorous play. All that was Puritan in Stephen shrank from the idea, but it was of Destiny that he now thought with anxiety. If the Earl had only realized the sort of influence to which he had consigned his innocent daughter! He had died too soon. Stephen turned back to his bedchamber, full of troubled fancies.

I must keep a close watch over my Lady Destiny, he thought sombrely. It is my duty to guard her from this kind of knowledge and conduct.

And his loathing of Lady Destermere increased a hundred-fold after this night.

9

DURING THE WEEKS that followed there was more villainy afoot in the house of Destermere than the painstaking young secretary with his integral character and his fine sense of honour, ever dreamed of. Only two things were evident to him—one was that Mahla soon tired of the red-headed groom, and started to pay attention to another lover. The other, the fact that an extraordinary barrier of hostility seemed to have arisen between Destiny and himself.

He saw her of course, daily. If at no other meal time, they usually dined together at night, with Lady Destermere. And sometimes there was some small elegant party arranged by Mahla to introduce the young girl, at quiet intervals, to some of her neighbours. It was Mahla's idea that the big dance for Destiny's first real public appearance should not be held until the end of July. Mahla wanted Destiny to meet "Prince Alexis" before then.

But each time that Stephen saw Destiny and tried to converse with her, she answered him only as briefly as possible and with the minimum of politeness.

"She seems to hate me," Stephen told himself quite simply.

The reason he concluded could not be that he had done her any harm, but must be because of the initial misery he had caused her when he separated her from her "little family." Once or twice Lady Destermere brought up the subject of the Barleys and in front of Stephen, declared that "poor dearest Destiny was pining for her darlings" and had not even had news of them to console her.

"I have told her that you do not think it expedient that she should bring them all here," Mahla had added with a sly look at the secretary, who flushed and turned from the mute appeal in the huge eyes of the younger girl. She turned from him sullenly. She found no sympathy.

"That is true," he nodded.

"There, my dear, I am so aggrieved for you," said Mahla.

Destiny turned on Stephen and blazed.

"I hate you!"

"Hatred will exhaust you and put lines on your charming face, my lady," he said bluntly, "and pray remember how many parcels you have sent by postchaise to the children since you left them and how much money you have sent to the Jupps to spend on their behalf."

"It is not enough," said Destiny, and ran from the room in tears.

"Our little Lady Destiny does not seem to fancy you, my dear Stephen," drawled the Countess.

"Are you putting her against me?" he asked furiously.

"Absurd!" exclaimed Mahla, full of injured innocence.

"Was it not you who expressed every sentiment against having the Barley family here? You agreed that it would cause local gossip about my lady's upbringing and injure her chances in life," said Stephen. "Besides, these children are no relatives of hers. We must make her see this. It would be her father's wish that she should cut completely adrift from her early life in Bath."

"I keep telling her so," said Mahla smoothly.

The young man looked at the Countess under frowning brows.

"I would like to see a list of the gentlemen you propose to bring here for her entertainment, before you send your invitations to the ball, my lady."

"If you wish, my dear Stephen," she said, shrugging her shoulders.

He remained silent, confused, well aware that he was no match for the feminine guile with which this woman abounded. He did not really know what was going on behind his back. He only knew that he hated the Countess and wanted more than he had thought possible, to be friends with Destermere's daughter.

Then Mahla glided towards him. They were alone standing in front of the fire in the morning-room during this particular conversation. Close to him, she looked up into his eyes and whispered:

"Am I not being a good devoted stepmother to Claud's daughter? Have I not done my best?"

"Yes . . . little doubt. . . ." stammered Stephen.

"Am I to receive no reward for my patience? For I do assure you, my dear soul, Destiny is not an easy creature. We have tears and scenes at every juncture."

"Your reward must surely be your own satisfied heart, madam," said Stephen stiffly.

She put her arms around his neck.

"Stephen . . . foolish one . . . do you not yet know how much I crave your regard? Lately I have seen so little of you except in the company of that child. . . ."

She got no further, for Stephen unlocked her hands and flung her away from him.

"I am no stable boy to be seduced by your charms," he said, his eyes blazing with contempt, and walked out of the room.

She stood still, trembling with rage. *So he knew about William . . .* and no doubt about the others.

He should pay for scorning her, she thought, he should pay through that girl whom he liked to think he was protecting. Hatred and rebellion should be all he would ever receive from Lady Destiny Frane, Mahla decided venemously.

Stephen went to his bureau, sat down, scribbled some words, and folding the letter, sealed it and sent for one of the men.

"Take this to Bath," he said. "By the fastest possible horse."

The missive was addressed to the innkeeper who had taken charge of the Barley family. It enquired after their health and well-being and demanded a detailed reply.

Stephen had suddenly felt stricken by the thought that he had been too harsh with Destiny over the children. He must try to comfort her with some immediate news of them.

A few moments later, looking through his windows he saw the slim young figure of my Lady Destiny walking through the grounds, accompanied by the Countess. Behind them, the blackamoor whom Stephen detested, capered and skipped, carrying a large bunch of flowers.

Stephen, hands behind his back, regarded the younger of the two women. Destiny wore a green velvet mantle and hood. She looked charming and for a moment she seemed engrossed in what her stepmother was saying. Undoubtedly these two were getting on together a lot better than Stephen had anticipated, but he could not attune his fundamental knowledge of Mahla and her true character, with her new maternal solicitude; nor reconcile it with the spite and anger with which she had first received the news of the girl's existence.

What was going on?

If he could have heard their conversation, he would have been even more worried.

"I have a little surprise for you, my dear," Lady Destermere was saying, "But I wanted to be away from the house where there is so much prying and spying so that I could tell you my secret in privacy."

"Oh, tell it to me, *pray,* Mahla," exclaimed Destiny, and slipped a hand through her stepmother's arm.

During the ten weeks she had been at Destermere House, she had grown to feel quite an affection for her dead father's wife. It was agreeable to have such a young fascinating stepmama and she could not complain in any way of the Countess's treatment of her. Everything was done to keep her amused and interested.

True, it was all a bit of an ordeal and at times the girl still felt dazed and fatigued. She must learn this ... learn that ... she must not use this language, or say that ... she must curtsy *so* ... lift her handkerchief or gloved hand to her lips and gaze over it provocatively, *so*. She must be able to speak about the politics of today; about the fashions and the scandals, and all the frivolities which she found amazing, and really rather a waste of time. Yet they were the things which Lady Destermere said a young lady must learn and do in her position.

Destiny had half-forgotten the miserable garments she used to wear. She was accustomed now to the tedious hours of being attired by her maid. She had grown to love the rich silks and satins and fripperies worn by a young gentlewoman. She had learned to hold herself with a pride and to feel less confused when the servants attended her or strangers, whom they met while she was out driving with her stepmother, addressed her. Already she had managed to acquit herself quite creditably at some of the little dinner parties that had been held here. She had been painstaking with her lessons. She spent hours with the dancing master—learned how to bow and smile and hold out her hand for some gentleman to kiss, without feeling that terror of contact with the other sex, which the Reverend Mr. Barley had inspired in her by his loathsome advances.

She had learned a little to control her quick impulses, her spirited temper, her individual attitude towards life, even though she remained in her heart, something of a rebel. She felt that she could never really lose herself so completely as to become a puppet such as most ladies of fashion seemed to be.

Fascinated, with her stepmother as her model, she listened endlessly to the older woman's graphic descriptions of London life as Destiny might soon be asked to lead it.

When alone, she wandered through the house, examining her father's treasures which were now hers. She had begun to add to her little store of knowledge of the arts and could name some of the great painters. She could recognize good music. The reading and writing which she already had learned, had improved. And although she felt she did not want to offend Lady Destermere by saying so, it was in books and in the arts that she was really interested, rather than in the endless empty recreations.

Lady Destermere's idea of how a woman should behave was that she should spend most of her time in a physical and mental state of indolence. But Destiny had a burning desire to improve her mind. On such occasions she would steal into the library. She had already devoured the plays of William Shakespeare and some of Sir Isaac Newton's work. She began to feel akin to the father she had never known when she was there in this world of books, which her grandfather had loved and collected.

Once Stephen found her there and had offered her a beautifully bound book of essays which he thought she would enjoy.

"It is a pleasure for me to find you in this room, my lady," he had said. "So often in the past your dear father and I browsed together here, studying the arts. Here, he encouraged me in my literary efforts."

For a few moments, Destiny forgot her hatred of Stephen which Mahla was fanning in her, and questioned him further about the late Earl. She even allowed Stephen to sit down and show her one or two drawings which had been made of the Earl as a young man, by contemporary artists. And then it seemed to her that she passed a very pleasant hour indeed, talking to Stephen. He had a depth of mind, a lucid conception of the arts which put her stepmother's frothy conversation into the background. They had even found some jest to laugh about together. Then suddenly Stephen had stopped laughing and said seriously:

"It would be a great happiness to me, my Lady Destiny, if you would let me steal a little of your time more regularly in order that we should enjoy a mutual discussion of the world of art."

But in the end Destiny had emerged from her dreamy state and instinctive admiration for her guardian, and remembered him again as her enemy. The anguish she had felt at losing the children had by no means abated even though it was less acute. She held Stephen to account for it. She bade him a cold *adieu* and walked out of the library, determined not to approach him again. She *would* not be friends with him.

But up till now she had met nobody else in the district whom she found at all diverting. Once she drove in the phaeton with her ladyship to the Ancasters' ancestral home and was dazzled by the magnificence of the place but wearied by the Duchess who was a stupid frothy woman, with less brains than Countess Destermere and only one ambition—to be a leader of fashion.

"Oh, you pretty child!" she had exclaimed when she saw Destiny. "We must find her a splendid husband, must we not, Lady Destermere?"

To which Mahla, with downcast eyes, had answered: "Yes, indeed, your Grace!"

But Destiny felt no immediate urge to enter the marriage market and suffered in scornful silence the extravagant attention of the Duchess's elder son. She thought him a young fop. On another occasion, she edged away from an equally silly young gentleman— the Marquess of Midhurstholme—who had driven with his mother and sister from Great Hampton especially to call on my Lady Destiny.

As for a female friend of her own age, she had also failed to find even that. Such young ladies as the Hon. Caroline Midhurstholme for instance, was a stupid vain miss of fifteen and a half, and an utter snob. She was quite pleased to talk to Destiny and share a few girlish secrets with her (Caroline's were mainly concerned with her own hopes of making a fine marriage) but when Destiny mentioned that she had been brought up "quietly" in a poor parson's house in the West Country, Caroline had stared, then withdrawn from her company. Destiny received her first lesson in class distinction.

She spoke of this during dinner in Stephen's presence. He expressed a somewhat ironic view of the matter.

"You will find that is how society behaves, my lady. It is not very attractive I fear."

Destiny looked at him with some interest, but immediately Lady Destermere put in her spoke.

"Do not let Mr. Godwin confuse you, my love. You are Destermere's heiress and must consort only with fine people of lineage and high social standing. It would be better if in the future, you did not mention your unfortunate upbringing to the ladies and gentlemen you meet at parties."

Destiny lapsed into silence. But she found herself wishing that things could have been different—that there was not such open hostility between herself and the secretary. She could not deny that his ideas and principles were far more to her liking than those displayed by her stepmother. But as soon as the meal was over and she was alone with the Countess, the older woman whispered in her ear that she need pay little heed to anything that Mr. Godwin said. His attitude towards life was not all that was to be desired, and his opinions of no value.

"But my father thought otherwise," Destiny protested—confused.

"Your father did not know our dear Stephen as I do, or he would never have left him in charge of your affairs, my dear."

Destiny had asked what her stepmother meant, and

if she thought Stephen had ever showed signs of marrying and leaving Destermere House; setting up a home of his own.

"Assuredly it is to be hoped that he will not always be here to snoop and spy on us," her ladyship answered glibly. "But I see little chance of his marrying." Then lowering her voice, she added: "He has poor taste. He consorts with wenches of the lowest order."

"Oh, how disgraceful," said Destiny with hot pink cheeks. She brooded over it all when she was alone. Nowadays, she was better able to judge for herself. She was more worldly wise. She could see that Stephen Godwin was a proud upright man. She could not reconcile such a nature with Mahla's picture of him indulging in amorous pleasure with serving girls. She was astounded, but saw no reason to disbelieve her stepmother, who had become her guide and mentor in all such things.

Now, on this bright June day when the beautiful gardens of Destermere House were beginning to wear the ardent green and bright floral colours of the summer, Lady Destermere played the first card in the game which she had been preparing for Destiny. A game which she had been wildly anxious to commence. But she had thought it best to wait until the time was ripe ... until the girl was a little more fitted for it. In her opinion that time had now come.

Over there to the west, on the other side of that forest, lay the Ancaster estates and Humbert sitting in the Lake House. Poor Humbert, bored beyond words, driven almost to distraction with impatience. On such occasions when Mahla had stolen over to visit him, he had agreed that it would not do to rush things.

When she had last seen him, Mahla had had plenty to say about Destiny.

"The girl is still so raw, I must mould her—soften the edges—or she will be frightened off by anything you say or do. Gradually but surely I am gaining her confidence. I have gleaned from her all that she has so far experienced which was no more than an attempt upon her virginity made by the fuddled parson with whom she lived. I have assured her that was unimportant and that he was just a lecherous old fool. I have told her that love, romantic and delicious, awaits her. I have prepared her mind for a Prince Charming. It has taken some little time for she is a strange fastidious creature, as you will discover, and as stubborn as her father was before her. I have often felt like striking her, maddened by her obstinacy. Even though not yet sixteen, she is a determined woman rather than a meek child to be easily influenced. You will have to go very carefully!"

The newly installed "Prince Alexis" announced that he had every intention of going carefully, but that if he had to wait much longer for a visit from his future bride, he would expire of ennui.

So today for the first time, Destiny heard about the "Russian Prince" who had been ill and was recuperating in the little house on the lake.

She had known him all her life, the Countess told her. Oh, but he was *charming* and so handsome and so clever. He had left Russia as a boy. He was now completely Europeanized, but he could not stand the fogs and miasmas of London; hence his retreat to the country. He was longing to meet Lady Destiny Frane.

"Why does he not come here to call?" asked Destiny, puzzled.

"He is not well enough to leave his home. In addition to this, Mr. Godwin, our dear secretary, does not like him, nor would he approve of you making his acquaintance."

"Why does he not?"

Mahla had an excellent story ready; how when Stephen had first met the Prince, he had made derogatory remarks about the Prince's Cossack blood and expressed a dislike of Russia, which had naturally, offended Alexis. He found Mr. Godwin a sanctimonious, priggish young idiot and had said so.

"So you see, poor Alexis would not be readily admitted to this house," said Mahla.

"I consider it very churlish of Mr. Godwin," said Destiny indignantly. "He takes far too much upon himself. Why should *he* give the orders? It should be your prerogative, dearest Mahla."

The older woman's heart leapt with triumph. She had indeed schooled the young girl to her liking. She said:

"Your championship of me is sweet, dearest child, but unfortunately your father endowed Stephen Godwin with certain powers of administration concerning you and I can do nothing unless his authority is added to mine. He has already made it clear to me that under no circumstances will he allow you to meet the Prince."

"Then I *wish* to meet him!" exclaimed Destiny.

"So you shall," said Mahla delightedly. "He is a splendid creature. I'faith, his playing and singing would soften the hardest heart." And she sighed.

Destiny began to feel intrigued. She had heard so much talk of a romantic nature—about the attentions she was sure to receive from infatuated gentlemen; and about her marriage (delicately and cunningly portrayed for her), so she had begun to take a faint interest in such matters. She had even begun to feel the power of her own femininity and to realize that men already found her beautiful. She had seen the way young Oswald Midhurstholme had languished his gaze at her. *He* had actually said he would write a poem to her beauty and send it to her.

At the time the young girl had thought him stupid, nevertheless it was quite diverting to be adored. In fact, her life had begun to be really amusing, and promised with each day to become more so. Were it not for Stephen's refusal to send for her dear children, she might have enjoyed her new exalted position. But Mahla regularly drove home the point that it was

Stephen alone, who stood between Destiny and her heart's desire, and that spoiled all her fun.

For a little while, as the ladies took the fresh air, Mahla talked constantly and insidiously of her friend Prince Alexis. Soon the young girl was all agog to meet him.

"But it must be a clandestine visit. You must not tell Mr. Godwin where we go," Mahla warned her.

"Ought I to be so deceitful?" asked Destiny doubtfully.

"When you have such a hard cruel person as Mr. Godwin to deal with, my dear, you must live your own secret life."

"Then I will visit the Prince who is your friend," said Destiny, and gave her stepmother that wide sweet smile that made her radiantly beautiful.

The elder woman noticed with satisfaction that ten weeks of good living and perpetual grooming, had truly made a beauty of the once pale emaciated child. She did not think that Humbert would be disappointed in his future wife.

Just before the two women re-entered the house, Destiny suddenly remembered the Maltese terrier which she had not seen today at her stepmother's heels.

"Where is Cou-Cou? I love him. I miss the animals I used to have as pets—even the old nanny-goat," she added with a laugh.

The Countess reprimanded her.

"It is better you should not refer to the miserable conditions under which you once lived. Goats, indeed!" she shuddered.

Destiny coloured but held her head high.

"I like animals. Let me take Cou-Cou for walks."

Mahla frowned. Yesterday, up in her own rooms, in a flaming rage, she had kicked the poor little dog once too often and it had died. It meant nothing to her. She had never really cared for it. Yet even the twisted nature of the blackamoor had more pity in it, for he had shed a tear when he carried the little corpse out to be buried.

Mahla fabricated a smooth story about the death of the terrier.

"We found him thus in his basket this morning. I did not mean to tell you for I know your soft heart," she said to Destiny with a hypocritical sigh.

The girl sympathized and thought sadly of the little, jumping, affectionate dog. But she said no more, innocently believing that it would bring grief to the heart of this woman who—had she known it—was utterly heartless.

10

THE MAN who now called himself Prince Alexis Malinkoff was seated at his spinet playing a plaintiff Russian folk-song and humming it in a warm pleasant baritone, when two lackeys opened the double doors of the drawing-room and announced the Countess of Destermere and the Lady Destiny Frane.

Humbert Faramund pretended not to notice the entrance of the ladies, just for a moment. His playing was so effective. Thus Destiny for the first time, saw to some advantage the man who was to influence her life in so sinister a fashion during the next few weeks. She took a quick look around the elegant octagonal room in this enchanting house which was quite different from the palatial home of her father, and much more to her liking. It had all the delicacy and *petite* beauty of French décor. Here, were thick white fur rugs and Louis Quatorze gilded chairs with lemon coloured satin draperies. A love-seat piled with velvet cushions. Exquisite china ornaments and marble statuary gave an air of charm, and through a little archway Destiny could see a tiny fountain playing in a jasper basin.

Around this fountain—the waters of which were scented with orange perfume—stood green malachite jars full of lilies. The sunshine of the hot June morning had been shut out by gold and silver brocaded curtains. Lighted candles sparkled in crystal and gilt sconces on the high mantelpiece over which there hung a single painting by an old French master; the subject a naked nymph lying under a green tree, playing with a pretty cupid. It was a room that at once spelt luxury, beauty and sensuality.

Destiny stared and stared. Never before had she seen such a place. Then the man at the spinet stopped playing and turned around.

Destiny saw in the kindly candlelight what she thought an extremely handsome and quite youthful gentleman. She was at once fascinated by his full-lidded blue eyes, and thought the chocolate-coloured ribbon tying back his peruke, very distinguished. He wore a fashionable brocaded suit of deep cream colour, with a great deal of frilled lawn at the neck, and a floral waistcoat with amethyst buttons. As she stood there, her heart beating slightly faster than usual with excitement, he put up a spy-glass and "quizzed" her which made her feel indescribably but agreeably shy, and sent the blood rushing to her cheeks.

Now he advanced slowly, placed a hand on his heart and bowed to the two ladies.

"My dearest friend, Mahalah," he murmured, using her name in full, "Lady Destiny Frane—your servant, ma'am."

"I . . . thank you, sir . . . and good day to you," stammered Destiny, deliciously terror-stricken.

Over her bent head, Humbert looked at his sister and they exchanged amused glances. The woman was quick to note the satisfaction on Humbert's face and she had to admire him, she thought, for the way he had sacrificed his meals in order to regain that slim figure. He really looked quite young and attractive this afternoon.

"Let me lead you to a chair and remove your cloak, Lady Destiny," said Humbert.

"Thank you, your Highness," she said trying to remember that he was a Prince. In her ignorance and innocence she felt completely overcome by the magnificence of such a title.

As he unfastened her cherry-coloured velvet cloak, the grace of her young thin body was revealed in a charming little flowered satin jacket, and she wore full petticoats over a domed hoop which had recently been made for her. A little feathered hat was perched on the side of her black smooth head; her long curls were tied back with a bow and she carried a tiny beaver muff.

Humbert was enchanted by what he saw. Of course his sister had told him that Destermere's heiress, now that she was becoming accustomed to good dressing and speech, was a very desirable prize—apart from her vast fortune. He certainly began to feel that all the boredom of waiting about and having to hide himself from the world, was worth while.

Once the ladies were seated, he clapped his hands. A lackey entered carrying a tray bearing sweet cakes, goblets and a silver flagon of wine. Another footman brought in tea.

Destiny sat back in her velvet-cushioned chair and started to draw off her embroidered gauntlets. She accepted a cup of tea and one of the cakes. Meanwhile she listened with respect to the conversation of the two older people; a seemingly artless froth of chatter about the Court, the Queen, and the latest news of Marlborough and Lady Sarah, his wife. Not forgetting an entirely fictitious story which Humbert began to pour out for Destiny's benefit about St. Petersburg and some Russian relatives and friends from whom he had heard.

"Ah, my dear St. Petersburg!" he ended, sighing.

"One day in the future I shall hope to see the wonder and beauty of her again, but my health has been so poor, my Lady Destiny—I could not stand the intense cold. I have been ill you know, and that is why I am convalescing here in this divine little house."

"I trust you are better now, sir," she said.

He noted the sweep of her long lashes and the brilliance of her eyes. There was going to be nothing difficult about making love to *her,* he thought with satisfaction.

She sympathized with his "delicacy."

"I trust that you will soon recover your strength and that the quiet English countryside will not prove too dull for your Highness," she said.

Mahla put in:

"Alexis could not be bored when he has such delightful company as yours, my dearest little one."

"The Countess has taken the words right out of my mouth," said the "Prince." "You bring with you a freshness and enchantment such as I have rarely met. I have moved in society in London, Paris, Rome and my native Russia, and grown weary of sophisticated women and artificial elegance."

Destiny who had a sense of humour, gave a little self-conscious giggle and twiddled her muff.

"To be sure my stepmother would tell you *I* am not sophisticated, sir, nor ever likely to be."

"We shall see," said Mahla, and then made an excuse to leave these two alone. "Ramilles is jumping up and down in the carriage. I have warned him that my new satin seat-covering will not stand his heels; the little demon," she said "I should not have brought him. Pray excuse me, for a moment."

"Allow me," said Humbert, and opened one of the doors. As his sister passed through, he bent and whispered to her:

"She is a trifle gauche but ravishing. I shall adore my job."

"And you will soon mould her to your own ways. She is a willing pupil and hates Stephen Godwin," Mahla whispered back.

The next half hour passed delightfully for Destiny. The Prince proved an admirable host and made her feel much more at home than Stephen Godwin had ever done. He treated her like a fine lady and yet there was a warmth and friendliness here that found an echo in her heart. He was enormously diverting, she thought, so full of wit and humour and so very interesting.

Humbert remained standing in front of the fire watching the girl as he sipped his wine. She had found a jewelled golden puppet on the table beside her. When she moved the hands and legs, little bells tinkled. She played with the toy like a delighted child. He thought how charming she looked in the fire-glow, jerking the jewelled puppet up and down.

"That is a toy Punchinello I bought in Rome. May I present it to your ladyship," said Humbert.

"Oh, I couldn't possibly—" she began, but he broke in.

"The Punchinello is yours, my Lady Destiny."

She fondled the puppet and smiled at him.

"Everything is so pretty here," she sighed, looking around her. "I love to watch how the candlelight sparkles in the fountain."

"Yet you come from the magnificence of Destermere House. My Lake House is poor in comparison."

"But I like it better here," she said. "It is not so gloomy."

"Then I hope you will come and visit me many times in the future."

"I would like to," she said eagerly, "And I would I could ask you to my father's house, but my stepmother tells me our horrid secretary has quarrelled with you."

Humbert grinned to himself but said with sympathy:

"Poor fellow. He is a fool. One must forgive him. And if you dislike him, I am truly sorry for him."

"Why?" the girl asked, puzzled.

"No man living but would be the worse for your disapproval," said Humbert in his silkiest voice.

She would not have been human and a budding woman if she had not been flattered. She liked that slightly foreign voice of his, mistaking the German accent for a Russian one. The Prince was proving all that the Countess had promised. A most romantic and handsome figure, in this romantic little house by the lake. It was deliciously simple to come here, too, without Mr. Godwin knowing. The duplicity gave it all a touch of wickedness which was thrilling.

Later on when it was time for Destiny to return to Destermere House with her stepmother, the latter impressed upon her the importance of keeping the visit secret. Besides which, in the Prince's delicate state of health, he did not want callers, Mahla added, and nobody knew about his life here. Even the Ancasters had never met him, for it was only through their agent, and his, that the lease had been purchased on the little French-built house.

The Prince played the spinet and sang to the two women again before they left. As he said good-bye to Destiny, he bent over her hand and said:

"For long I have been a wanderer. I have felt the vexations of solitude. Now you have solved my problem sweet lady, and if you do not find me too tedious a host, I pray that you will come soon again to lighten my darkness."

She was enthralled. She had passed a strange dreamy afternoon in his presence. Impulsively, she answered him:

"If my stepmother will bring me, I shall come soon again and with great joy, your Highness."

As she stepped into the carriage, Mahla lingered a moment to toss a few whispered words to her brother. "You play your part charmingly, Humi. Almost I am persuaded to believe that you are indeed Prince Malinkoff from St. Petersburg. You have laid the foundation stone for the castle of our dreams. It will not be long, I am sure, before this girl is wax in your hands."

He smiled and answered:

"Mind that you continue to feed her dislike of dear Stephen Godwin."

On the drive home, Destiny spoke with the enthusiasm of a deluded and infatuated young girl about Prince Alexis. She realized today why it was necessary for her to learn to be a great lady. She had felt untutored and uncivilized in the presence of a great nobleman like the Prince who knew everything.

"I will pay extra attention to my lessons now. Promise that we can visit the Prince soon again."

The little fool, thought Lady Destermere scornfully as she gave the promise.

"Alexis has never so far wanted to marry," she told Destiny. "He has the nature of a recluse, yet he has such infinite charm and grace that with the right wife beside him he would blossom out and make a splendid husband."

"He will have to marry some great lady," said Destiny reverently.

"My dear, make no mistake—he found you as charming as you found him," said Mahla, tapping Destiny's cheeks with a gloved finger.

"Oh, no, no, he could not have done," breathed Destiny, her cheeks on fire, her lashes fluttering.

Mahla said no more. She thought she had said and done enough for one day, but she was quite sure that she and Humbert between them had touched the heart of Destermere's daughter with that gilded arrow which was poisoned at the tip and which would eventually slay her.

Now Destiny's resentment against Stephen increased. She began to look upon him as a gaoler as well as a guardian. When that evening, he sent a message to her asking that she should grant him an interview in the library, she had half a mind to be wayward and to say that she had a headache and refuse. But at heart she was neither a coquette nor malicious and she tried to remember that she owed Stephen Godwin quite a deal of her present good fortune. It was, after all, he who had searched for her and taken such trouble to bring her here. He who had been her father's trusted friend and protégé.

Her feelings towards him were conflicting. Her stepmother hated him but those who had served her father in the past seemed to love and respect the young secretary. Mrs. Perkins could not speak well enough of Mr. Godwin.

"He is a sweet gentleman with great thought for others and little for himself. My dear master used to look upon him as a son," once she had told my Lady Destiny.

The girl, sometimes nostalgic for her homely past, used to creep into the housekeeper's tiny parlour and talk to her there. She learned more from Mrs. Perkins about her own father and grandparents, than from anybody else. Once, quite humbly, Destiny said to Mrs. Perkins:

"Do people look down upon me because nobody was acquainted with my poor mother, and because I have been so badly reared?"

The old housekeeper had dabbed the corners of her eyes with her handkerchief and exclaimed:

"Bless you, my lady, no, not a soul but is pleased that your little ladyship has come to Destermere House, and hates to see you sorrowful."

"I am sorrowful only because I grieve for my little brothers and sisters," had been Destiny's reply. For she had told the housekeeper all about the little Barleys, and the good kindly creature sympathized with my lady's feelings and was the only person in the house with whom Destiny could discuss them.

But when she spoke of her stepmother and expressed

an admiration for Mahla's astonishing beauty and wit, and said that she wished that she resembled her, Mrs. Perkins remained silent. But she gave Destiny the impression that the Countess was not popular with the servants.

A great deal took place in this house that puzzled her. She was beginning to grow up, and now she was not quite so much like that passionate, headstrong child who had once threatened to murder Mr. Godwin. She had grown reserved and cautious. Her hands had lost their redness. Her manners were charming. She was becoming accustomed to the flowery exaggerated speech of the day. She had, in fact, become in truth, my Lady Destiny.

Yet there remained that simple-hearted girl who had grown up with the parson and his wife—who had been neglected and often ill-treated but managed to lead an inner idealistic life of her own. She was still easily shocked. The faint sweet breath of corruption threatened to taint her innocence whenever she was with Mahla, yet she never lost the fine bloom of her modesty. She could no longer be ignorant of the world, but she remained essentially pure of heart.

She decided to grant Stephen his interview in the library and joined him there after dinner.

Stephen was garbed as usual in sober grey with spotless Steinkirk and neat bob-wig. He bowed as she approached. He, himself, always found it hard to believe that she had ever been the wild shabby Destiny he had first seen and rescued. She entered that library with all the grace and distinction of a well-bred lady. A little uneasily he noticed the enigmatic smile that curved her lips and wondered what lay behind it.

"Thank you for coming, my lady," he said, bowing.

Destiny seated herself, spreading out her hooped satin skirt which was of powder-blue satin. She began to play with one of her black glossy ringlets—herself quite at ease. She had decided to feel no conscience about keeping secrets from Stephen even though he was partially her guardian, and with her father's bankers and notaries, seemed to have more power over her future than the Countess. She even felt a childish thrill of pleasure because she was playing truant behind his back.

"Pray tell me any business that you may wish to impart to me, Mr. Godwin," she said in a deliberately languid voice.

He felt sudden anger, and coloured. He could sense the Countess's teaching behind the rather scornful indifference which this lovely child showed him tonight.

"It is no dull dry document that I have for you to sign this time, my lady," he said coldly. "It is something more to your liking."

She pouted at him.

"What can that possibly be? I have listened for so many hours to your dull discourses on money and estate accounts, and of what I may or may not spend, or where I should or should not go. I am growing a little weary of your attempt to act the tyrant."

Stephen, red as a turkeycock, bit his lips and stood before her, hands clasped behind his back, inwardly fuming.

"Are you then treated as a prisoner in this house, my lady, and am I so monstrously tyrannical?"

She looked away from him. In here where there were hundreds of beautiful leather-bound books on shelves from ceiling to floor—such an air of quietude and study—she felt really more at home than she did in her stepmother's over-hot and scented boudoir. She knew that deep down within her she longed to talk more fully to Stephen, to exchange words with him on all the subjects that her father had loved. The music, the painting, the literature to which her eyes were only just being fully opened.

She said:

"I do nothing much at Destermere House but learn things, do I?"

The faintest smile touched Stephen's lips, making him look, she had to admit, at once more winning and sympathetic.

"It was essential that you should become acquainted with such subjects as are familiar to all young ladies of birth and breeding," he reminded her.

She shrugged her shoulders.

"The Countess thinks that young ladies need some diversion and that I need more money to spend on pastimes. I would like to live in London for a Season, and drive every Sunday in the park and go with the *beau monde* to great men's levées, or be carried in a sedan chair to the fashionable coffee houses—or some pleasant rendezvous," she said, and for the first time there was coquetry in her smile, and a look in her great eyes which appalled Stephen.

Dear heaven, she is a true woman now. How fascinating she has become, he thought. What an influence the Countess is having upon her—a baleful one, devil take it. It is as I feared. . . .

He found it difficult to express what he felt in suitable words, but managed to convey to Destiny that life was not all frivolity nor must a very young lady of her standing listen to too many wild stories which should be of interest only to married women.

"The Countess is a woman of the world. You are still a pupil," he finished lamely.

"How dull you make life sound! You are so sober and righteous. You recall to me the lectures I used to receive from the late Mr. Barley!" exclaimed Destiny.

Stephen turned away. He was hurt to the quick. The young girl looked at his stiff back and was suddenly remorseful. She had not meant to be so cutting.

"That was unkind of me. I am sorry, Stephen," she said. I know that you work hard on my behalf and often late into the night. How goes your own work—your essay on Marlborough?"

"Well enough when I have the opportunity to write, but there is too much to be seen to concerning his lordship's estate," was the reply.

"I know you served my father well," said Destiny, her eyes softening.

"I did my best, my lady."

The warm-hearted child in her suddenly superseded the cruel capricious female that Mahla was trying to make of her.

"You are angry with me, Stephen. With reason. Forgive me," she said.

At once he swung round. There was a new richness and friendliness in her voice which he found strangely attractive. He looked into her eyes. They were no longer mocking or resentful. They held a sweetness he had not dreamed of ever seeing there. His heart seemed to knock. Memory swept him back to a day when Claud Destermere had treated him unfairly over something and then with rapid warmth and this same sweetness, had held out a hand and told him that he regretted being unjust and called him his "very dear boy."

"Sometimes I find it difficult to understand you," went on Destiny, and she was being sincere and for the moment forgetting Mahla (and the little French house by the lake). "There has been such a great upheaval in my life. A complete change from all I ever knew. Sometimes, frankly, I do not know whether I want to stay here or return to my old harsh life in the parsonage."

"I understand," said Stephen gently, "I sympathize."

"I still pine for those who were once my whole world," she added, her eyes swimming suddenly.

"You mean the children?"

She nodded.

He felt troubled. She had swept away all the antagonism between them. That heart of his was beating faster than it had ever done for any woman in his life.

Destiny Frane had a magic in her voice and in her eyes, and he was touched by it. A little giddily he said:

"My lady, it is about the children I wish to speak to you and why I asked you to come here tonight."

Up shot the dark proud head.

"You have news for me concerning them?"

"Yes. I sent a servant to Bath to ask expressly for your sake how the little Barley family are faring."

She sprang up, her cheeks peony-bright.

"Oh, Stephen, that was kind of you. Oh, Stephen, what does the man say? It is only a matter of weeks since I left them with Mr. and Mrs. Jupp, but to me it seems an interminable period of time."

"Be of good cheer, my lady. They are all well, except perhaps the small boy whom you called Matt, who suffers continually from earache."

Destiny clasped her slender fingers together.

"Poor little Matt! His ears were delicate from infancy. Always he has had pains in his head. Oh, I should never have left him, for I, alone, understood him when he had these times of suffering and used to put hot cloths about his head."

Stephen sighed. One of the girl's chief attractions was that strong maternal streak which sat so strangely upon one so young and virginal. It seemed as though she had been born with the desire to nurse, to protect.

She drew nearer him—so near that he could smell the fragrance of some perfume which had been sprayed upon her hair.

"Tell me more. Tell me everything that your servant said," she begged.

"I fear he brought no great detail of information. Merely that Mr. and Mrs. Jupp say the children eat well and are content, and send you their thanks for your presents and their dear love."

"If I could but send for them," she choked.

The sight of those tears ravaged Stephen's heart in a way he had not thought possible. He prided himself

123

upon being calm and stoical but who could remain so in the face of Destiny Frane's tears for a band of little children who were not even her flesh and blood? He felt a deep respect for her, and sadness for her grief; and at this moment something more which sprang to life within him (like a madness he thought which would never again allow him to be quite sane). He took out a handkerchief and wiped his forehead. The warmth of the room was too much for him.

"My lady, if that is not possible, perhaps you could take a trip to Bath and visit them quite soon."

Now, with none of the antagonism she was supposed to feel towards this man, she put out both hands and gripped his arms.

"Thank you, Stephen, for suggesting it. I will hold you to that idea, whensoever you can carry it out."

He stood rigid.

I must be mad, he thought wildly, to feel as though my past life is as nothing and that the future does not matter but that the present stands out like a radiant fabulous star. *The present,* when she smiles upon me and touches my hand.

"I am glad my plan pleases you," he said in a suffocating voice.

"I will never forget your kindness in sending your man to visit them," she said. "It was a gentle thought. I fear I have been most disagreeable to you since I came to Destermere House, and am sorry for it."

"You have no need to be. Things have been difficult for you. I ask only to serve you as I did your father," he said, and tried wildly to remember her as she was— the thin pale child who threatened to shoot him if he took her from her brood—rather than this fascinating young woman, slim and graceful, in her beautiful gown.

He walked to a walnut secretaire bureau, and unlocking a drawer, drew out a case.

"Yesterday I came across this among your father's things and feel sure you would like to have it," he said.

She reached out her hand, opened the case and saw a miniature. It was of a young girl—a delicate face not much like her own, yet there was a faint resemblance about the winged brows, and the way the luxuriant hair curled about the slender neck. Destiny breathed.

"It must be my mother."

"Yes, my lady, and it is signed, as you will see on the other side."

Destiny turned the miniature over. Written on the back in faint purple ink were the words:

"For my belovèd from his wife, Amabel."

"Oh!" gasped Destiny, and back came the tears, "My poor little mother!"

"Yes," nodded Stephen, "Your father greatly regretted the whole tragedy. But you must never hold it against him, my lady, for he was much oppressed by his dominating parents and a sick man when he tried to follow your mother."

"You are very loyal to my father," said Destiny raising her streaming eyes to Stephen's pale face.

"As I trust I shall always be to you," he said with a deep bow.

She thought:

There is something noble about Stephen Godwin. A reason why my father had such confidence in him. My stepmother must surely misjudge his character? Can it be that she is in some way personally prejudiced against him? Perchance she is wrong and he is right.

And Destiny decided that there must in future be less of hatred and misunderstanding between herself and her father's secretary.

Then she remembered—rather guiltily now—the secret that she shared with her stepmother. The visit to the fascinating Russian Prince in that golden glamour-filled house. Almost she was on the verge of telling Stephen about the Prince and the house by the lake, when the doors of the library opened and the Countess, splendidly attired and bejewelled, as usual, swept in.

Mahla had been standing behind the closed door for some little time. She had heard every word that had been spoken between Stephen and her stepdaughter. She was furiously angry that Stephen had managed so far to ingratiate himself into the girl's favour and was terrified that Destiny would give away the secret of the Lake House. She interrupted the two just in time, perhaps, she thought cynically.

Stephen bowed to the Countess, unsmiling. Destiny walked quickly towards her and said:

"Oh, Mahla, is it not kind of Mr. Godwin? He sent down to Bath to bring me news of my darling children."

Mahla put up a quiz glass and looked through it at Stephen as though he were of no account.

"Indeed!" was her acid comment.

The long look that passed between Lady Destermere and the secretary was of pure hatred—unnoticed by the happy Destiny.

PART TWO

11

A CONVERSATION BETWEEN Lady Destermere and her
stepdaughter that night brought little satisfaction to
either of them. It failed to bring gratification to the
older woman because Destinẏ, who had always threatened to have a mind of her own, would not be entirely
turned against Mr. Godwin. Mahla glibly denied that
she had ever refused to have the children to live at
Destermere House and persisted that it had been
Stephen and Mr. Finch who remained inflexibly determined not to allow Destiny's life to be spoiled by bringing the Barleys here. She maintained that she, Countess
Destermere, was forced to agree because after all her
word had little influence nowadays. She had to bow to
the will of these gentlemen who dealt with the Earl's
family affairs. She denounced Stephen as being sly and
double-faced.

"He hoodwinked Claud, my poor dear husband. See
to it that he does not get around *you* with his suave
tongue and sanctimonious ways, my dear," cautioned
Lady Destermere. "I am of the opinion that our dear
secretary is out to feather his *own* nest."

When Destiny, who had an awkward way of wanting
to know facts, asked for an explanation of this, Mahla
had not a suitable one to offer, but mumbled:

"I warn you, my dear, that if you confide in him, for
instance, about the dear Prince and our little jaunts
down there, he will put a stop to them."

This of course, at once fired rebellion in Destiny.

"How can he, if I *wish* to have the Prince as one of my friends?"

"He would write to the Prince, or see him, and tell him that such an intimate little friendship was not suitable because you are about to be launched into English society. And the Prince, being an honourable man, would at once take himself far far away," was Mahla's glib retort.

Then Destiny thought of her delightful hour this afternoon, and the Prince's dazzling smile and the sweet plaintiveness of his voice when he sang to her. Her girlish heart yearned towards him. She brushed aside the thought of Stephen, although she still felt a sense of gratitude because he had brought her news of the children.

"I will keep our secret and see more of the Prince. I like being with him," she said.

So there was no further discussion about Stephen. But that night while her maid unclothed Mahla and placed her between the silken sheets of her exotic bed, the Countess feasted her own thoughts upon Stephen Godwin, and felt mad with rage and thwarted desire. He behaved to her as though she hardly existed in this house. His chill formality enraged her. With all the sensuality of her nature she wanted this man if only to be able to show that she despised him once he had weakened towards her. She could not bear his every effort to repulse her. The other more crude young men whom she took to her arms gave her little but physical satisfaction. She was not an unintelligent woman and it was Stephen's searching mind that fascinated her as well as his aesthetic face. Also she was shrewd enough to guess that his thoughts were turning towards Lady Destiny. He would never dare say so. But he was ready to adore the late Earl's daughter. Of that Mahla was positive.

Early next morning, Mahla, hooded and cloaked, took

herself down to her brother's retreat and confided her troubles to him.

He smiled and soothed her.

"A little patience, *liebling,* and the bird will be snared. Just bring her here again, often, and leave things to me."

"She must be married to you ere long, or that monkish devil of a secretary will find out and poison her against us. She is fascinated by you and by what I tell her of life but she has a prudish streak. She would not be pleased to hear that you are my brother, Humbert."

"She will not hear it until after our marriage."

"And when will that be?" asked Mahla gloomily.

"Leave it all to me," said Humbert again, patting his sister's hand. "A little more romance in this idyllic setting and I will soon have her running away with me to the nearest priest. Then when it is *fait accompli* we will face the 'monkish devil' as you so amusingly call him; with the wedding ring on your stepdaughter's finger. After that the destiny of my Lady Destiny . . ." he laughed softly . . . "will rest with me."

Mahla returned to Destermere House only half satisfied. She was impatient and apprehensive. She could only vent her bad temper on the blackamoor whom she beat with a cane until his eyes rolled in his ugly little face and he squealed like a stuck pig—all because of a trifling offence.

She screamed, too, at her maids. She dismissed, at a moment's notice, the young handsome groom whom she had made her lover, and later when she heard that he had drowned himself in the river, she laughed and called him "a love-sick fool."

The servants knew of these things and whispered amongst themselves but Destiny did not know. To Destiny, Lady Destermere remained a sweet and sympathetic stepmother. To the socialites of the district she showed herself a charming hostess, and she began to make arrangements for the big ball which was soon to take place at Destermere House now that the weather was warmer and the gardens ablaze with flowers.

Meanwhile Destiny went on with her learning. At times she felt overwhelmed by the greatness that had become hers and at times did not know whether to admire this new world in which she moved or feel contempt for it.

The young men with whom she conversed or who drove with her or walked with her often, seemed like spaniels, fawning and servile. The women were callous and avaricious. To own the largest diamonds, the richest furs, the finest Arab horses, seemed their main ambition. Things which in the spiritual sense were cheaply purchased. But Destiny had in her the seeds of something finer. She was not sure that she altogether enjoyed this empty world of the wealthy. At times it was distasteful—even frightening. But every day now, Lady Destermere arranged that Destiny should go down to the Lake House to visit the "royal invalid."

Once in that golden octagonal little room with Alexis, Destiny was dreamily content. In the light of the wax candles, in the warmth of the fire which "the Prince" still kept burning, even though it was summer, she slipped into unreality. She found the fruit that he gave her was always sweet. He charmed her endlessly with scenes of his former triumphs in the palaces of St. Petersburg, or at the state balls and operas in Vienna and Paris. Through his eyes, she travelled through Asia, India and Africa. Humbert cunningly painted for her a vision of romantic splendour in which he, the Prince, was always the figurehead and *she* was "the Princess." Without actually calling her so, he conveyed to her the fact that she was born to reign—to be royal. He piled the gorgeous colours on the canvas of her thoughts.

"You are far too beautiful and too young to be incarcerated in a grim castle like Destermere House," he said one day as they sat by the windows which opened into the small but perfect garden. (As usual, Mahla had found something else to do, while her brother charmed his unsuspecting guest.) "If only I were younger—stronger—I would like to ride upon a white horse and pick you up and dash with you to freedom. Ride like Icarus through the clouds. Away from England—from Europe—until we could drop down into the gossamer golden cities of Persia. I would show you the glories that are there, teach you a thousand Oriental delights."

Destiny listened, as always, with reverence and awe to the Prince's whimsical stories. He never let her see him unmasked. He was careful to stand in the shadows. He did not allow the sunshine to fall too clearly upon his ageing face. He became a sad lonely figure to Destiny which, of course, touched her maternal heart.

"I am too old for you!" once he cried.

"You never seem old to me, sir!" was her reply.

The Baron's full-lidded eyes rested on the girl with a burning desire which he found difficult to conceal, although Mahla had warned him not to be too impetuous, in case he scared the little bird away. Mad with impatience, he had said to his sister:

"How much longer am I to remain restrained and bored, leading this damned hermit's existence? When will the time for *her* be ripe?"

"I will tell you," was Mahla's reply.

Today, the Baron thought that Destiny looked particularly charming in a new costume of olive green over a butter-yellow petticoat which suited her admirably. For weeks he had watched her gain in poise and grace. He wanted to take her slender child's form with all its promise of budding womanhood in his arms; to devour her with kisses; to stop this romantic talk and show her what real passion could be. But he controlled himself. He read the innocence in her dreamy eyes and knew that she was not yet ready for an elopement.

While he played the spinet to her and she sat there looking at his handsome face and figure and listening to his beguiling voice singing an old love song from his true Fatherland—Germany—she was completely enslaved.

Everything here was tempting and seductive. Poisoned honey, which she drank without suspecting the evil in the charming satin-clad figure of the so-called Prince.

And day after day it was like this. Now, at his request, she no longer addressed him as "Your Highness"—to her he was *Alexis,* and to him she was just *Destiny.*

Always he had some little gift for her. A Fabergé trinket box; a charming golden dagger for her hair; a little Russian jewel-case, made entirely of precious stones (which, he told her, had belonged to his mother).

When Destiny protested that she must not take presents from him, he bent over her hand and murmured:

"I have nobody else in the world but you to whom I can give these trifles. They are not really worthy of you, anyhow!"

When Destiny was with Mahla, the woman added the poison of her own influence.

"You need not frown upon his gifts, my dear. Alexis has only you in the world to spoil. He finds you a most enchanting and precious new friend."

Destiny coloured with pleasure. She then asked, innocently enough, why Alexis had never fallen in love with *her,* as she was so beautiful, whereupon Mahla's lips curved into an ironic smile and she answered that they were and always had been "friends" alone.

"Although I think he is most fascinating and most women would find him so."

"But when can we ask him to our home?" Destiny asked impatiently. "It is not right that he should always be the one to entertain us. Let us be bold and tell Stephen that we are going to invite the Prince to Destermere House; let us insist upon it."

"No, no," said Mahla hurriedly. "It would never do. You will spoil everything."

So Destiny allowed herself to be guided by the older woman. And the belief that Stephen disliked him made her feel less friendly towards the secretary. Nevertheless she felt guilty and awkward in his presence and sometimes betrayed the fact. He, now utterly at her feet, was deeply unhappy. But nothing would have induced him to show it nor did he make any efforts to steal one moment more of time than she wished to give him. They seemed to meet only during meals or on the occasions when matters of business concerning the estate, demanded her presence or signature. He knew nothing whatsoever of those visits to the little Lake House. Nor did it enter his head that the Countess's brother was in England again. So far as Stephen knew, he was still in Germany. Stephen was thankful that her ladyship appeared to have no wish to invite her brother to reside under her roof as she had done in Geneva.

Meanwhile Destiny's admirers continued to call upon her. The Marquess of Midhurstholme sent flowers daily but Destiny found him a foolish fop. Indeed, none of the so-called eligible bachelors to whom she had been introduced interested her. Not even young Lord Fencham who was considered the finest horseman in the county, and although small, was good-looking. But he cared nothing for books or music. He bored her. There was the Hon. Esmond Culthorpe, too. With his mother he drove frequently from their big house in St. James's to visit the young girl who had become a fashionable prize. But Destiny found him unintelligent after Alexis.

Mahla now showed a new cunning. One day when Destiny announced that she was looking forward to the usual visit to the Lake House, she was told she could not go, because the Prince was ill. Immediately Destiny was all concern.

"Should we not send or take him flowers from our gardens?" she exclaimed. "Would he not like me to call on him?"

"He does not want anybody," said Mahla.

"Oh, poor Alexis!" cried Destiny.

"Why not write him a little note?" murmured the older woman, "I am sure that will console him."

"Do you think I may receive one in return?" asked Destiny with a hand on a heart that beat faster, full of romantic yearning.

"Little doubt, my dear soul."

So Destiny, on violet paper, in violet ink, wrote a careful letter of sympathy and of regret that they could not meet today.

Mahla made her wait a day or two for the answer which further intrigued and worried Destiny. She was so afraid that the handsome delicate Prince might be seriously afflicted and that she would never see him again. So concerned was she, that she actually confided in her stepmother about the health of the youngest of the Barley children.

"I am reminded of days when Matt was ill and I used to be the only one to soothe away his pains. If only I could do the same for Alexis," she sighed.

Sentimental little fool, thought Mahla contemptuously, but she patted the girl on the cheek and bade her be patient. Alexis would soon send for her.

Then came the reply from the Prince. It was in the form of verses which the wily Baron had copied out from a book of poems, and which expressed undying devotion. Lines written by Robert Herrick a hundred years ago:

> "I dare not ask a kiss
> I dare not beg a smile.
> Lest having that or this
> I might grow proud the while.

> No, no, the utmost share
>   Of my desire shall be
> Only to kiss that air
>   That lately kissèd thee."

The letter ended:

"These words were written to Electra by the poet, but I send them to thee, my sweet Lady Destiny, without whom I am so empty and forlorn."

It was signed "*Your devoted friend Alexis.*"

It was the first love-letter that the young girl had ever received. Quite naturally she was dazzled by it. When she showed it to her stepmother, the woman curled her lips and thought that brother Humbert was doing well. She said:

"How charming, my dear. It is obvious he misses you."

Destiny read the poem again, half terrified.

"But he cannot mean that he wishes to kiss the very air which I have breathed. I *cannot* mean so much to him."

"Who knows? He has to my certain knowledge never been so charmed by any female as he is by you."

Destiny went to bed that night thinking over the Prince's words, reading and re-reading her poem.

The separation was a little more delayed by the designing Mahla. Destiny wrote again to the Prince. She received in reply yet another of Herrick's poems:

> "Bid me despair, and I'll despair
>   Under that cypress tree,
> Or bid me die and I will dare
>   E'en death to die for thee.
>
> Thou art my life, my love, my heart,
>   The very eyes of me;
> And hast command of every part
>   To live and die for thee."

Stronger words this time—especially chosen to ravage a young female's heart.

After she had received this letter, Destiny went about with a glazed look in her eyes which satisfied her stepmother. If the little fool was not already madly in love with Alexis, she was well on the road to it, the scheming woman decided.

Stephen also noted that new, rapt look and wondered at it, but said nothing. It was not his business—nor was he privileged to question my Lady Destiny about her secret thoughts.

Stephen was entering now upon a period which marked for him a private and personal anguish. For try though he had been doing to think of Lady Destiny Frane only as his charge—his ward—the sweet object of his administration and care, she had come to mean much more to him.

Each day she grew more desirable—and inaccessible. At no time did his feelings of loyalty and devotion diminish even when she frowned on him or, which was more often, ignored him. When she deigned to smile even in passing, he felt a tremor of the heart which brought him more misery than pleasure. He worried over her future and he mistrusted the Countess who seemed to have such complete control over the girl. He was exceedingly anxious lest her influence was not for the best. But he could not guess what passed between the two. He could only try to watch from afar and hope for the best. He found it a thankless task trying to guide a young girl's footsteps. Anything that he planned seemed to be altered and taken right out of his hands by the Countess.

Came the day before the big Destermere ball, to which everybody who was anybody in the county, had been invited. Many were even coming down to Richmondwyke by fast carriages, from London.

A lovely July day, glorious sunlight, a profusion of roses, promised well for the gathering. Now Mrs. Perkins marshalled her army of servants. There was much polishing of the marble staircases and vast galleries. Preparations in kitchen and pantry for a banquet. Dressmakers and hairdressers, in and out the rooms of the Countess and her stepdaughter. The whole place teemed with activity, for tomorrow Lady Destiny Frane would make her first real impact upon Society, and during the following month, she was to be received at Court by the Queen.

But Destiny had little interest in the glittering dress she was going to wear or the Destermere jewels which had been brought up from the vaults by Stephen and sent to her for choice. She only knew that for the last four days she had not seen Alexis. She was frantic with worry about his health. She loved him now as only a young inexperienced girl can love and adore a man much older than herself. She was full of excitement when her stepmother took her down to the little house again, having received word that the Prince was now recovered.

"Can he not come to my ball? It is only with him I wish to dance," Destiny sighed as the two women drove to their clandestine meeting with "Alexis."

"My child, you know the reasons why he cannot come."

"But I want no other gallant!" cried Destiny.

Mahla smiled—a slow cruel smile.

This time it was not in the house that the Baron received the infatuated girl, but in his lakeside pavilion—a small charming Folly built by the Frenchman, on the water's edge—in the silver quiet of the summer evening.

He received her alone—handsome and imposing in pearl-grey satin with a black ribbon tying back the well-powdered wig which he was now wearing because he thought that it gave him an air of distinction and added youth. He had put on new high-heeled red shoes and lace hose, with silver clocks. He looked a dandy, yet serious-eyed and tender as he welcomed Destiny.

There was a silken couch bearing many cushions in the pavilion. A statue of Eros, bearing aloft a little oil lamp which shed a romantic glow. A table set with delicate china bowls of fruit, with crystal decanters and wine, a silver canister of Lisbon snuff, a golden crystal smelling bottle, a few sheets of writing paper and a quill. And, of course, a book of poems. Somewhere in the distance, music was playing. The violinists were hidden in the shrubbery. Hungarians—playing wild sweet dances.

The scene was set. The young girl, all in white today, with a sapphire blue hooded cloak, came towards the "Prince" timorously, yet wild with excitement.

"Oh, Alexis, are you better?" she began.

Then he held out his arms.

"My dearest little one," he said, "My sweet consoler. Without you it has been like death. You have become the Light of my Life."

Destiny was completely seduced, feeling that the devious roads in her short life had led to this one hour. She could be grateful now even to Stephen who had pulled her out of the old misery and made it possible though he did not know it, for her to come to this pavilion and be with her adored Prince. Alexis spoke again in that deep thrilling voice of his, with the foreign accent which fascinated her.

"My belovèd child! . . ."

And now Alexis took a great bunch of violets from a bowl beside him and crushed them into her hands.

"Take them. They are as sweet, as innocent, as fragrant as you," he said.

In delight and terror, she held the dewy purple violets and went into his arms. Her eyelids closed as she felt the joining of his lips with hers.

Humbert Faramund in this moment of triumph felt little but mad cruel passion for Destiny Frane, but he was clever enough to control it. It was with a youth's gentleness, that he kissed this beautiful trusting creature. He kissed her lips, her eyes and her hands. He told her that for years he had been a Prince without a palace or hope of a crown. A sad man alone, believing that love would never come to him. Now he knew that she was his star and had brought back to him all the colour and sweetness of life. .

"Let me dedicate the rest of that life to you," he begged, passionately.

She leaned her full weight upon him. He was agreeably pleased by the warmth of her response although all this "dallying" was distasteful to a man of Humbert's gross nature. For he was as likely after a kiss to turn like a serpent and strike a woman to the ground. Cruelty was a part of him—like desire. But his need for money was greater. To gain control of Destermere's fortune and all that Destiny's inheritance entailed, was the most important thing of all. He must play his cards well and remain the gentle delicate Prince a little longer. He could see that he had this girl completely fooled. He must hand it to his clever sister, he thought, and he admired his own histrionic ability.

Now, when her brilliant eyes implored the kisses she was just beginning to accept and enjoy, he let his arms fall away from her.

"This cannot be," he exclaimed emotionally. "You are a child and I am an old man in my thirties. I cannot hope that you should love me."

"But I do!" she exclaimed. "I love you with all my heart, Alexis."

"It cannot be true," he breathed, stepping back in well-simulated astonishment.

"It *is* true! You are my first love and you will be my last," she said.

"No, no, I must not touch you again, you sweet belovèd creature, but I must admit that the days have seemed long without you," said this man who was an abominable fraud.

"I could not sleep," she ' said with shyness and

warmth in her eyes. "I longed for my stepmother to bring me to you again."

"But I would not be a true man if I did not respect your youth and try to conceal my passion for you," he said grandly. "I had no right to send you those verses, but I was mad with longing."

"Why should you not love me?" she demanded. The first strong passion of her life gave her confidence and strength to say it.

"My Dear One, they are even now preparing the ball for tomorrow in order that you should meet and dance with a younger more suitable man who will eventually be chosen for your husband."

"Never. They can never force me to marry where I do not love."

Humbert smiled to himself.

"Are you sufficiently experienced to know whom you truly love, dearest?"

"Yes, and it is *you*, Alexis."

So immensely flattered and victorious did the Baron feel that it seemed now all the weeks of work were rewarded. A reward that was being offered to him on a golden platter. He could not resist taking the charming girl in his arms again.

Destiny was lulled to a stupor by his passionate yet restrained caresses. She assured him with all her generosity and kindliness uppermost that she did not despise him because his health was not good. He was, to her, the most handsome gifted man she had ever known. Prince Alexis had become her Prince Charming.

"Whatever Stephen and the others say, I shall marry no one but you!" she declared.

His eyes narrowed. He laughed low with triumph. When she was in his arms again, he pressed her face against his shoulder and she could not see the avarice or cruelty that convulsed his handsome face, nor how old and haggard he was. She did not realize that the delicate "Prince" became a dangerous panther—strong—

snarling—anxious for the kill; enjoying the sense of power in anticipation of slaughter. But strangely enough Destiny did not immediately concur with everything that he wanted her to do.

When she came out of her daze of enchantment for a few moments, the Countess joined the lovers and the three of them discussed the future. The young girl then expressed a strong desire to tell Stephen and her father's financial advisers exactly how she felt.

"I do not really care for lies and deception," she said, almost apologetically, and holding fast to the hand of the "Prince." "I would rather be married to the man I love in open rebellion than continue in secret."

Brother and sister exchanged glances. At once Mahla entered upon a long dissertation on the madness of such an idea. To be frank, to be good, yes, one must be, of *course,* said the woman glibly, but there were times (and this was one) when it was necessary to deceive. If Stephen so much as guessed that Destiny intended to marry Prince Malinkoff, he would do as Mahla had already warned her and prevent the marriage.

"But why, *why*?" Destiny kept arguing, "Alexis is a man of title and distinction . . . surely Stephen and my father's advisers would be pleased for me to make such a marriage."

Again brother and sister looked at each other. Then the Baron lifted the slender hand he held, kissed it from time to time and added his own persuasion in his rich rolling voice.

A Russian Prince was of no particular account, he said, and he had only humble means these days in comparison with what he used to have. His vast estates in Russia had been long since sold or destroyed. Mr. Godwin would certainly want the heiress of Earl Destermere to make a more brilliant marriage.

"So you see, my darling, we must marry first and tell Mr. Godwin after," Humbert finished decisively.

"But if Mr. Godwin disapproves could he not follow

us, in league with Mr. Finch of London and M. Bertian from Geneva, and force me back to Destermere House?" asked Destiny anxiously.

The Baron passed a perfumed lace-edged handkerchief across his lips to conceal a scornful smile.

"I shall see that they do not. Anyhow I do assure you they will prefer to leave you in my care once we are man and wife, my belovèd child," he said.

Mahla tapped the toe of her right foot impatiently against the ground. She knew what Humbert had in mind. Part of their scheme had been that Humbert and the girl would be well away before Stephen found out and followed and that Destiny, once she had spent the night with Humbert—her reputation ruined and her honour gone—would never find a young respectable man in England to propose to her. They would realize that. She would *have* to remain married to her "Prince." Only at a later date would he disclose the fact that he was her stepmother's brother—Baron Humbert Faramund.

But Destiny was not to be as easily conquered as the Baron and his sister had anticipated. They discovered that Claud Destermere's daughter was no mere pawn to allow herself to be moved about the chess-board. Her senses were beguiled and enslaved by her lover but her spirit of rebellion was not yet weakened even by these two experienced people.

"I must have time to think," she kept saying. Mahla's pansy-purple eyes flamed with a sudden hatred of the stubborn young girl. Almost, that strong dislike broke through her façade of honeyed sweetness and spoiled everything. But the Baron was quick to see what lay on his sister's face and bundled her out of the pavilion.

"Leave me to talk alone with my little wild bird," he murmured. "I will arrange everything."

Once alone with her he took Destiny in his arms again, and tried to alter her mind. She assured him of her eternal love and her desire to marry him at once.

But she must think awhile, she said, before she could agree to an elopement behind the back of the man in whose care she had been entrusted, and those others who were her father's friends.

"Maybe," Humbert said in an injured voice, "you wish to wait and see if you find a younger and more attractive suitor during the ball tomorrow night."

That hurt Destiny. At once she put up her face to be kissed and stroked Humbert's cheek with a tender hand.

"Indeed not. I love *you* and only you. There could be no other man. But just let us get through tomorrow's festivities. I will think things out. Maybe *you* will come round to my way of thinking and allow our marriage to be announced. Something—I know not what—persuades me not to agree to a secret runaway match."

The Baron could willingly have strangled this obstinate child. Then suddenly a brilliant thought struck him with all its new cunning.

"Whom do you love most in the world?" he asked in a silky voice.

"You," said Destiny with all the ingenuousness of youth, combined with her newly-roused passions.

"Who else?" he persisted, watching her closely.

"My four babies—my little adopted brothers and sisters," she said hanging her head, "but alas, I do not suppose you will want them to live with us any more than Stephen does."

"Ah, but that is where you are wrong!" exclaimed the Baron. "Come here, my angel, and let me tell you something—"

He led her back to the sofa and sitting there, he with one arm around her waist, and she with her head on his shoulder, he enchanted her by opening up a new vista of happiness. This time *perfect* happiness. Grandly he said:

"Not only do I want you to have your heart's desire but I will become a guardian to your little sisters and brothers. In a week from now, they shall be here in my house for you to join."

She caught her breath—cheeks burning with excitement.

"You cannot *mean* that, sir!"

"But I do. I shall send my coach and my servants to Bath—is that not where they are living?"

"Yes, with Mr. and Mrs. Jupp, an innkeeper and his wife."

"I shall send also a good nurse to care for them," continued the Baron. "Then once they are here in this house, will you believe how dearly I love you, and agree to a secret marriage?"

"Alexis!" gasped Destiny, but paused as though her mind was still confused and troubled.

"Do you not see that if you told Mr. Godwin all these things he would put a stop to it," persisted the Baron. "Has he not told you, himself, that you may not have the children at Destermere House?"

"Yes, yes, he has."

"Then give me your word that if I have the children here to greet you in six days' time—you will stay with me, and marry me before saying one word to Mr. Godwin."

"And I need never leave my darling children again?"

"Never," said the Baron carelessly.

Now she was conquered completely. All her heart went out to him. Whatever doubts she had entertained about deceiving Stephen Godwin were swamped in a flood of ecstatic happiness. She even seized one of the "Prince's" hands and touched it with her fresh moist lips.

"You have my adoration and gratitude for ever, sir."

He smiled triumphantly over that bowed pretty head.

"I want no gratitude, only your love. And pray do not call me 'sir.' I am your humble slave."

"Oh, Alexis!" she exclaimed, "what heavenly bliss, to come here to this darling little house and live here with you and my brothers and sisters. My sweet little Matt who is always ill and needs my care. Dear Jem, dear Luke, and dear Lucy!"

It was as well she did not see the expression of horror and disgust on the face of the man who bent over her. When she left the Folly a few moments later, rosy from his kisses, she felt irrevocably bound to him because he had proved his true love for her.

As she was about to drive back to Destermere House with Mahla, the Countess made an excuse to return to the Lake House and speak alone with the "Prince."

She patted his shoulder—an evil grin on her lips.

"You are a genius, Humi!" she said excitedly. "You now have the girl eating out of your hand. I never *thought* of sending for those awful children."

The Baron removed his wig and scratched ungracefully at his bare itching pate. Now he looked old and unattractive, but he popped a sweetmeat into his greedy mouth and munched it.

"Yes—was it not a brilliant idea, my *liebling*? She will willingly consent now to go on deceiving our friend, Stephen. The trap is baited. And, of course, the brats will remain here in hiding only until the priest has tied the nuptial knot and the girl is mine. Then they can all go drown themselves in the lake so far as I am concerned. But *she* will be with me on our way to Paris while you tie up the finances and see that the money belonging to my dear little wife passes instantly into our hands."

Mahla smiled. She kissed her brother on both cheeks.

"Thank heavens," he said, mumbling over another sweet, "that I shall soon be able to eat and drink once more as I used to, and put an end to this 'slim youth' nonsense. My dear wife will have to put up with my natural corpulence."

Mahla laughed again, and returned to the phaeton. She was sweet and sympathetic to Destiny.

"Do not forget, my sweeting," she said, "that we

must keep this plan a deadly secret, or all will be lost and you will never see those children again."

"I shall not breathe a word," said the girl. She turned dreamy eyes upon her stepmother. "I cannot get over this sweet surprise, dear Mahla. To love and be loved by Alexis and have the children with me, too—oh, I think he must be the most noble man in the world to arrange this for me."

"Indeed he is," said Mahla. "Did I not tell you so?"

But for the first and perhaps the only time in her life, the older woman turned away from Destiny's shining eyes, and was ashamed.

12

THE BALL WHICH was held at Destermere House for the début of Lady Destiny Frane was whispered about among rich and poor for many days afterwards. Certainly nothing so splendid had been seen in the village of Richmondwyke for the last twenty years—since the old Countess, Destiny's grandmother, was alive. Then, there had been a fine ball to commemorate the birth of William, Duke of Gloucester, who had, alas, followed the rest of Queen Anne's family to the grave. But it had not been as fine a social event as this.

The weather remained calm and beautiful. The sky was luminous with stars. A full moon shed an unearthly brilliance on the dimpled waters of the river and the glorious grounds. Down the main road from London to Richmondwyke, down the chestnut drive, came the dashing equipages of the wealthy families who had been invited to Destermere House.

Many of the more sedate matrons of the season had

accepted the Countess of Destermere's invitation more out of curiosity to meet this hitherto unheard of daughter and heiress than any desire to become friends with the widow. Nothing much good had been said about Mahla and nothing much was really known about her as the Destermeres had for so long lived in Geneva.

Came magnificent coaches with their uniformed and bewigged postilions. Smart phaetons with their high wheels and fast trotting horses, bearing two gentlemen at a time. Sedan chairs carried from houses in the vicinity.

Footmen ran with their flaming torches down the drive clearing a way for their grand masters and mistresses. All the lights of the great castle-like house shed welcoming lustre into the purple darkness. Outside, in the tossing flame-light, the handsomely dressed men and women stepped from their vehicles and entered the house to be greeted by the Countess of Destermere who stood at the foot of the staircase with her stepdaughter at her side.

Mahla looked regal enough tonight, her red hair piled high on her head and well-powdered; her dress of black damask satin over a purple silk petticoat overlaid with gold lace. A rich, unusually sombre attire for her which gave her voluptuous beauty some taste, and was the envy of the older women who were anxious to criticize her.

For the moment my Lady Destermere, in excellent spirits and smiling, was playing her part as a grand lady and devoted stepmama, to the best of her ability. Wondering what all these decked-out, painted, fashionable ladies with their good little daughters and dandified sons and stout claret-faced husbands, would say if they knew how far she was really removed from being a respectable lady; or what little hope they had of marrying any of their sons off to the wealthy daughter of the house.

But it was not so much at Lady Destermere, as at the Lady Destiny Frane that most eyes were focused.

Destiny had hardly believed her own sight when she had seen herself upstairs, earlier this evening, in the long cheval mirror of her robing-room. She wore purest white satin over which there was a green, silk-knit waistcoat embroidered with silver flowers. The skirt was wide and hooped, covered with yards of delicate lace. The blackness of her hair had been powdered with silver dust. She scintillated from the top of that lovely head to the tips of her green slippers. The corsage was cut low, in the fashion of the period. Around the long slender neck sparkled emeralds set in old gold, of Italian design. The famous Destermere emeralds. They sparkled too, in her tiny ears and about her wrists. She wore white embroidered gloves and carried a little silver-framed posy of lilies-of-the-valley.

She knew that she was a success but she had not really looked forward to tonight. She would so much rather have put on a cloak and run down to that little Folly by the lake into the arms of her lover. She had refused to do so of her own accord; she knew that she remained here, because she wanted time to think, and she wanted above all to see the four children there in the Lake House before she finally broke away from her father's house.

One young man, who looked into Destiny's large eyes and at the rich curve of her mouth, afterwards confessed to his best friend that he was quite overcome.

"I as near as could be, swooned, my dear soul, when I bent over her hand," he said, "I' faith, our Lady Destiny is a rare prize."

"With those emeralds and the rest of the state behind her—very rare indeed," murmured his friend, who was a cynic.

Two by two the guests were received by their ladyships. The sonorous voices of the footmen echoed through the great hall.

"Lord and Lady de Coverley . . ."

"The Countess of Luxborough and the Hon. Miss Estella Luxborough. . . ."

"Her Grace the Dowager Duchess of Grafton. Lord Roger Grafton . . ."

And as each man bent over Destiny's hand murmuring some fulsome compliment about her dress, the beauty of the house, the flowers, or the music, Destiny answered with a shy smile and a few stammered words.

Oh, if my father had been alive to see my triumph, she thought, thinking more kindly of the Earl tonight. If it were not only my stepmother here beside me! If my own mother had but lived and borne her rightful place and title. If only my brothers and sisters were here, as well, to see all this splendour!

So many *ifs*.

Destiny was excited. She was pleased by her success, *yet in some dim inexplicable way she was frightened.* It was all such a change from her old life—from the summer of a year ago. Deep down inside her soul she felt alone in the grand crowd. Yet only a few miles from here, her darling Prince Alexis waited to take her away. Why should she feel apprehensive? She wondered. . . .

Perhaps I am tired, she thought. I have studied too much and I am laced so tightly tonight I can hardly breathe. And I don't really like the way all these men look at me. I want nothing but Alexis.

Then she saw standing alone by the big carved stone fireplace, the familiar figure of Stephen Godwin.

Tonight the secretary was garbed in a slightly more fashionable manner than usual, having forsaken the sober grey for a brown satin square-cut coat and breeches, with long flapper pockets and waistcoat of a light corn colour, cuffs edged with lace.

He looked strange to her in such a splendid attire, but worthy of note, of a sudden. Truly he had a fine face, she thought, and straight proud bearing.

She caught his gaze. He was looking straight at her. She gave a half smile and then immediately looked away again. Her lashes hid the guilt in her eyes. For she did indeed feel guilty whenever she looked at Stephen and realized how she meant to deceive and leave him. A dozen times or more since yesterday she wanted to run to him and tell him all about her wonderful Russian Prince and her intended marriage.

She had rehearsed what she would say.

"However much you object—whether you like him or not—I intend to marry Prince Malinkoff immediately."

Aloof from the crowd, Stephen continued to watch his lady. His heart was heavy within him. Every time he looked at her, his depression deepened.

She was so breathtakingly beautiful, he thought, in her white, green and silver dress, with her lilies, he could hardly tear his gaze from her. Last night he had not slept. All day, although busy with preparations for the entertainment, he had found his thoughts straying to her. Every time he passed her—looked into her eyes—his heart had seemed to turn over.

He was faced with a terrible truth; he was madly in love with Destermere's daughter. Madly in love with the ugly duckling of the past who had turned into the beautiful swan of tonight.

Of course, he knew that his was a hopeless love and he must stamp on it, ruthlessly—and obliterate it—but Lady Destiny had become the ruling passion of his mind.

He watched young Lord Midhurstholme crook an arm and bear Destiny off to the ballroom to open the cotillion.

Bitterly the young secretary watched her go. After a moment he turned and walked into his belovèd library where there were only a few candles burning. Here it was darker and cooler, more to his liking. For a few moments he stood with the back of his hand to his burning eyelids.

Destiny! Oh, God, what a name, he thought. Such as she was—she might become any man's destiny (but never his!) What was Stephen Godwin but the paid, humble servant of her father; and the chancellor of her exchequer?

God grant that she chooses the right man tonight and that nobody hurts her, he thought.

Then he heard a low voice murmur his name.

"Stephen!"

He swung round and saw the magnificent figure of the Countess standing before him. Her extraordinary, pansy-purple eyes held a faintly malicious look, he thought. She glided towards him, holding up her hooped satin skirts between her fingers.

"Well, Stephen," she murmured, "and why is our gentle studious secretary not enjoying the party? Why is he alone in here? Why has he not found some charming girl to flatter?"

"I want no girls and I do not flatter people," he answered curtly.

Mahla's long eyelashes flickered from side to side. Her eyes grew restless and avid. Her tongue touched her lips like the fang of a serpent, he thought. She was regal—splendid—with diamonds in her powdered hair, but tonight he admired her no more than he had ever done.

"If you will pardon me, I have work to do, my lady," he said.

She barred his way.

"What work?"

"Something I must do," he stammered.

"Always so anxious to get away from me. Foolish boy, I wonder whether you realize what you are missing by your refusal to be friends with me."

"I do not object to being your *friend*, my lady," he said coldly and with meaning.

Mahla drew nearer him. She tapped his shoulder with the end of a jewelled feather fan she was holding.

"You are not flattering, are you?"

"I repeat I do not easily flatter."

"Not even my Lady Destiny?"

The red blood flowed into his cheeks. The woman saw it and knew that there was hidden passion in this cool aloof maddening young man. But it had taken the child, Destiny, to rouse it.

Mahla was filled with furious jealousy. The sooner Humbert got hold of that spoiled chit of a girl and taught her who was master, the better pleased she would be. She had had about enough of "mothering" Destiny Frane. She was bored, bored, *bored* by playing the grand matron. She was still young herself, and she wanted colour and ardour and excitement. She wanted, too, to possess this young man.

She put her arms around Stephen's neck and pressed her body against his. The musk of the heavy scent she used assailed his nostrils. He was appalled to feel the hot hungry taste of her kiss. She whispered:

"Stephen, *Stephen,* do not reject me . . . *love* me . . . Destiny is not for you. Anyhow, she is much too young and inexperienced. It is *my* love you need. *I want you.* Come to me tonight, Stephen. When the ball is over, *come to me,* and I will open your eyes to pleasures such as you have never imagined."

He stayed rigid, unbending, and sweating. He was wholly disgusted. At last he unclasped her hands from his neck and pushed her rudely away from him.

"If your ladyship permits . . . I have other and better things to do. . . ."

He strode away. Mahla stood for a moment, her face a white mask of fury, her eyes sick with disappointment. She could see that she was further than ever from conquering Stephen Godwin. Further, because of that obstinate brat with all her virginal purity.

She shall be made to pay for this, Mahla thought. Humbert will see to *that*.

After he had left Mahla, Stephen felt weary of his whole life. With the late Earl, he had lived in peace and happiness. Here in this house at Richmondwyke there was an atmosphere of antagonism—bitterness—distrust. And *she* whom he loved so hopelessly treated him with an indifference that cut him to the quick.

The ball went on. Some of the men grew a little drunk. Some of the women, for all the fact that they were high-born ladies, also were flushed with wine and looked a little dishevelled and amorous.

Lady Destiny Frane saw it all. Wondered at it and decided that it was a waste of time and money. The compliments paid her were false, of that she was sure. She did not enjoy the bubble-light conversation, or even the dancing.

On with the whirl; the music becoming a little more frenzied as the night wore on; too much food, far too much wine. The laughter grew a little more shrill—couples disappeared from the ballroom and were found whispering in dark corners, or coming, giggling out of the shrubberies in the moonlit grounds.

It should have been so different—have seemed glamorous; amusing. The glitter and pomp might have made Destiny proud of her heritage and fortune. She was warmly congratulated on the success of the evening wherever she went, and to whomever she spoke. But the whole affair held little charm for her. She knew of course, that soon she would be leaving it all. It was her first and last public appearance. Soon she would say farewell to Destermere House for ever. She would wait with feverish anxiety for the summons from the Lake House—and go to Alexis and her children.

Destiny received six proposals of marriage that night and refused them all, stammering and embarrassed. Some of the mothers who had brought along eligible sons looked at the dark-haired golden-eyed girl in her lily dress and whispered among themselves.

"She isn't going to be easy to get. Whoever her mother was and whatever her breeding on *that* side, my Lady Destiny has quite the grand manner. Chilling, in fact."

But they made a mistake. There was nothing really chilly or "grand" about Destiny Frane. She was a warm-hearted passionate child; a woman's deepest emotions stirred in her for the first time, she had little admiration for the sort of frivolling and coquetry which she saw among so many of her female guests tonight.

In the early hours of the morning these people showed no signs of leaving. Grooms and coachmen and postilions yawned their heads off. The footmen and serving maids were run off their feet.

Destiny suddenly broke away from the side of a young heir to an earldom, who had been telling her that she had the most glorious eyes in the world, and fled to the library. Somehow, her footsteps were always directed to that particular room when she felt world-weary, for she knew it would be quiet there, and a little austere. But as she ran breathlessly into the room and shut the door behind her, she was unprepared for the sight of Stephen Godwin sitting at his bureau, arms folded, forehead resting upon them.

For a moment she stared at his back, confused. She had not seen him for several hours; not even at the supper. In fact, she had thought he was sulking and had gone to bed. She knew that he was a strange man and far from gregarious. She felt suddenly remorseful at the sight of him in this attitude of despair. What was wrong? Why was he here, alone, instead of taking some charming woman by the hand and dancing with her, or going for a walk in the moonlight, like the rest? Why should he stay friendless and alone?

She remembered, too, with a throb of shame how

badly she was treating him. Her elopement would be a terrible shock when he learned about it.

"Ought I not to tell him the truth tonight?" she asked herself.

Now Stephen turned his head as though conscious of another's presence. Seeing Destiny, he sprang to his feet, his white face colouring.

"My lady—" he said, then stopped as though speechless.

She came towards him. She moved beautifully, he thought. She had certainly learned much from the dancing master who had put her through her paces every day. She carried her small dark head with the true dignity of the Destermeres. His gaze travelled over her and rested only for a single second on the snowy curve of bosom, showing in the daring *décolletage* of the day.

It was not heaven but hell, he thought, to love this girl—with all the first vivid passion of his manhood.

"Stephen," she began and paused. (Even the way she spoke his name, cut him like a knife because of its intrinsic sweetness.) Despite all her radiant beauty— her enchanting attire—her emeralds—her success tonight—he still thought of her as a desolate child, as she had been when she first came here.

"My lady—" he began again, the muscles in his cheeks working.

"Surely you're not working at this hour?" she reproached him.

"No," he shook his head.

"Then what are you doing in here alone? Why are you not dancing with the rest?"

"I am only the secretary, my lady," he reminded her with a sudden bitterness. "I do not take active part in such entertainments."

"That is not strictly true," she corrected him, and looked at him with puzzled eyes. All hostility between them had died—as it so often did in this quiet room when they were alone and they talked together; apart from the Countess. "At several of the soirées or dinner parties," she continued, "you have been as one of the family and helped me to entertain, and, so far as I could see you are ever a favourite conversationalist with many of the gentlemen."

The compliment pleased Stephen but he tore his gaze away from her, trying to quell the tumult of his senses. He said curtly:

"I like to talk to those gentlemen who share my interest in history and literature, Lady Destiny."

"But you do not care to talk to the ladies?"

"No," he said, "not in particular. I do not understand women."

"And you do not give them a chance to understand you," she said impulsively.

"I apologize if I have not behaved as you would wish with your guests, my lady," he said in a harder voice.

Now suddenly she was angry. She marched to the bureau and picked up a small gilt stiletto which was used as a paper knife. She tapped it on the blotter.

"How difficult you are, Stephen. No one can get to know you. You seem bent on remaining apart from the rest of the world."

He gave the ghost of a smile.

"The world of fashion and froth does not appeal to me, my lady."

"Nor does it really to me, Stephen," she said quickly, and in a low tone, she looked at him now with eyes so gentle, so unusually full of understanding that his whole body trembled. He tried to hold his back more stiffly.

"Maybe you will soon grow more accustomed to Society and enjoy it," he said.

"Like my stepmother does? She dances with all the gentlemen so gaily, and they tumble over themselves to win one smile from her. It is easy to see why my father was carried away by her," Destiny sighed.

Stephen said in a violent undertone.

"God forbid that you should ever become like Lady Destermere."

Destiny dropped the little stiletto on the blotter—shocked.

"Why do you say that? Why do you hate my stepmother so much? I never can understand why you two should be such antagonists."

He wondered what this young girl would have said if he had told her how Mahla had behaved towards him just now, in this very room. As he remained silent, Destiny went on:

"I think you do the Countess an injustice. She may lack some of the qualities you admire—because she is worldly and you are an intellectual quiet man; but she has been enormously kind to *me*. I need not have feared a cruel stepmother."

Stephen could not begin to tell her the manner of woman Mahla really was. He muttered:

"I am glad that your ladyship finds the Countess helpful."

Destiny was silent a moment. Again and again it was on her tongue to tell Stephen about Alexis and the sweet intrigue which had ended in the proposal which she had accepted. She gave him a grave look and said:

"If I . . . I . . . f-found a gentleman who pleased me . . ." she was stammering, ". . . and my s-stepmother liked him but you did not approve—what, then, would transpire?"

Stephen began to walk up and down the library restlessly, unable to stand and face the young girl with equanimity any longer. He tugged at the laces at his throat. He felt hot and uncomfortable in his new splendid suit and wondered why he had bothered to have it made. He replied at length:

"It is to be hoped that that day will not come, my lady. It would be better if your guardians and your father's advisers should all approve the gentleman in whose hands the control of the Destermere fortunes and estates must fall."

Destiny bit her lip.

"Does it mean that when I am married that everything I own will pass to my husband?"

"Yes—at least, into his control."

"You and the Countess will no longer be my guardians?"

"Not once you are married."

So, Destiny thought. Alexis will handle everything as my husband and sole guardian. That will be wonderful. He wants only my happiness. He will help me, too, to build a splendid future for my dear children.

Stephen stopped in front of Destiny and looked at her uneasily.

"Can it be that you have already met a young gentleman here tonight who has taken your fancy?"

"No. . . ." Destiny could at least answer that truthfully.

Stephen felt relieved. He knew that she must eventually take a husband and that it was both mad and impudent of him to suffer one single pang of jealousy. But somehow he could not bear to think of her in any man's arms.

She asked him a few more questions.

What would happen, she wished to know, if, indeed, her guardians disagreed over her choice?

"Unless he was utterly unsuitable, I am sure everybody will wish you to marry the man you love, my lady," Stephen muttered.

She persisted:

"What would make my choice unsuitable in *your* eyes, for instance?"

Stephen clenched and unclenched his hands. What had got into the girl that she should want to know all these things tonight? Hitherto she had seemed to show little interest in the idea of marriage. Indeed, he could remember that once she had seemed repelled by it. When she repeated her last question, he answered:

"No one, least of all myself, my lady, would wish you to unite yourself with a fortune-seeker, for instance, or a rogue."

"Is such a man likely to come my way?" she parried.

"No, I do not think so, I see the lists of your friends and they are carefully chosen," he said uneasily.

She blushed and looked down at the ground.

For the fraction of an instant it was her turn to feel uneasy. What *would* Stephen think of Alexis? Of course Alexis could not be a fortune hunter, and certainly was not a rogue. He was an old family friend of her stepmother's; a Russian prince of great distinction. Mahla had told her that he was only fifth or sixth in succession to the Czar himself. No, she need have no qualms about Alexis. Alexis was the type, surely, to appeal to Stephen once he got to know him and they would patch up their misunderstanding. Alexis lived a quiet, solitary life dedicated to his music and his books.

Shall I confide in Stephen? Destiny asked herself for the hundredth time.

But her courage failed her at the end. She dared not spoil everything now, and she had given both Alexis and Mahla her word. But suddenly, in a wish to bridge the gulf between herself and her father's secretary who appeared so dedicated to his duty towards her, she drew near Stephen and held out a hand to him.

"Would you not like to come into the ballroom and dance a step with me, Stephen? Believe me, we may not see eye-to-eye always but I never forget that my father loved you. In all his letters which you have given me to read, I have learned that, and must ever be grateful to you for the way you served him. Indeed, for the way you serve me, now."

He hesitated for a moment, then gripped the hand

between his and fell on one knee as he would have done to a queen. He kissed the back of the slender hand. He only touched it with his lips then dropped it, but she felt how those lips burned. A queer startled feeling shot through her whole frame. She caught her breath. She heard him murmur:

"My Lady Destiny . . . *oh, my Lady Destiny!*"

Then before she could answer, he rose and walked out of the room at a great pace as though anxious to get away.

Puzzled, she stared round the empty library for a moment, wondering what this was all about. The cool, solemn Stephen who usually spoke to her so abruptly and in a businesslike manner, had never before done such a thing as kneel at her feet. It flung her into complete confusion. She had thought that he disapproved of her and even at times disliked her being here. To-night—or, rather, in the early hours of the morning—he had shown another side. He had proved that there was quite another Stephen—human and warm and vulnerable.

As Destiny walked slowly into the hall and heard the lilt of the violins from the musicians' gallery and came into the gay lights and dancing crowds again, she did not know whether she wanted to laugh or to weep. Stephen, of all men . . . to become emotional and rush away from her as though possessed! She wondered if she should tell her stepmother about it. But she said nothing. She was learning tact, among other things. It would be best not to mention the one to the other, since they were so unsympathetic towards each other.

Yet when morning light filled her beautiful, perfumed bedroom—and after her maid had undressed her and put her to bed—Destiny pressed a hot cheek against the cool silk of her pillow, and found her thoughts straying not only to her handsome romantic Prince, but to Stephen. For a long time she would remember his lips against her hand; his voice, so full of desperate urgency, whispering:

"My Lady Destiny . . . *oh, my Lady Destiny!*"

13

DURING THE NEXT few days following the ball, Destiny did not go down to the house by the lake. Once again Lady Destermere used her diabolical cunning and made the girl wait.

"Soon your dear children will be there. Until then, let us pay a great deal of attention to people and things at Destermere House and so divert Mr. Godwin's attention completely."

Destiny complied with her stepmother's wishes, and each night, in her innocence, she prayed for the return of her darlings and for heaven to bless the love that she bore her dear Alexis.

She saw rather more of Stephen than she wanted. For, twenty-four hours after the ball, he summoned her to the library for a business conference. Godfrey Finch had come from London, and the good Monsieur Bertian who had travelled from Geneva attended, and two venerable, bearded gentlemen—Sir Edgar Landseer and a Mr. George Featherly—both of whom were at the head of the Bank which dealt with Destiny's huge fortune.

The gentlemen were served with Marsala wine and cracknel biscuits once they were gathered together around the table.

Destiny refused both. To Stephen she looked very young and subdued and thoughtful; no longer the gay, radiant young girl he remembered last night in her lily-white ball gown and sparkling emeralds. This morning she wore muslin with a white fichu and sprig-muslin mantua with pale pink ribbons. She looked very charming, and strangely pure. Stephen thought. Young and delicious, thought the three older gentlemen as they gazed benignly upon their client.

The Countess had not been invited to this conference, neither had Mahla shown any wish to attend it. It concerned the boring details of the estate which she was sure she would soon be handing over to her brother.

She had laughed to herself when she greeted the gentlemen and bade the footman conduct them to the library. Let these old fools talk and argue about this allowance, that stipend, and the other wage. What cared she? Anything that they arranged today would be cancelled within a few days—yes—as soon as they were informed that Lady Destiny Frane had become the Baroness Faramund. What a shock awaited them, the Countess had reflected—all such pious, God-fearing sober-sides, who looked slightly down their aristocratic noses at *her*. The sort of look that reminded her that she had German-Jewish blood in her veins and came from an aristocracy which they believed inferior to their own.

But Destiny gave the gentlemen the respect due to such personages and listened attentively to all that they, who had been her father's advisers, had to say. They were discussing the workers—a subject which held her attention, for once *she* had been poor and needy. Once *she* had slaved like a servant. She pitied the lower classes. She would be glad to improve conditions for labourers on the Destermere estate. She said so, frankly. She also told herself, guilelessly, that sweet, kind Alexis who could never say "no" to a request from her, would soon be standing by her side, to help her look after her people.

Sir Edgar Landseer, this morning, had come from London to discuss the Law of Settlement which had been passed ten or twelve years ago, to remedy the evil of the people who sought employment where they had practically to starve on a parochial pittance.

"Our peasantry depend upon such landowners as yourself, my Lady Destiny," he murmured. "I am sure that you wish to help break these chains of the old feudal system."

"I do indeed, sir," she nodded.

Sir Edgar glanced at a paper which Stephen had placed in his hand.

"I see that the average wage for your labourers varies between four and six shillings a week."

"That is so," said Stephen.

Destiny drew in her breath. Her cheeks grew pink.

"Indeed. I think that is far too little when they have to feed themselves and their children upon it."

"Make a note," said Sir Edgar, "that her ladyship would like to raise these wages. I feel in sympathy with her."

"I, too," said George Featherly, an honest and genuine banker, who had known and cared personally for Destiny's father as a close friend.

"In France they get less," put in Monsieur Bertian, shrugging his shoulders.

"Much as I love France, Monsieur," said Sir Edgar, "I feel the day will be not long before there is a revolt in your country against the wealthy classes who have so much more than the others. They are, after all, human beings."

"Oh, I agree with that," exclaimed Destiny, clasping her hands together, "for I, myself have known for instance, what it is to long for wheaten bread. But Mr. and Mrs. Barley could not afford it, nor could we buy anything like tea or sugar which I have in such plenty here, in my own home. Fresh meat we ate only twice a week. And once, when the parson caused one of his labourers to cure a pig's flesh for us, it was unwholesome and made everybody ill and. . . ." she broke off, crimson, looking shyly from one gentleman's face to the other.

They looked back with sympathy and kindliness, thinking that Lord Destermere's daughter was a most angelic young lady. How much more did they approve the fact that it was she who would inherit her father's fortune rather than that shocking widow of his.

Stephen, alone, did not look at Destiny. She noticed that. Not once did he raise his eyes to her. He sat very pale indeed, and with a frozen look on his face which troubled her exceedingly. She was still unable to forget the amazing moment of revelation in the library.

More business matters were discussed. Two of the gardeners and their wives lived in a cottage with a thatched roof and crumbling walls which offered miserable shelter. This must be put aright. The bank would willingly allow Mr. Godwin the money to direct such operations. Wages in general were to be raised a shilling per man.

Destiny had seen some of the men on her estate working till half-past-seven at night, and been told that they started at five o'clock in the morning and rested only an hour during the day. For every hour's absence other than that they were fined a penny. Some of the work—the haymaking, for instance—was done by small children unequal to the task. They were all sturdy enough to start with but became pinched and miserable-looking.

"If you will excuse me for being dictatorial, I will not have this on my estate," said Destiny hotly.

The gentlemen all stared at her, feeling that this was the late Earl, himself, speaking; for Claud had never favoured slavery nor agreed with those who worked his employees until they dropped.

Before the conference was over, Destiny had ensured that some of the dreadful misery of the poor would be mitigated by her financial aid. And she thought:

I must remember to tell Alexis all that has been

agreed. I know he will approve. And she looked a little sadly and timorously at all these gentlemen; her inherent honesty made her long to tell them now, this instant, about the Prince, and her intentions.

It made her feel even worse when Sir Edgar turned the conversation to the subject of her marriage.

"All London talks of the magnificence of your first ball, Lady Destiny. We wondered if you had met any charming eligible man who took your ladyship's fancy, for of course, all of us who are behind you look with interest and hope towards your ladyship's personal future and happiness."

Now, for the first time, Stephen looked up at Destiny. He watched her face grow crimson and her eyelids droop so that he could not read what lay in her eyes. Her reply was confused and almost inaudible but accompanied by a shake of the pretty dark head. Why did she blush so violently, he wondered. What had she in mind? Dear God, if only he were not so shaken with longing for her! He got up abruptly and with his portfolio under his arm, begged to be excused from the gathering, saying he had a meeting with the head bailiff of the estate.

After he had gone, Mr. Featherly said:

"A most estimable young man upon whose loyalty you can count, Lady Destiny."

"Indeed, yes. The late Earl entrusted everything in Geneva to him, as to his own son," put in the Swiss notary.

"There could be no better champion for her ladyship's cause," added Sir Edgar. "I like Stephen Godwin greatly and always have done. He is not only conscientious but of a high intelligence."

To all of which Destiny listened, growing somehow more and more ashamed of her duplicity. So moved was she that when the gentlemen had gone she went at once to her stepmother's boudoir. That indolent lady was lying on her couch being fanned by the blackamoor whom Destiny found so hateful.

"Mercy on us but the August day is grilling," complained Mahla, keeping her eyes shut.

"I must speak to you," began Destiny.

"Now don't tell me any of the boring details about the business which has just been discussed without me," said Mahla rather spitefully, "for I am not of a mind to listen."

"Bid Ramilles go. I wish to speak to you alone," said Destiny.

Now Lady Destermere lifted her lashes and cast a somewhat startled look at her stepdaughter. It was not usual for Destiny to use such a peremptory way. Remembering what was at stake, Mahla immediately sweetened her tone.

"Pray be seated, then, and let us discourse, my dear soul," she said languidly; and to Ramilles: "Get out of here; you black limb of Satan!"

Ramilles retired. Outside the door he made a frightful grimace. He was the slave of the red-headed milady but there was a malicious streak in him that resented her treatment of him. He never knew where he was; either she was patting his head or kicking him as though he were a dog. And, if anything, he disliked the younger lady even more because she openly disdained and ignored him.

He waddled on his short fat legs off to the kitchen to ask for some pastries with which to console himself.

Alone with her stepmother, the girl made a final appeal to be allowed to tell Stephen and her father's friends the truth. She did not want an elopement. She wanted to send for the Prince and introduce him now, this moment, to the household.

This brought Mahla to her feet. She no longer succumbed to the heat of the day. Quelling the desire to strike the obstinate girl across the face, she argued and wheedled and brought out all the old warnings. If

Stephen knew he would try to forbid the match because the Prince was Russian and much older than Destiny, and he would most certainly put a stop to the children coming here.

"And at this eleventh hour—why, they may even now be here in the district waiting for you!" added Mahla. "Why spoil everything by your desire to be so honest with Mr. Godwin?"

"He has been good to me," muttered Destiny.

Mahla pushed back the heavy waves of her red hair. She fixed her stepdaughter with her hypnotic gaze whilst her lips smiled in a freezing manner.

"So for the sake of being grateful to our dear Mr. Godwin, you will risk not seeing the little ones for whom dear kind Alexis has sent his coach. You are mad. I thought you loved and trusted the Prince."

"I do—indeed I do!"

"Then think only of him and not that canting secretary, and pray do not tell me that Stephen is trying to win your favours. I would not put it past him to make a bid for you *and* your fortune," said Mahla spitefully.

"Oh, *no!*" breathed Destiny and drew back horrified.

Mahla seeing the impression she had made, went on eagerly.

"Let me tell you in confidence, my dear, that that humbug would like to see your fortune entirely under his control, for only the other day he licked his lips when speaking of you and said what a prize you were, and why should not he, being young, consider himself in the running for your hand? What of *that* for a hypocrite?"

Destiny gasped. This was so contrary to the noble character those gentlemen in the library had just given Stephen Godwin. Indeed, so hard to believe, when she thought of his general conduct—she found it incredible. Yet she had to remember how he had knelt at her feet and kissed her hand and called upon her name. Mahla's words cast a new and less attractive light upon the gallantry.

What am I to believe?! Destiny asked herself help-lessly. Where in this life that I am now leading, is the *truth*?

And she felt a desperate longing to see her lover— her fascinating, wonderful Alexis who had taught her the meaning of love and in whose arms she could be lulled to a sense of security and rapturous delight.

"Oh, I want to see Alexis!" she broke out involun-tarily. "I want to talk to him about everything. . . ."

It was at this very moment that a knock came on the door and the dwarf, Ramilles, thrust in his be-turbaned head. Grinning, he held out a silver salver, bearing a letter.

"This has just been delivered to me," he piped in his falsetto voice, "to be handed to no one but my young lady."

It was to Destiny that he held out the salver.

Mahla saw the writing and her heart leapt. From Humbert. Good old Humi! . . . He had sent this note at the psychological moment. For now Destiny broke the seal, unfolded the letter and read the only words she wanted to read—

"Come to the Lake House. They are here. Alexis."

She forgot Stephen and all her doubts concerning him. She forgot her desire to be truthful and open about her love affair. She rushed at her stepmother and hugged her.

"Oh, they are *there*. My little darlings are there! Oh, Mahla, think upon it!"

Mahla smiled, a slow cruel smile. Without speaking, she fondled the girl's dark tumbled curls, and congratu-lated her.

Within a short time, both ladies were dressed and in the phaeton which my Lady Destiny drove herself, for she was accomplished with horse. Two smart, high-stepping greys pulled them rapidly through the grounds of Destermere House to the Ancaster estate.

The charming French-built house drowsed in the hot August sunlight. The lake was a sheet of gold. Up in the high trees the rooks cawed and flapped their strong black wings. The sky, today, was a deep Italian blue. It was one of the loveliest afternoons of the summer.

Humbert, his gaze meeting the amused eyes of his sister, clasped Destiny in his arms and kissed her warm, red lips.

"Yes, they are here, my belovèd. You will find them all four in the pavilion. Go and enjoy their company."

Eyes blazing with excitement, Destiny paused a moment to question him.

"Will not everybody in the district know now that they are here?"

"Not at all," said the Baron, blandly. "I have arranged things so that they came well hidden in my coach and they are to be given over to the care of my German housekeeper who is an old devoted servant of mine and will speak not one word unless I bid her to. They will sleep and eat in her rooms and take the air only in the enclosed garden, guarded by my wolf-hounds."

"Can I not have them with me?"

"As soon as we are married, of course, my little dear," said Humbert, and raised her hand to his lips.

She was enchanted. She felt that he had done more for her than anyone in the world by giving her the bliss of this reunion. From the pavilion she could even now hear childish voices, laughter recognizable to her hungry ears. Dear Jem laughed like that when she was pleased.

It was Destiny's turn to seize Humbert's hand and kiss it.

"I will never forget what you have done for me, Alexis. Let me quote now that poem you sent to me:

" 'Thou are my life my love, my heart
   The very eyes of me
   And hast command of every part
   To live and die for thee'."

"Not die but live," said the Baron glibly, pressing a fond kiss on her glowing cheek.

But after the girlish figure had fled down the rose-filled garden to the pavilion, his smile vanished. He turned to his sister.

"Now to make our plans. The marriage must be at once—tomorrow. I will speak to the priest tonight and pay him well for his silence and services."

"I agree, for she has a mind to tell Stephen all."

"Not now with the children hanging over her as a threat. If she does not do everything I say, she shall be told that she will never see them again."

Mahla frowned.

"Easy, my dear; no threats of that kind until the nuptial knot is tied or you will scare her off completely."

"Leave all to me. She is wax in my hands. You heard what she said. She will *'live or die for me'* now."

Mahla nodded. Looking towards the pavilion she twisted her lips in an ugly smile.

"To live or die for thee, eh? Well, once you have command of Destermere it would not really matter very much if the little darling did, indeed, give up the ghost."

"When I am tired of her," said the Baron lazily. "But until then I fancy we might lead quite an interesting life together. She has much to learn."

Down in the pavilion, Destiny, deluded and wildly happy, clasped the four Barley children in her arms. They had thrown themselves at her with screams of delight. Only little Matt of the retarded mentality stood by, shyly sucking a thumb. At his age children soon forget and he had grown accustomed to the good Mrs. Jupp's motherly care. But it was not long before he was seated on sister Dessie's lap, munching sweets and the others were following suit, talking nineteen to the dozen.

Destiny asked endless questions and they answered them all. Yes, they were quite happy at Bath. Yes, Mrs. Jupp was very kind. They had lovely cakes and creamy milk and played games with the other children and had been to a fair and it seemed that everyone was good to them. Certainly, Destiny had never seen her little adopted brothers and sisters look so well. Matt still had a sickly mien but had put on weight. Jem was a fine tall girl and had grown an inch. Lucy was taller, too. Luke had lost his hollow cheeks and listlessness and was going to be a strapping boy. They were all neatly clad in good clothes with fine hose, and leather shoes. They were not the ragged, verminous, miserable brood who had almost starved with her at the parsonage.

She was enchanted—full of nostalgic memories of the old days, which even though spent in poverty, had been happy because Destiny had made them so. She had baked and sewn for the children, invented games, read to them, protected them from the last sad months of their mother's life, and the unkindness and illtemper of their wretched father. But now, she thought happily, she was rich. She could give them everything in the world that they wanted, and educate them. They would belong to her and to Alexis, once she was Princess Malinkoff. They would eventually live with her at Destermere House—whether her stepmother or Stephen Godwin wanted it or not. She would be a married lady then and able to decide things for herself. And she was sure Sir Edgar and the other advisers would be on her side.

She could see that dear Alexis had given them everything; toys, books, bonbons. But they clung to her and begged her not to leave them again.

"I will not," she promised them. "That dear, sweet gentleman who made it possible for you to come here is a Prince who is going to be my husband," she said shyly, "and I am going to become a Princess and then you can live in my fairy kingdom—happily ever afterwards.

Starry-eyed, the four children stared at their "sister" who was so magically changed, so wonderful; yet the same dear, loving Dessie whom they trusted and adored.

"You will be Princess Dessie," piped little Lucy, and all the others fondly echoed the name.

Never had Destiny felt so proud. A little later a plump German woman, whose chubby features made her look amiable enough, joined the happy little crowd in the pavilion. Her smiles disguised the small, puckered mouth and mean eyes. She curtsied to Destiny and in broken English murmured that she had come to take charge of the little ones as His Highness wished to see her ladyship.

Destiny kissed all the children and promised to return to them.

"I will take them to the house now, my lady," said the woman respectfully, "to eat their dinner."

Back with the "Prince" and her stepmother, Destiny chatted to them in tremendous spirits. She kissed her lover like an excited child rather than a passionate woman, and even kissed, impulsively, her stepmother's delicately painted cheeks. She did not as a rule feel so demonstrative towards Mahla.

"Oh, I shall never stop loving you both for making me so happy!" she exclaimed.

Humbert and his sister exchanged satisfied glances.

"And now, my darling," said Humbert, his spirits as high as Destiny's, "we must make arrangements for our elopement tomorrow."

A shadow fell across the girl's bright face.

"Tomorrow?"

"Yes, my darling—the sooner the better," said Humbert, "and then we can confront all these dreary, conventional gentlemen whom you received this morning and tell them that you are the Princess Malinkoff and that in future you can dispense with their services."

Mahla was quick to see the girl's forehead pucker. She was quick, too, to realize that Destiny did not find it easy to be ungrateful or ungracious.

Hastily she said:

"Those things will come later, Alexis. Do not confuse our little dear with matters of business now. All that concerns us is her personal happiness with you."

Destiny hung on to her lover's arm and looked trustfully up into his eyes.

"You have made me the happiest girl in the world, Alexis," she whispered.

"And I am the happiest of men," he said, beaming; and thought: *Ach!* what a relief it will be when I need not utter such foolishness but can be myself again. She will rebel at first but she will soon find out that I am her master.

Now Destiny listened with a growing excitement to the plans Alexis had made for her.

Tomorrow was the ideal day, because Stephen was driving to London on business at the invitation of both Sir Edgar and Mr. Featherly. She would be able to pack her boxes and without being seen by any of the servants, drive, alone, down to the Lake House. The "Prince" would have a fast carriage waiting to take them on to the neighbouring village of Little Hampton. There they would be wed, and then rest the night at The Mitre Inn on the river. Already the "Prince" had arranged for rooms at The Mitre to be placed at the disposal of himself and his bride.

"But the children—" began Destiny.

To Hades with these miserable brats, thought Humbert, but he gave Destiny a charming smile.

"For just one night they must stay with Gretchen who will care fondly for them, my love. The morning after we can return and re-join them here."

Of course he had not the slightest intention of doing

any such thing. Once Destiny was his, body and soul, she would have to be told the truth and accept it. That damned secretary and his friends would realize that to save her honour, she must be permitted to remain with her lawful wedded husband, whether they considered she had been tricked into the bridal or not.

Humbert was completely callous. In his nature sadism and sentimentality went hand in hand. He could sing songs of passionate love to little Lady Destiny, he thought drily, but once she was the Baroness Faramund, she would have to dance to another sort of tune. He would be in control of her and her fortune and Stephen Godwin could do nothing about it. As for the girl's feelings—they did not come into it, with Humbert. What a terrible shock it would be to a sensitive highly-strung girl to learn how she had been duped and to whom she was married—Humbert did not care. As for those four children—they would be put away in the Poor House long before she returned from her brief "honeymoon."

It was with mixed feelings that Destiny finally bade good-bye to her "Prince" and returned to Destermere House. So quiet was she on the way home that Lady Destermere glanced at her uneasily and asked her what was amiss.

"Come, cheer up, my dear. Surely you cannot be sad on this the eve of the happiest day of your life. You are going to the man whom you adore, never to be parted from him again."

Destiny gave a long sigh.

"I know. I know. But—"

"But what?"

Destiny hesitated for a moment. She could not quite explain to her stepmother but a queer, apprehensive feeling had come over her just now when she kissed the four children good-bye. Little Matt had started to cry. It had always hurt her to see Matt cry, because he was backward; such a sad, sickly little thing. She used, in the past, to defend him from his horrid, impatient father, very often at the risk of getting a beating, herself. Alexis had been sympathetic—sweet about the children, she thought. He had reminded her, just before she left them, that it was only good night, and not goodbye, for she would see them tomorrow. She ought to be satisfied.

But she was not at all sure that she wanted to shelve all those good gentlemen who had been her father's advisers. She could tell Alexis these things tomorrow after the wedding.

The wedding! Could it be true that she, who a short time ago had been a complete nonentity, was now about to become the bride of a Prince? Her cheeks coloured hotly at the memory of his passionate farewell kiss.

"I live only for tomorrow, my own belovèd," he had whispered, and it had made her tremble deliciously.

Mahla's insidious propaganda continued.

"I am your stepmother and I promise you have made the right decision. Leave everything in my hands and the hands of dear Alexis."

It did not take long for Destiny to be reassured and convinced. But she felt that she did not want to come face to face with Stephen again because that look of respect, of deep quiet trust in his grey eyes, made her feel so guilty.

Stephen approached her later that evening. He sent word that he wished to speak to her when he knew that Mahla was busy with her robing (which always took that lady a couple of hours). But Destiny was quickly dressed and came downstairs long before her stepmother.

Stephen felt a pang of hopeless love as he watched the young girl descend the stairs. She looked marvellously beautiful, he thought. But when she reached his side he saw that she seemed unusually pale and heavyeyed and that she had a nervous air.

"I trust all is well with you, my lady?" he said anxiously.

"Oh, yes, very well," she said, but her cheeks blushed. He cleared his throat.

"I want to thank you, my lady, for this morning's work and for troubling to interest yourself in the business affairs of this estate. It would I know, have greatly delighted your father."

Her colour increased. He was certain now that she was unhappy and disturbed about something and emboldened by his great concern for her, added:

"Are you sure there is nothing distressing your ladyship?"

Her head shot back. Her large gold-flecked eyes met his for the fraction of a moment, then turned away again.

"Why should there be?"

Her voice was cold and not encouraging, but he persisted.

"If there was anything . . . I would always try to serve you . . . if I could win your confidence—" he broke off stammering.

Heavens, she thought, why does he speak like this? What does he know?

"There is nothing," she muttered aloud, but was conscious again of a sickening feeling of guilt and distress which all Mahla's influence could not entirely smother.

A painful pause between them, then Stephen said:

"I have been thinking about your adopted family. . . ."

"What—what have you been thinking?" she demanded.

He could not help noting the way her eyes dilated and how she moved her head like a startled fawn.

What is wrong with her? he asked himself. There is some mystery here but she hates me and will not give me her trust.

He told her that he had been troubled by the thought of her distress over the long separation from the little

Barleys so he had wondered if he could find lodgings for them at not too far distance, so that she could visit them sometimes.

She thought scornfully: You are too late. Someone who truly loves me has already brought that to pass—and more besides.

Aloud she said:

"Thank you. I—will consider what you say."

She turned and walked away from him. He looked after her. She wore one of the fresh crisp sprigged muslins with hooped skirt which suited her so well, and in which she looked cool and fresh on a hot summer's night like this. How slender her waist was, with its sky-blue velvet sash and the blue velvet ribbons in her satin-black hair, and around her throat! Oh, God, how madly he loved her and how impossible the whole situation was becoming. He felt as though he would go out of his mind with the pain of it. He had for a desperate moment, considered handing in his resignation and begging that she would allow the other guardians to direct her footsteps. Then he remembered what the dying Earl, her father, had said to him after he had heard this young wife revile his name. *"Destiny,"*—the dying man had gasped that name in Stephen's ear, *"never . . . leave her. . . ."*

Stephen walked away with bowed head knowing that he could not break that trust, no matter how bitter the cost to himself.

14

DESTINY WOKE to a morning of wind and rain. A sudden and typical change in the variable English weather.

Ten degrees cooler than yesterday. A sunless, lowering sky. Indeed, the rain was heavy and threatened to ruin the roses. Soon the velvet sweeping lawns of Destermere were puddled and the tall delphiniums, soaked and battered, bowed their haughty heads.

Destiny had not slept all night. She had felt far too troubled! At one moment she thought of Alexis with all the excitement of a young innocent bride-to-be. In the next she wondered what had led Stephen to speak to her as he had done last night. What he had said must surely be coincidental, yet how strange it was that he should have mentioned bringing the children to the district.

She was up and wrapped in one of her velvet, fur-edged dressing-robes when Stephen drove away on his three-hour journey to the City of London. She watched him enter his coach in the courtyard and heard it clattering over the flagstones towards the archway into the drive.

Once he was gone, she knew she would have no trouble about getting away to Alexis. Now she would not be found out. She ought to be glad. She supposed she might never see Stephen again; that Alexis would soon be her husband and that he would look after her and cherish her more tenderly than Stephen had ever done. Yet when she looked down at the secretary in his cocked hat and grey travelling cape, it was not without regret. Destermere House without Stephen would definitely lose something. Was it a sense of security? So many conflicting feelings rent her peace of mind that finally the young girl concentrated on her future husband and the joy of seeing her little family again. She would only be parted from them one more night. Tomorrow she need never leave them again. That would make up for everything. If Stephen saw her and reproached her, she would say:

"*You forced me away from my children in the first place. It is your fault if I have deceived you and if I leave you now and go to one who understands my true feeling.*"

After she had taken her morning chocolate, she descended the staircase and wandered restlessly through the great house. It seemed very empty and quiet this morning and very cold. The lashing of the rain against the windows and the howl of the gale that had sprung up in the night, gave her a depressing feeling. She shivered and drew her robe closer around her, and pouted to herself. At least, the sun might have shone for my wedding day.

She paused under one of the many paintings of her father and looked up at his proud, handsome face a little wistfully. Would you approve of what I am doing this morning, I wonder? Do you see me from your heaven, and know that I am the happiest woman in the world, and soon to be a Princess?

She entered the library at last, after a reluctance to do so, for it would be filled with memories of the secretary who was now on his way to London. So quietly did she move that Ramilles, the blackamoor who was standing on a stool in front of Stephen's bureau, did not hear her come. So an astonished Destiny saw the hateful little dwarf busily engaged in trying to force open the top drawer with the end of a broken knife. She uttered his name with furious indignation:

"*Ramilles!* What are you doing! *How dare you!*"

When he turned and saw who spoke to him, he fell off the stool in his agitation. He picked himself up, his eyes rolling with fright. He tried to waddle on his grotesque legs past the young lady of the house, but she caught him, knocking his pink and silver turban off as she did so. He looked horribly evil, she thought, thus denuded of the turban, with that black, woolly pate. She shook him as she would a rat.

"Villain! How dare you attempt to rob Mr. Godwin in his absence!"

"Oh, my lady, my lady, let me go! I meant no harm, let me go!" Ramilles implored.

"Not until you have told me what you were searching for," said Destiny.

He began to blubber and whimper.

"Let me go. I will not tell you."

"Oh, yes, you will!" said Destiny in a fierce voice.

He let out a howl, trying to release himself from her strong young fingers. Both of them leaned down simultaneously to snatch at the dwarf's turban. It was then that a piece of white paper fell from a pocket in Destiny's gown, but in her anger she did not notice it. He, however, saw and picked it up and stuffed it quickly inside his tunic. He had a natural cunning. She caught him by the collar and he started to howl once more.

"What on earth is all this about?" asked a voice from the doorway.

Lady Destermere marched in, her red hair flowing down her back. She, like the younger girl, was still in her dressing-robe. She looked languid-eyed. She had not slept too soundly, herself, and was in a vile mood, fearing lest anything should go wrong with Humi's plans. When Destiny started to explain what she had found the dwarf doing. Mahla listened, her temper worsening. Of course she knew all about it. She, herself, had ordered the dwarf to go down and open that desk the moment Stephen was gone, thinking that her stepdaughter would still be abed. She had never expected the girl to wander round the house so early, for it was not yet ten o'clock and very often the ladies did not descend until midday.

Destiny was full of indignation and demanded that Ramilles should be expelled from the house. This was too much for Mahla even on this important day when she must be (for the last time) beholden to the girl.

"You're making a mountain out of a molehill," she said pettishly. "Ramilles was merely being mischievous and I do not intend to expel him. He is a rare specimen in this country. The Duchess of Ancaster, herself, asked me to sell him to her and I refused. He amuses me."

Destiny looked disgusted.

"Well, he does not amuse me, and he is a thief," she declared.

"I will have him whipped," said Mahla carelessly.

Ramilles, who was a craven coward, flung himself at his mistress's feet, seized her hand and tried to kiss it.

"Mercy, my lady, mercy!"

Mahla hissed at him meaningly:

"Don't dare utter a word."

"But, your—ladyship—"

"Keep you ugly mouth shut," Mahla screamed in a rage and sent him sprawling on the floor with the tip of her toe, adding viciously: "It will be ten lashes for you and I shall get the strongest groom in the stable to administer them."

"I do not wish that," began Destiny, feeling suddenly sick.

The blackamoor picked himself up and scuttled as fast as he could out of the library. Outside the door he adjusted his turban, wiped his face and made hideous grimaces at the door. He hated my Lady Destiny and he hated his own mistress. She had ordered him to open that desk and find whatever papers there were relating to the late Earl's fortune. Now she had betrayed him and was going to have him whipped. He would get his own back on her somehow.

He went off, hid himself in a cupboard, and read what was written on the piece of paper that had fallen from Lady Destiny's pocket, the only thing he had had time to steal. As he did so, he began to grin, and he thanked his lucky stars that it had been my Lady Destermere's whim to teach him how to read. Sometimes when she lay resting on her couch he would read aloud to her—lewd poems from the licentious writings of the medieval poets which excited her and caused her special amusement coming from the dwarf's lips in his falsetto, squeaky voice.

That note was fated to be a powerful and important weapon of revenge in the hands of the slave. For it was the one which the "Prince" had sent Lady Destiny yesterday and which Ramilles himself had delivered.

"Come to the Lake House. They are here. Alexis."

The diabolical dwarf who had been with the Countess long enough to know most of her private affairs—and Lady Destiny's too—was quite aware that this meant that her young ladyship was in the throes of an affair of the heart outside this house. He had accompanied Mahla on one of those journeys to the Lake House. Prince Alexis had actually spoken to Ramilles that day and had pinched his ear which the blackamoor had found excrutiatingly painful, and called him an "ugly little animal." The dwarf had a revengeful nature and an absurd vanity. Always dressed up as he was in fine silks and satins, he was used to being spoiled and pampered by some of the coarser-natured maids in the establishment.

He was bitterly aggrieved by the injustice that his mistress had just done him, and he was terrified of being whipped. For a long time he brooded over his wrongs and wondered how he could get back on these fine ladies—particularly the Countess.

Obviously, there was only one way. He would show this note and tell all he knew, to Mr. Godwin when he returned, and ask for his protection.

The cunning little negro raided the larder, crammed a selection of stolen cakes and tarts into a basket, and hid himself in a loft over one of the stables, where he intended to remain—out of sight of his terrible mistress. He would hear the horses bringing Mr. Godwin's coach back tonight. Meanwhile he must stay hidden and escape the lashing Lady Destermere had ordered for him.

At midday the two ladies left the house and walked

down the drive together, wrapped in hooded cloaks which soon got wet in the drenching rain. They took a short cut through a wooded dell, which led them out on the main road, beyond the main gates. Mahla, who hated her feet getting wet, shivered.

"This will cause my death . . ." she grumbled, pettishly.

The younger girl hung on her stepmother's arm, looking pale and frightened now that the hour of her elopement had come. She did not even notice that her dainty boots soon became splashed with mud or that the rain beat cold little arrows against her face. She kept saying:

"Oh, Mahla, I pray that this wedding will have God's blessing."

The Countess—bored and impatient with Destiny— kept her temper and replied:

"Foolish one, have no fears. You will soon be in excellent hands and far away from this dreary old place."

She had laid the plans cleverly. None of the servants was permitted to enter Destiny's room while the girl, aided by her usually lazy stepmother, packed a small box for the night with a few necessities. Tomorrow the rest of her wardrobe would be sent on to the Lake House. Meanwhile one of the grooms—another wretched boy, fascinated by Lady Destermere's red curls and seductive lips—had stood beneath my lady's window while it was still dark, received the box (let down on a rope) and carried it away. He was carrying it now, well beyond the lodge, on to the road. There, a smart little phaeton waited which had been sent from the Lake House with the Baron's German coachman and a footman, who had orders to pick up my lady and drive her to the "Prince."

As the ladies reached this coach, and Destiny watched her heavy leather-studded box being lifted onto it, she hung back and looked appealingly at the older woman.

"Will you not come too, Mahla?"

The Countess shook her head.

"My angel, I dare not leave home today. I must be there to cover up your tracks. I shall tell everybody that you are ill and in bed and forbid them to open your bedroom door, so that there shall be no hue or cry—nothing to send Stephen and his sleuthhounds racing after you, should he return unexpectedly and find you gone."

"I cannot go like this—" began Destiny, her stubborn blood asserting itself, but to Mahla's relief the coachman pulled from inside the vehicle a great bunch of pink roses tied with silver ribbons. Attached to them by a little diamond arrow was a note.

Destiny pinned the brooch to her corsage and took the flowers in her arms and inhaled their fragrance, then she read the note:

"Come, my Light, my Love, My bride. . . ."

The shadows and doubts fell from her like dark phantoms, chased away by a shaft of sunlight. She stood a moment longer in the rain and smiled at Mahla.

"Dearest Alexis! You are right, Mahla. I must go to him. I must be with him always."

She stepped into the coach. The elder woman kissed her—a traitor's kiss—then Destiny was gone. Lady Destermere stood waving gaily until the phaeton was out of sight.

Now the obstinate little idiot will be safely in *his* keeping. I am sick of her, thought Mahla.

She was prepared for a furious storm to break over her head once Stephen returned and learned the truth, but what did she care? The fortune would be in Humbert's hands, which meant in hers, also.

The young groom who had carried Destiny's box, and had been bidden to keep his lips sealed, waylaid her ladyship on the woodland path along which she returned to the house. He dropped on one knee before her, as to royalty.

"I hope I did right and I wish to serve you always, my lady. . . ." he said in a hot, hoarse voice.

Mahla, shivering in her damp cloak under the grey skies was not in a romantic mood, but the sensual side of her could not help but be stirred by the lad's servile homage and the burning ardour in his eyes. Sparkling, handsome eyes, with long curly lashes. He was not more than seventeen years old; tall and well-built. He had only been in her service since the death of the unfortunate William.

Trying to remember the new groom's name, Lady Destermere motioned him to rise, then lifted one of her jewelled fingers and touched his brown, rain-wet cheek.

"You shall indeed serve me always if you so wish it, Jack . . . is it not Jack you are called?"

"No, my lady . . . Adam."

"Ah yes, Adam," she nodded, and ran her fingers through his curls which were the colour of cowslips. How blue his eyes were, she thought. She could see his strong body trembling and knew that he was mad with desire for her. One of her rings caught in his long curls as she pulled her hand away, and he winced. She gave a low laugh.

"Poor Adam—he doth not like having his hair pulled. Never mind, he shall be compensated for the pain. . . ." And she added in a low voice: "Outside my balcony window tonight, Adam . . . there is a strong vine . . . you can climb up in safety once the house is in darkness and all are asleep."

He dropped on his knee again, covering her hand with mad kisses. Laughing, she left him there kneeling in the rain, babbling. This was what Mahla liked—this feeling of feminine, pantherine power over men—and especially those of the lower order.

It would be amusing tonight; with neither Stephen nor Destiny in the house.

She walked home, humming an old German melody. She barely remembered the existence of the young girl whom she had betrayed into the hands of one of the worst men alive.

This man, the Baron Faramund—gorgeously attired in a manner fitted to a bridgegroom—received Destiny with much pomp and ceremony when she arrived at the Lake House.

More bouquets were waiting for her; more poems, and flowery speeches.

In the elegant French drawing-room, Destiny looked at her "Prince" and her heart stirred at the sight of him. He had well concealed all his natural arrogance and brutality. He wore blue and silver today, and a small three-cornered blue and silver hat laced with silver galloons and trimmed with feathers of the same blue; his handsome damask coat had black buttons, and he wore fine, black silk hose and silver-buckled shoes.

Destiny looked at him with shy admiration. She began to feel less apprehensive. Especially once she was clasped to his heart and she felt his kisses warm, yet restrained, against her lips. He could lull her so quickly into a false sense of security. As her spirits rose, she became less inhibited—more feminine and anxious to coquette. She flung off her damp cloak and hood and stood arrayed for him in the fine dress that she and Mahla had chosen for the bridal. It was charming—with a tight white jacket edged in buttercup yellow, laced on either side over white satin petticoats. She had refused to powder her hair and tied it back with a yellow ribbon. She wore a most becoming little white hat with a curved yellow feather on the side of that glossy dark head.

Around her neck hung a necklace of twisted gold and a beautiful gold locket shaped like a heart.

"Do I please you, my prince?" she murmured, curtsying to Alexis and smiling at him through a tangle of lashes.

The Baron had to admit, even to himself, that he had never seen the girl look so enchanting. He could span that small waist with his two big hands, he reflected. He had been lucky to get hold of a fortune that was backed by both beauty and innocence. It was going to be no hardship to make this child the Baroness Faramund. The only thing he feared was her fighting spirit, which his sister had warned him would not easily be quelled once it was roused.

So he must play his part for a while longer. He covered her hands with kisses, telling her that she was the loveliest thing on earth and much too sweet and young for him, which immediately had the effect of making Destiny anxious to flatter and reassure him.

"Indeed, no. It is *you* who are too good for me, dearest Alexis. Oh, I cannot wait to show Stephen the ring that you will so soon put on my finger."

Humbert grinned to himself. He could not wait for that moment, either, he thought viciously.

Destiny ran to the window and looked out.

"The rain is ceasing to fall. Look, Alexis, there is a chink of blue in the sky. The sun will shine after all upon our marriage."

"Delicious thought," murmured the man.

"Are my darlings down in the pavilion?"

"No—er—they are with Gretchen in the—er—servants' quarters." He coughed. "I, er—allowed them to go there—er—because the maids found your little angels so charming—they begged to be allowed to play with them."

"But of course, the children love to be in the kitchen. They used to enjoy cooking with me at home," said Destiny in a merry voice. "I must go to them."

Humbert scowled. He was not amused. The dainty gilt clock in its glass case on the mantelpiece told him that it was time they started for Little Hampton. The parson would be waiting. But he dared not disappoint the girl just now, so (for the last time, he thought spitefully) she could go to them.

Destiny, full of excitement, quite forgot her qualms

and embraced her four darlings again. They seemed to have had a happy enough evening with their German nurse. "Mr. Prince," they told her, had showered them with presents. He had even given them a little gold cage with four white performing mice in it to amuse them.

Now Matt burst into tears.

"Why is he crying?" asked Destiny, going down on her knees and caressing the little boy, unmindful that her white satin petticoats trailed on the floor.

The other servants, who had not much idea of what was going on behind all this, watched and whispered amongst themselves, and thought how lovely and kind the young lady was. But Gretchen flushed and looked embarrassed because Jem, the spokesman of the family, told "sister Dessie" that they had come down in the morning to find that the cat had eaten the mice. Someone had opened the door of the cage.

"We think it was Gretchen," said Jem, whispering in her sister's ear, "because she said she could not bear mice. Was it not cruel of her?"

The German woman's sharp ears heard this, and immediately she plunged into denials and explanations, to which Destiny listened gravely. She tried to comfort the little boy. She would soon buy him some more pet mice, she said.

Gretchen stood by, her mouth tight, vowing to herself that she would make that girl, Jem, pay for what she had told my lady, once she had left the house.

Gretchen, herself, had made the arrangements for an attendant from the Poor House to come and take the wretched foursome away later this afternoon. The Institution had been reimbursed by the "kind Prince," who had told them that the children were the offspring of a former servant, and that he had clothed and befriended them.

Once more, the children whined and looked tearful when "Dessie" said that she must leave them for yet another night. But she soon persuaded them to smile again. She promised that tomorrow she would return, for by then Prince Malinkoff would have become their dear brother—or their uncle—or whatsoever he chose they should call him.

It amused the Baron to play up to this. He, too, embraced the children, fed them with bonbons and expressed a great fondness for them.

"Be good, little dears, and do all that Gretchen tells you until we return," he said gaily.

So Destiny was bluffed and knew no sadness this time when she waved good-bye to them. They drove away from the Lake House towards the village of Little Hampton which was two miles further on from Richmondwyke.

Her hand was tight locked in that of the Prince. Her lap and the padded seat beside her were covered with roses. Yellow roses, this time, to match her gown. That was one of the nice things about Alexis, she thought, he always added such charming touches. The moment he had seen the predominating colour of her bridal attire, he had ordered the gardener to produce a yellow bouquet.

"I can scarce credit my good fortune that I shall soon be your very own wife," she exclaimed.

"And I shall be your husband and your devoted slave," he said, giving her an ardent look from under his heavy lids.

She gazed excitedly out at the countryside. As she had thought, the sun was shining now, sparkling over meadow and forest. It all looked deliciously green and refreshed. She gave a sudden cry.

"Look, Alexis, there is a rainbow! That is a happy augury!"

The Baron made a suitably poetic reply and applied a pinch of snuff to his nostrils. He was so bored with this whole procedure that he could barely hold out until the morning, he thought; but until he had this girl firmly under control he must continue to act the adoring lover.

Destiny chattered to him in her artless manner as they drove towards the church. She told him all that had happened since they last met and how she had found the blackamoor trying to break into Mr. Godwin's desk.

The Baron frowned. He was surprised. Obviously, the little black devil had been acting under orders from Mahla, who should have waited until the girl was out of the house, too. Women were so infernally impatient, he thought. Why must his sister choose to pry into details of her late husband's money affairs now? What did it matter? Once *he* was husband to this girl, he would automatically take over control of the Destermere money, and there was nothing the dear secretary could do about it.

15

THE WEDDING WAS OVER.

The bogus "Prince" had taken the Lady Destiny Frane for his wife. The bride, pale with emotion, walked out of the little church on her husband's arm and stepped into the phaeton which was to drive them on to "The Mitre Inn."

It was her wish as well as his that the "honeymoon" should be so brief. She longed, she admitted, to get back to the Lake House and her "family" so that they could all be immensely happy together.

The Baron Faramund kept his thoughts to himself. He had thoroughly disliked the church atmosphere and the elderly parson and the vows he had taken (and never intended to keep). Now, alone with his bride again, he reaffirmed his undying adoration for her.

"My belovèd Princess," he called her.

Strange, thought Destiny, that now that the secret wedding was over her feelings of confusion and guilt crept back. She felt uneasy. Perhaps that was why she longed to get home again. She hated changes. She liked people and places she knew. She wanted to tell Stephen, and the others, the truth, then there would be no further need for lies and subterfuge and hiding-places.

She was silent during the drive on to "The Mitre Inn." She tried to forget her sudden uneasiness. She felt a thrill of pride when the innkeeper and his wife ushered them into the stone-built, creeper-clad inn on the banks of the river. They bowed and curtsied and addressed the pair as "Your Highnesses." It was quite fun, Destiny thought in her innocent child's way, to be treated as a Princess. If only some of the old people—friends of the Barleys—down in Bath, were here to see her triumph.

The rooms upstairs which had been especially prepared for the bridal couple had none of the grandeur of Destermere House nor the sensuous beauty of the little French retreat on the Ancaster estate. But much time and trouble had been taken to make the "suite" as luxurious as possible for the wealthy "Russian Prince" and his bride.

Ever since the orders were received by the proprietor, Mr. Henessey, there had been a scrubbing and a polishing and a rushing around by Mistress Henessey to collect her best articles of furniture and any treasures she owned to adorn the rooms.

Most of the stuff was oak, dark and old and shiny. Fresh white muslin curtains had been hung and tied with white ribbons, as befitted a bride. Mistress Henessey was a sentimental creature.

The huge four-poster had clean red damask curtains. The big bed had been made up with silken sheets and quilts which had been especially sent by the Prince. There were flowers everywhere, *and* mirrors. The

Prince had particularly ordered that as many mirrors as possible should be hung in the rooms. He had a passion for them. Mr. Henessey had found two silver candelabra which had belonged to his grandparents, in which tall wax candles burned tonight on the mantelpiece. There was a little powder closet for the bride and an adjoining room in which His Highness could robe. The private parlour was full of heavy oak decorated by blue willow-pattern plates and shining pewter. On a round table was spread a lavish supper. The best Rhine-wines in the Prince's cellar had been brought along by his Highness's men. They were now being cooled until the meal was served.

Mistress Henessey had not forgotten to make a bridecake, a monster, glittering with sugar, and festooned with sugar roses and cherubs made of icing.

"Oh, how charming it all looks! So fresh, so homely, so simple and just what I really like!" Destiny exclaimed, clapping her hands together.

The Baron groaned to himself. The whole place disgusted him. He had no use for sweet simplicity. He preferred the gilded, exotic type of salon to which he was more accustomed. He found this inn dull, and the atmosphere boring. But once alone with his bride, he set to work to captivate her afresh. He untied her little hat. He caressed her smooth bare throat. He complimented her on her exquisite proportions and soon, under his experienced fingers, she began to melt in his embrace.

But suddenly Humbert Faramund was seized with a terrible spasm of uncontrollable desire and the desperate wish to become himself—to put an end to farce. His kisses, his caresses, grew avid and passionate. His fingers began to tear more roughly at his bride's corsage. His language grew more coarse.

The young girl was at first startled then appalled. He was so different from the gentle Alexis she knew and loved. She was frightened now and repelled. She gasped:

"No—please—Alexis—let us wait awhile."

"Wait for what?" he asked. His face looked florid and he was sweating.

Her eyes glanced away from him. She gave a nervous laugh.

"At least until we have had supper and the candles are lit."

"Nonsense," he said.

"But, Alexis—the innkeeper or his wife will be serving the wine. We shall be—interrupted."

"We can soon settle that," said "Alexis"—marched to the door, clapped his hands and called for Mr. Henessey to bring up the bottles.

The innkeeper and a serving boy rushed up the stairs with trays bearing wine and goblets.

"Open six of the bottles," thundered the Baron in his most authoritative voice. "Then leave us undisturbed."

"Yes, your Highness; certainly your Highness. . . ."

While the innkeeper uncorked the wine, Destiny stood by, clasping her hands nervously in front of her. Her heart beat fast. Her eyes were scared. Her spirits had dropped to zero. It was as though she was beginning to see her Prince for the first time as he really was, instead of through a haze of romanticism. In this strange coffee-house away from everybody she knew, and quite alone with him, she felt dreadfully nervous and unsure of herself. Perhaps, she thought, it was natural for a bride to feel so. Oh, but *why* did Alexis seem so different this evening? He looked somehow much *older* and coarser. That angry flush and irritable manner did not suit him. He was not at all like the tender lover who sang sweet, sad, Russian songs dreamily to her, and caressed her so gently.

Her trembling fingers went to the locket at her throat and clung to it as to a talisman, while her big grave eyes watched this man who had just been made her husband, and had become a stranger.

The servants left.

Humbert threw himself into a chair, stretched out both legs and began to loosen his clothes. He felt they were too tight for him.

With the full light upon him now, she stared, wondering if she had ever noticed before what a big stomach he had, or that there were such pouches under his handsome eyes. He did not seem either handsome or desirable to her like this.

He drank noisily—one, two, three glassfuls of the Rhinewine—smacking his lips after each one. Then with a sudden return to the smiling jovial Prince, he poured out a glass for Destiny.

"Come, my pigeon. Do not stand there staring at me. This is our bridal night. Let us drink and be gay, little one."

She swallowed and shook her head.

"I . . . I do not care for wine."

He swallowed the drink himself. Then he looked up at the pale, beautiful face. That touch of dignity which made her hold her head so high and which reminded him of the late Earl who had been his mortal enemy, suddenly aggravated the Baron's bucolic temper. He was so sure of his prize now that he allowed himself to slide back into what he really was—a bully and a brute. He thrust a goblet into her unwilling fingers unceremoniously.

"Drink!" he repeated angrily, shouting the command.

She held the wine but stood as though frozen, staring at him. She could scarcely believe her ears. *Her Prince,* her romantic adoring Alexis, *shouting* at her . . . but this was dreadful! She grew even paler but she shook her graceful head.

"Please, Alexis, no. I do not wish to drink."

And she set the goblet down on the table.

Humbert had by this time swallowed his fifth glass of wine. It was fast mounting to his head for he had eaten no breakfast in order to get into this suit. Enraged, his fingers tore again at the buttons of embroidered waistcoat and shirt. These damnable clothes! He wanted to hurl them across the room. He wanted to tear the white and golden gown off that girl, too, and show her who was the master.

He got up and advanced towards her. Then pulled off his wig and threw it on the floor. Now, in a lightning flash, the truth was revealed to Destiny. The scales fell completely from her eyes. For he was revealed to her as a plump, middle-aged man with an almost bald pate. With that leering expression on his face he was no longer even good-looking, but quite ugly, she thought. Every vestige of romance was sunk in her extreme terror at this sight.

She began to back away from him, trembling so that she could hardly move.

"No," she said, under her breath. *"No!"*

"You will learn not to say 'no' to me, my dear," he said with a laugh that froze her blood.

She tried to escape—to reach the door, but he bounded after her at once, moving like a great cat. His fingers closed around her wrists and pulled her back to him.

"A little maidenly reluctance may be charming but surely you could not mean to walk out of this room, my little bird?" he exclaimed and laughed and put his hot lips against her pulsing throat.

She gave a bitter cry. For in yet another flash of terrible revelation, she remembered the moment when Sextus Barley had tried to seduce her; how she had loathed him and thought of him as a miserable, lecherous old man. This man was the same—with the one difference *that she was married to him.* But he was equally repulsive to her. His expression, his actions, brought back all her old disgust and terror of men.

The music, the poems, the tender love-making, the romantic elopement, all such things had been mere illusions. She realized that this present nightmare was reality. Oh God!—surely this balding, heavy-handed man with his wine-laden breath, grabbing at her neck and bosom, could not be the Prince Charming whom she had loved—to whom she had bound herself for life? *Could not be.*

She gave another despairing wail. And this time she instinctively called upon a name which made the Baron grow livid with rage.

"Stephen! *Stephen!*"

He hit her across the mouth, felling her to the ground.

Downstairs, the innkeeper and his wife heard the two sharp agonized cries, through the ceiling, and glanced up and then at each other; and, being good Catholics, crossed themselves.

Destiny was knocked senseless by that savage blow. When she recovered at first she did not know where she was. Then her eyes focussed, and she saw the red fringe of canopy around the pelmet on the four-poster bed; also that it was dark, for the white muslin curtains had been pulled across the casements.

She was lying on top of the quilt. Her bodice was torn, otherwise she was still fully clothed. She felt hot, sticky, and rather nauseated. Lifting the back of her hand she drew it across her mouth, looked at it again and saw blood. Gingerly she felt her teeth with her finger-tips. One of them was a little loose. Her whole head ached.

Two candles in pewter sticks burned on the high mantelpiece, casting grotesque shadows on the white-washed ceiling. It was quiet. Later she heard voices from below, and out in the roadside. Men laughing. The clip-clop of horses and a coachman shouting *"Whoa there!"* Then more shouting and laughter. She remembered that she was in "The Mitre Inn." She remembered this bedroom, too. *And she remembered Alexis.* The man who had been made her husband this afternoon in the eyes of God and man.

In the eyes of God? Her whole body shivered. Again

she examined the blood on her hand and touched her
bruised mouth, remembering that blow and how the
pain and terror of it had caused her to swoon.

Oh, dear heaven, she thought, *dear, dear Christ our
Saviour,* what have I done?

Suddenly she heard a steady rhythmic snoring from
the adjoining room. The dizziness in her head cleared.
Soon she was alert, heart pounding madly as she sat
up. That must be Alexis snoring. She had heard Sextus
Barley make sounds like that many a time in the old
home, when he had too much of the mulled hot wine
that poor Mrs. Barley used to make for him.

Destiny swung her legs over the side of the bed, and
moved on tiptoe to the door. She saw her husband—
(her bridegroom, she thought, with horror and a grief
too deep in one so young). He lay sprawling on the
sofa, an unlovely sight, chin dug into the wine-stained
lawn ruffles at his throat. That balk pate made him look
so elderly, so different from the elegant Russian Prince
with his silver wig and black ribbons. He was asleep.
He resembled a plump pig, she decided with disgust.
He was not, *he could not be,* the man with whom she
had fallen so romantically in love.

Too late, she regretted her elopement and secret marriage, and wished that she had had faith in Stephen and
confided in him first. She recalled his pale, aesthetic
face, all the cool dignity and austerity of the young
secretary, and how those old gentlemen had told her
that Mr. Godwin had always been well beloved by
her father and deeply trusted. How well he had served
her since she went to Destermere House. She recalled
that night when he had knelt in homage at her feet like a
chevalier at the feet of a queen. The difference between
Stephen and this man she had married was bitterly
apparent to her now.

Why, *why* had Lady Destermere encouraged her to
marry such a man? She was well acquainted with him
and must have known what kind of temper he had. All

Destiny's recently acquired affection for, and confidence in, her stepmother fell away from her—just as her sweet love and belief in Alexis had fallen.

I must get away, she thought in a frenzy. But even as she turned, the Baron Faramund opened his eyes and saw the slim dishevelled girl standing there in the doorway—a girl whose long black hair fell about her shoulder in wild disorder, and whose lips were bruised and bleeding.

The fumes of alcohol cleared from Humbert's brain. He glanced at a grandfather clock which the Henesseys had painstakingly brought up to help adorn the bridal suite.

Ten o'clock. *Ach gott!* he thought, how time flies! He must have been asleep for over three hours. It had been nearly seven when they had arrived here and he had started to drink the wine—drink in a way he had not done for long months because he had felt it worth his while to abstain and appear youthful and moderate enough to attract a young girl.

Now he could see that he had been an imbecile to lose control so quickly—before he had done more than caress the little stupid. (So his thoughts raced on while he held her with his bloodshot gaze). What had possessed him to strike her like that and scare her off so early in the evening? Before the real entertainment had begun. It was unlike him to have acted so carelessly.

He got up, bent down, picked up his wig, put it on and tried to rearrange his clothing. But as Destiny turned and began to move away, he darted after her and caught her in his arms.

"No, no, do not leave me, my little wife. I implore you not to leave me. . . ."

Once more he was using the old tactics. Once more pretending to be the gentle adoring lover. Pulling her round to face him, he went down on one knee and looked up at her with imploring eyes. He babbled of remorse for what he had done. He had been intoxicated, he declared. He swore to God he had not realized whom he had hit, but in his inebriated frenzy had blindly struck her. A thousand, thousand pardons! He kept sobbing the words and actually squeezed tears from his eyes. They rolled down his flabby cheeks. Yes, she could see now how flabby they were and see too, all too clearly his corpulence, his loose, sagging muscles.

She was still puzzled as to how she could ever have been so blind. It must have been that she always saw him in the twilight or by the soft glow of candles, or *something,* she thought in despair. His hot fingers made her tremble violently again. She could not overcome her repulsion nor forget how he had hurt her mouth. As a child she had often been cuffed but to have been treated thus by *him,* her bridegroom, that was different. It was unpardonable and terrible.

Looking down at Alexis she remembered again that other man who had knelt at her feet. *Oh, how different!* How respectful Stephen had seemed, scarcely daring to touch her hand with his lips. Now she could see, too, the difference in age between the men. How young and clean and *nice* Stephen was by comparison. Despite all the efforts that Alexis had made to regain her favours, he left her cold as a stone. It was no good, she told herself dully; nothing could ever revive the old blind worship. Her love had been a fantasy. Her lover did not exist. And the most terrifying thing was the fact that she had married *this* man. The long, long years with him stretched before her. And if she stayed with him tonight (and she supposed she must) there would be more between them than the kisses.

Oh, God, she inwardly whispered the name, if only You would let this be a nightmare so that I might wake up and let me find myself back in my own bed in Destermere House knowing that this had never happened!

The Baron lumbered on to his feet, struggling against

the fumes of the drink (he had still eaten nothing and drank for the sheer joy of intemperate drinking). But he tried not to let his evil temper betray him again. Not yet, he thought savagely; first he must try to win a little natural response from his bride. So he pulled out his handkerchief and wiped his eyes as he stood before her. A sorry spectacle, she thought, with his wig not quite straight, and those maudlin tears. They did not make her feel at all sorry for him.

She remembered how once, years ago, down in Bath, she had found a schoolboy tying a stone around the neck of a puppy which he intended to drown. At that time, Destiny was aged eleven, a strong child, full of spirit. She had not hesitated to fight the boy, then release the puppy. She had twisted his arm, and made him blubber but she had felt not the slightest vestige of pity for him. He had been cruel to the dog. He was bestial. She felt exactly the same way about Alexis. He was an old beast. She doubled her fists and gasped at him:

"I hate you. I wish I had never married you."

He tried to laugh.

"Come, come, my dove, you are just being hysterical."

But all Destiny's old courage and spirit flared in absolute revolt. She backed away from him.

"I will not let you touch me again."

"Come, come, my little wife, my bride. . . ." he contorted his features into a foolish smile and ambled towards her with outstretched hand, "do not hold the liquor against me. Be tolerant of a man's weakness."

"You hit me!" she exclaimed. "You hit me so hard that it knocked me senseless. Then you flung me on the bed and left me to lie alone whilst you returned to your drinking. I see you now as you are—old and horrible. I must have been mad ever to have loved you. And I hate my stepmother for allowing it. *She* knew what you were like, assuredly."

The Baron nearly exploded—hissing into his lace-edged handkerchief. He wanted to strike her again in fury and hurt vanity. Calling him old and horrible, indeed! She would pay for that tomorrow. But first this night's pleasure must be completed—then they could never take her from him.

He made another effort to apologize and woo her after a fashion. As she continued to reproach him and call him names, he was half inclined to be amused. Mahla had warned him that this child was no meek weakling under her façade of romance. Well, all the more intriguing, so long as she did not keep up this attitude too long.

At last, seeing that she refused his every effort to kiss or caress her—she was darting around the room and he followed in a most humiliating, inglorious manner—he grew sullen and furious. As he glowered at her, Destiny read the hot ugly look in his eyes.

He resorted to compromise.

"Maybe you do not feel well, my love. I blame myself. I am still overcome with remorse because I hurt your pretty mouth. Go to your bed and rest there alone awhile. I will not disturb you. Drink the wine, then sleep, my beauty. I'll come to you later on."

She burst into tears.

"I want to go home. Back to my own home and my children."

He raised his hands as though in horror.

"You cannot. You are my own true wife and only just wedded to me. You are the Princess Malinkoff—do you not recall your vows to me?"

"I do not want to remember them," she sobbed.

"You will get over this feeling. Come, I say, dry your eyes and behave in a more agreeable fashion. You are scarcely proving yourself a loving or a willing bride."

Her eyes blazed with tears. She stormed at him:

"You have scarce proved a loving bridegroom, sir. You struck me cruelly."

"Oh, I am sick of this. Pray go to hell," said the Baron, his patience gone.

She turned. He ambled after her, anxiously:

"I did not actually mean you to go to hell, my love, but I am losing my temper again. Pray go to bed and let us have done with scenes. Later I know you will feel differently towards me."

I will never feel differently, she thought in despair.

"Think," continued the Baron, "if you try to run away, it will cause a fearful scandal. You do not want it to reach the ears of your—er—guardians. Mr.—er—Godwin," he cleared his throat, "would not like to hear that you have made a mistake in your choice of a husband."

That was a clever move.

Sobbing to herself she pushed the heavy black masses of her hair back from her face. In bitterness she thought of what Stephen might say, if he knew. No, she could not admit that she had made such a terrible mistake. She must be proud. She must try to live with Alexis even if she could not forgive him. She could not, she supposed, untie the nuptial knot. And if he was really sorry . . . if it had really been the drink.

The Baron saw her hesitation and eagerly put in his spoke.

"I will become your own true lover again—your own Alexis—only give me another chance, dearest child. Sleep awhile, then wake and welcome me."

She shuddered and turned away, and walked slowly into the candlelit bedroom.

"Very well," she said under her breath.

He let her go, sighing with relief. She lay down on the bed and buried her bruised face against the cool pillow. The tears ran silently down her cheeks. She wondered how she was going to endure the rest of this night.

16

IT WAS NINE O'CLOCK that evening before Ramilles, the blackamoor, dared leave his hiding place in the loft and creep out to search for Mr. Godwin.

By now the wretched little negro was hungry and cold. He wanted his own comfortable bed. He generally slept on a mattress in a powder-closet communicating with the Countess's bedchamber.

So far nobody had come to search for him. He could only presume that my lady had other things to think about this evening.

He waddled into the kitchen quarters and bumped into a pantry-boy called Ned. He asked if Mr. Godwin had returned. Ned said that he had. The secretary returned an hour ago.

Ramilles trotted on through the pantry and into the kitchen where Mrs. Perkins stood talking to other members of the staff.

She turned and saw the hated little negro whose pink and silver tunic, breeches and turban looked stained and crumpled. She put her hands on her hips and eyed him sternly.

"Imp of Satan, where have you been? Her ladyship has been calling for you everywhere."

"Never mind," muttered Ramilles, "it is Mr. Godwin I wish to see and not my lady."

"Why so?"

Ramilles tossed his head.

"That is my affair."

"Do not give me your impudence—" began Mrs. Perkins. "We've had enough trouble in this house without being bothered by you."

"What trouble?" asked the dwarf suspiciously.

"Do you not know?" put in the Swiss chef who was watching an under-cook baste a pair of birds that he was roasting for Mr. Godwin's supper. "That the Lady Destiny Frane is missing?"

The negro's heart leapt. He grinned ferociously. Yes, he knew all about that but he was not going to say so to the kitchen staff.

"Lor, what a to-do," murmured the old housekeeper, shaking her head. "Mr. Godwin has been like a madman asking questions and no one, including the Countess, seems to have seen Lady Destiny. She has just vanished as though she has been spirited away. Mr. Godwin has questioned all in turn, but the last to see her was my Lady Destermere herself, who said that her young ladyship had a bad headache and had retired for the night. Since then not a soul had set eyes on her. The postilions have been out with torches searching, because Mr. Godwin feared she might have left the house to take a walk and been attacked or robbed or fallen into the river."

And Mrs. Perkins started to weep into her handkerchief for she had grown dearly to love the late Earl's daughter.

As for the poor secretary, she continued, exhausted though he was by the long day's journey to and from the City, he had not ceased to walk from one end of the great house to the other, opening every door, running through the gardens, calling and calling for dear life on my Lady Destiny! The dear, devoted, young man. How ghastly pale he looked, and overcome with fear for her ladyship and with astonishment because he could not understand why my lady had left like this—or whence she had gone.

Ramilles listened to all this, then, tapping the stolen note in the pocket inside his absurd little coat tails, he slid out of the kitchen unnoticed and made his way towards the library.

His main object was to reach the secretary before his hated mistress, who wanted to have him thrashed, could waylay him and take that note away. First he was going to confide his story in Mr. Godwin, then ask for his protection and a reward.

Full of spite and for no other reason, Ramilles crept into the main hall. To his horror he came at once face to face with the Countess.

Looking exceptionally handsome in gown of pale-blue satin with black lace draped over her red curls, she stood by the great stone fireplace, talking to the secretary. Before Ramilles could escape she caught sight of him. He stood on his stubby legs, trembling, terrified, too scared even to run away.

"Where have you been? Come here you monster, you abortion!" hissed her ladyship.

He squeaked and would have turned and run now, but Mahla darted after him and seized hold of his arm.

The first of her schemes had gone awry. She had been all set to greet Stephen charmingly and attempt yet another *tête-à-tête* with him, telling him that Destiny was indisposed and in her bed. But after learning this, Stephen discovered a few minutes later, and by sheer accident, that it was not so. Coming out of his own room, he had heard two of the young serving maids laughing, and found the pair giggling and gossiping together in the corridor. He had upbraided them.

"Do you not know your young mistress is ill and sleeping and must not be disturbed?" he had asked them reproachfully.

"Oh, no, she is not, sir," Peg, the youngest of the two had answered artlessly. She was a raw country girl without much subtlety.

Mrs. Perkins had told the rest of the staff, as ordered by the Countess, that the daughter of the house was indisposed and abed. But Peg had not heard for at that moment she had gone to the privy and by the time she came out, Mrs. Perkins had forgotten her existence. The good woman had also forgotten that the maid who generally attended her young ladyship's bedroom was off-duty and that it was Peg who on such occasions took a warming-pan to my lady's bedroom just before six o'clock. Peg had cheerfully opened the door of her young mistress's bedchamber and found it empty and the bed unused. So, shrugging her shoulders, she had turned away. Now, unthinking, she gave Stephen the news that Destiny was not abed, whereupon he rushed to the bedchamber and found indeed that there was no one there. He rushed back to Mahla to acquaint her with this fact.

Mahla expressed astonishment and denied that she knew anything of Destiny's movements. Stephen hurled more questions at her, none of which she answered to his satisfaction. Finally she had grown tired of it and stormed at him.

"I am not Destiny's keeper. If she has chosen to go out alone, how should I know? Perhaps, like one of the servants she is meeting a scullion behind a bush," she had added spitefully.

White to the lips, Stephen had then started to organize a search throughout house and ground. He could not believe that the girl had left her home of her own accord. For some psychic reason, he felt that Mahla was lying and that she *did* know but would not disclose her knowledge. As for that insult about Destiny meeting a scullion—that was sheer nonsense and just spoken in malice by the older woman.

All his dislike and mistrust of Lady Destermere returned. And it returned again in full force after he had cross-questioned every member of the staff. For a pantry-boy swore that he had seen both the ladies—the Countess and Lady Destiny—together in the grounds. Mahla dismissed this as a lie. Then a postilion swore that he had seen Adam, the new groom, carrying a leather box, richly tooled, on his shoulder into the woods. The postilion at the time had been gathering nuts. He had later mentioned the box to Adam and asked if it was full of gold and if he was going to bury it. But Adam had laughed and said it was no treasure but contained a lady's garments. He offered no further explanation.

At once Stephen sent for Adam and questioned him. He looked scared at first but became more self-confident and cunning, denying the whole thing. He called it a delusion on the part of the other boy. He, Adam, had never carried a box nor seen such a one, he maintained (savouring the thought of the reward her ladyship would give him this very night).

Stephen had just been discussing these things with Mahla when Ramilles made his appearance.

"Can it be possible that Destiny had eloped and that Adam lied and that he did, indeed, carry her box out for her?" he had asked my lady.

"How should I know? I keep telling you I know nothing. I am sick of all this to-do about the silly child," was her pettish reply.

Sick at heart and fatigued, Stephen lapsed into a hopeless silence. If she knew anything, Mahla was not going to betray it. By this time he did not know who in the house had lied and who had not. He only knew that it was impossible for Destiny to have vanished into thin air, never to be seen again. He was also sure that she was in great danger. *He felt it.* He must follow and find her immediately.

He was unconcerned with the blackamoor—his mind was still full of the missing girl.

Ramilles yelped because the Countess had taken hold of the tender lobe of his ear and pinched it.

Things were going none too well for her. She was beginning to dread the moment when Humbert arrived to face Stephen and tell him the truth. She was quite sure now that the secretary was in love with Destiny. Why else should he be raising such a storm? And when he learned about the marriage, Stephen would be worse than he was now. It was as she had always imagined, she thought sullenly, there was plenty of fire under the cool exterior of the studious young man. It had only needed rousing. Half her rage was because she personally had been unable to raise it. But Destiny had managed it. Mahla was also furious with Adam. There would be no amorous episode with *him* tonight. If he attempted to climb up to her room she would throw a bowl of slops down upon him for allowing himself to be seen by that damned postilion. She had warned him to take infinite care.

There was little at the moment that she found pleasing.

Then to her perturbation and some bewilderment, Ramilles wriggled out of her grasp and rushed to Stephen.

"Mr. Godwin, save me, save me from her ladyship. Only let me speak to you alone and I can help you find my Lady Destiny."

Stephen stared down into the dwarf's goggling eyes.

"*You* can do that?"

"Come here you abomination. Do not listen to him, Stephen," put in Mahla and her guilty heart gave a jerk of fear.

In God's name what did the little horror know and what did he mean to tell Stephen? But, of course now Mahla remembered that she had once allowed him to accompany her to the Lake House. At the time, Humbert had reproached her for it and told her that she was growing too careless. But she had argued that Ramilles was her most adoring slave. It had never entered her head that the blackamoor might turn on her and betray her. She had certainly given him warning that she would flay him alive if he so much as mentioned the "Prince" to the secretary. Now, too late, she saw that she should never have allowed the dwarf to accompany them and that she had done herself no good by promising him that thrashing. The blackamoor was terrified of the lash and would do anything to escape it.

Ramilles hid behind Stephen, gripped the flaps of his pockets, and peered and grimaced at her ladyship.

"I will help you," he squealed, "and tell all I know, and I can show you proof, Mr. Godwin, sir, only do not let my lady condemn me to a beating. Save me, kind sir. Help me to get away from here and enter the services of her Grace the Duchess of Ancaster, who wishes to buy me."

Mahla made a dart for him, her face livid.

"You belong to me. Do not dare—" she began, but paused as Stephen held up a warning hand.

She had a tired, worried man to deal with tonight and he looked upon her with more than ordinary dislike and mistrust. He backed towards the library, pushed the blackamoor into the room and followed. Without another word he bolted the door behind them.

The Countess, losing her temper completely, beat her fists upon it.

"Let me in. Stephen I command you! The Earl may have given you certain privileges but you shall not behave as though you are head of this house. *I* am the mistress of Destermere. Let me in. What Ramilles tells you will be a malicious pack of lies, to spite me. *Let me in, I say. . . .*"

The pounding went on, and the shrieking, until the servants heard and glanced at each other, raising their brows.

Stephen took not the slightest notice of Mahla's screaming. He had but one burning ambition; to find Destermere's daughter, and if the dwarf could help— so much the better.

It took him only a matter of seconds to drag some of the truth from the gibbering little blackamoor.

First of all, Stephen swore that he would not give him back to her ladyship. He would keep him in safety tonight and offer him to the Duchess tomorrow. Stephen had never liked the blackamoor being in the house. He would be glad to be rid of him.

But after Stephen had heard the story that Ramilles poured out, he was wholly mystified. A *Russian Prince*

... occupying that little house on the lake on the Ancaster estate? Yes, of course, Stephen knew the place—he remembered it well in the old days when the Frenchman lived there. Vaguely Stephen remembered, too, having heard that there was a new tenant in possession but the news had not interested him.

Now he heard that every day, a phaeton had taken the two ladies from Destermere to see this unknown stranger, the Prince Malinkoff.

Stephen's worst suspicions broke into flame. He had halfguessed that Destiny was having a secret love affair. Now he knew she had been meeting this unknown gentleman, aided and abetted by her stepmother. Stephen felt disgusted. Who was Prince Malinkoff? Some Russian upstart. What wicked deceit! He had always known that the Countess was a vile woman who had resented Destiny's coming to Destermere. Obviously she wished to hasten the girl into marriage.

Oh, heavens, thought Stephen. Can it be that my Lady Destiny has already wed this man, before even her father's friends, or I, have met him and approved? Will I be too late when I *do* find her?

Ramilles held out a crumpled sheet of paper. Stephen, his heart beating fast with anxiety, scanned the words:

"Come to the Lake House. They are here. Alexis."

Who were *"they"*? What did this mean?

In a fine rage and without worrying his head about formality, or with any respect for the Countess, Stephen marched into the hall and confronted her. She sat sullenly on the edge of a chair tearing a handkerchief to shreds between her nervous fingers, her face blotched and unbeautiful.

"Well—have you finished gossiping with my nigger?" she asked venomously.

"I have finished nothing," said Stephen, "and I have only just begun to realize what a vile woman you are."

She changed colour but managed to laugh.

"You are insolent, Stephen. You had better be careful."

"It is you who must take care," said Stephen and thrust the note in front of her. She recognized it as the one Humbert had sent to Destiny.

Where in the name of heaven did the blackamoor get hold of *that*? she wondered; but she laughed again.

"It makes no sense to me."

"Oh, yes it does. You know everything," he exclaimed, doubling his hands. "But what you refuse to tell me, I shall soon find out. It is *you* who must beware. Tell me—what have you done with your late husband's unfortunate young daughter?"

Mahla shrugged her shoulders without answering. He added:

"I know now that every day you took her to the Lake House to meet some Russian stranger named Malinkoff."

My God, that little horror has most certainly betrayed me, thought Mahla, and her eyes sped to the clock on the high mantelpiece. Oh well—whatever Stephen discovered now, it would be too late, she thought spitefully. Doubtless Humbert, at this very moment, had his bride safely locked in his arms.

Stephen said:

"To deceive me, her guardian and her friend, and encourage her to do likewise—to let her conduct a clandestine affair outside the house—and she barely sixteen years of age—great God, madam! You have sunk very low. I wonder that the thought of the great name you bear and of the trust the late Earl put in you, does not bring a blush to your cheek."

The Countess gave her low, malicious laugh again.

"The girl was bored. I just helped her to find amusement."

Stephen felt chilled by nameless fears.

"Where is she now?"

"I do not know."

And Mahla thought: He can find out for himself. It won't be easy.

And she thought, too, that tomorrow she would leave Destermere House, take the Packet across the Channel and go to Paris, to the late Earl's residence there. She would stay in the French capital until Humbert and his wife joined her. They could all three then set out for Hanover. But first, Humbert must secure the money.

Stephen could see that the guilty woman had not the slightest intention of telling him any more. True to his oath to safeguard the treacherous little dwarf, he bade Ramilles follow him and sent for a footman.

"I want the fastest horses and the best coach in the stable to drive me to the Lake House," he said.

The man bowed and retired. Ramilles darted after him. He was hungry and thirsty and wished to stuff his stomach with food before he accompanied Mr. Godwin on this chase which he imagined would be quite diverting. It was a relief to him to know that her ladyship could not dig her pointed nails into his flesh any more, and that he would not now be beaten.

Alone with Stephen, Mahla changed her whole tone. All her old sense of frustration and desire to conquer this determined young man returned. She walked up to him and gave him a beseeching look from her strange purple eyes.

"Have you no feeling for me at all, Stephen? Why are you worrying so much about the child? I will admit that she was secretly married to Prince Malinkoff today. Why not? Let her go. Come with me—to Paris, to light and laughter—away from this dreary old place, and the mists of the English autumn. I love you. I will even consider marriage if you will take me no other way, Stephen. Would it not satisfy your ambition to step into Earl Destermere's shoes?"

Stephen looked at her as he would have done at a viper.

"I would rather be dead," he said.

He marched out of the great hall towards the door. There came a noise from the stables. Men shouting; horses whinnying. Drawing aside the curtains, Mahla saw the flicker of torches. She knew that one of the coaches was being prepared for Stephen's journey. He would be aided by the fact that it was a fine night with a full moon.

Mahla clenched her hands until the nails dug into her flesh. Rage convulsed her.

After the coach had driven away and all was quiet in Destermere House, she went up to her own room. She dismissed her maid. She did not wish to retire. She marched up and down the huge, handsome bedchamber, restless and tormented with her frustrated passion, and her guilt.

Stephen, she knew, had been in a rage because he imagined that Destiny had married "Prince Malinkoff." What, then, would happen when he learned who Alexis Malinkoff really was? All hell would be let loose, she thought gloomily. Things had not gone as well as she had hoped. It was touch-and-go now as to what would happen if Stephen found the pair tonight.

She had completely forgotten the existence of Adam, the groom, when after midnight she heard a furtive tap on her window. In her present mood she had no soft feeling towards the stupid, handsome youth to whom she had promised herself. She opened the window and looking down found Adam dangling below her balcony on a heavy vine. He looked up at her with a foolish grin on his face.

"Get down and go back to your stables where you belong," she hissed at him.

His expression changed from eager hope to one of astonishment.

"But, my lady, you said—"

"I said nothing," she interrupted. "You have made a mistake. Begone!"

The fellow hung on to the vine, looking up with bitter disappointment at this beautiful exotic lady who wore such revealing diaphanous draperies. For the last few hours he had been conjuring up visions of what was going to take place in her bedchamber—of the reward he would receive for the help he had given her.

He wished now that he had told Mr. Godwin about the box. Still clinging there beneath her window, he dared threaten Mahla, for he was a lad of spirit—not meek or weak like her previous victim, the groom, who had drowned himself.

Mahla cursed him—vanished and came back with the bowl of slops which she poured down on him, laughing spitefully.

The youth let out a howl and dropped to the ground, wet and malodorous. He had put on his best suit for the tryst with my lady. Now it was ruined. He was enraged, and bitterly resentful. His thwarted desire filled him with madness. Shaking himself like a dog, he picked up his cap which had fallen from his head, put it on again, then reached for a knife which he had thrust in his belt.

I will show her what I think of her, the proud bitch, he thought. I will do her in if I swing from the nearest tree for it.

And with the madness shaking his limbs like an ague, he started to climb up the vine again.

Were it not for an accident which had befallen the gentleman who had arranged to collect the four children at the Lake House and take them to the orphanage, Stephen might never have traced Destiny to Little Hampton. But the coach in which the man was due to arrive lost a wheel when going at full pace, and turned over, seriously injuring the unfortunate occupant. So Gretchen had waited for him in vain and faced the fact that she might have to keep "the brats" for yet another night.

The servants whom the Baron had brought from

London were all of German birth, well-paid and sufficiently incorruptible to refuse to answer any of the
questions that Stephen put to them. The nurse, Gretchen, appeared to be chief spokesman. She, who had
received Mr. Godwin in the hall, mumbling and grum-
bling, had nothing whatsoever to tell him except that
the "Prince" was not at home. Neither would she admit
that Lady Destiny Frane had ever been here.

It was just as Stephen was about to leave, defeated,
that he heard a wail. The long drawn-out cry of a child
in distress.

Gretchen heard it too. She glanced up at the ceiling,
her small tight mouth pursed, her eyes full of fear. She
had threatened those four not to make another sound,
after beating the lot of them, and leaving them unfed.
She had taken no heed of their pathetic, continued enquiries as to why, yet again, they were to be taken from
Destiny's keeping or why Gretchen had so suddenly
begun to beat and ill-treat them.

It was Jem, the eldest girl, who cried out so loudly.
Somehow that voice gave Stephen a queer, psychic feeling. Surely he had heard it before. He questioned
Gretchen sharply. She stammered that the cries came
from a child belonging to a married woman who worked
here.

At this point Stephen doubted again. Then suddenly
he heard a name being called upon in bitter misery.

"Dessie! Dessie! *Dessie!*"

Then he knew.

White to the lips, he turned back to face Gretchen,
whose cheeks had grown ashen.

"*They are calling for Lady Destiny.* I know them.
Her little brothers and sisters are upstairs. Good God,
how came they here?"

The woman, none too intelligent, was nonplussed
and knew not what to reply. Stephen rushed up the
stairs two at a time and broke into the room whence

215

he heard those wailing calls for Destiny. He had to hurl himself against the panels to break the lock open.

He saw before him a piteous sight. The youngest child was stretched out on the floor. The elder three knelt beside him. Stephen recognized them immediately, and although they looked better nourished and clothed than when he had seen them first, their faces were streaked with tears. They seemed badly frightened.

When the eldest girl saw Stephen, she, in turn, recognized him. She cried:

"Oh, sir, sir, where is our sister? Matt is dead. Poor little Matt is dead!"

Stephen, muttering under his breath, knelt down beside the prostrate boy. All too quickly he realized that Matt, the delicate and backward one, had indeed ceased to breathe. It was a small corpse there on the floor where the other children huddled.

Shocked and distressed, Stephen tried to comfort and soothe them. Bit by bit, he dragged the whole story from Jem. Matt, she said, must have had a fit after he had been thrashed by the horrible nurse. Mrs. Jupp had said once in Jem's hearing that the poor, backward little boy had a heart-weakness. That heart had not stood up to the brutality of the Baron's servant. Between choking sobs, Jem described how, as soon as sister Dessie had left, Gretchen had changed, locked them up in here, given them no more food and told them that they were all to be removed to the Poor House this night. And when Jem asked where Dessie was, the woman had told her that my Lady Destiny had gone to be married to the Baron and that when she returned here, it would be to find them vanished and that they would never see her again.

"Oh, Mr. Godwin, sir, save us, take us back to Dessie," sobbed Jem.

"Take us back to Dessie," echoed little Lucy and Luke.

"You shall be returned to her. Have no fear," said

Stephen grimly, and wondered if he were crazy or if he heard aright. *The Baron*. What did the girl mean?

"Has Dessie not gone away with Prince Malinkoff?" he demanded.

"Gretchen said that he was a Baron," piped up Lucy innocently.

This did not sink very deep with Stephen. For the moment he was too agitated and puzzled to think clearly. He only knew that the children had been brought here from Bath—no doubt as a lure to Destiny; that much he could presume. It could be no act of kindness otherwise why should this Prince (or Baron), or whoever he was, have ordered his servants to remove the children as soon as Destiny departed.

"Come with me," said Stephen tersely.

"But what of my little brother?" began Jem with a heartbroken sob.

Stephen folded poor Matthew's tiny hands on his chest. Looking at the waxen, pinched face he felt the deep sadness that any man must feel over the death of a child, and a horror that Matt had been driven by violence to his end. Yet he knew that the child's brain had been afflicted and he could never have grown into a normal man—he was best in his grave.

"I will see that Matt has a fine burial, my dear, but now come with me," said Stephen gently. He experienced nothing but sympathy and pity for the little Barley family whom he had thought to be in Bath living in comfort, adopted by the Jupps. Someone should pay for this night's work, he thought grimly as he took the children downstairs.

Gretchen, they found cowering in a corner.

As Stephen approached her, she began to talk to him half in English, half in German, trying to excuse herself.

Stephen said:

"The youngest child lies dead up in that room. You are his murderess, you vile woman."

"I did not kill him, sir," she shrieked.

"His heart gave out after you had most cruelly handled him."

Gretchen was a coward. She sank on to her fat knees, blubbering.

"Do not have me taken away and punished, sir. It was an accident. I did not mean it to happen. The Baron gave me my orders."

Stephen stared. Again, *the Baron*.

"Is your master a Prince or a Baron? What is this that you do not know the correct way to address your master?"

She stayed silent. Tears of fright began to run down her greasy face. The children cowered behind Stephen. Instinctively his arms went out and were folded protectively around them. He thought:

They are no flesh and blood relations of my lady's, but *she* loves them. From this night forth, whate'er betide, I shall see that they remain with her.

First he must find her. God alone knew whether or not she, too, needed protection this night.

Now he, the most gentle and peace-loving of men, with a burning faith in justice and right, threatened violence.

He pulled out the pistol without which he never travelled in these days of hold-ups, and advancing towards the shivering Gretchen, aimed the weapon at her heart.

"You will tell me where to find my Lady Destiny or I will shoot you!" he said between his teeth.

"No, no, *mercy*, sir!" she shrieked.

"Where has Lady Destiny gone?"

"With the Prince . . . with the Baron. . . ."

"Prince or Baron. Which? Answer me."

"I cannot."

"Answer, or I pull the trigger, woman," thundered Stephen.

In an agony of terror, she stammered:

"The Baron Faramund."

That was something Stephen had never imagined in his wildest moments. The name cracked as sharply as any pistol shot throughout that quiet candle-lit room on this late summer's night. The children clung to Stephen and stared goggle-eyed at their inhuman tormentor, but giggled a little, as children would, to see the woman on her knees, weeping.

Stephen felt his imagination boggle. *Baron Faramund*. So this clandestine lover of Destiny's was not a Russian Prince named Malinkoff, but Lady Destermere's brother—Humbert; that most hated, licentious and unscrupulous of all men.

"Christ in Heaven!" said Stephen under his breath, and shut his eyes a moment as though to ward off a fearful evil. He felt sick to his stomach. *She,* his lovely adored lady . . . the high-spirited, enchanting, intelligent Destiny who had been entrusted to his care . . . *she had eloped with Humbert Faramund.*

Now that Gretchen had given the truth away, she offered further information, hoping to get into Mr. Godwin's good books. She told how the Baron had brought all of the servants (Germans like himself) down to the Lake House from his London establishment. How they were all paid well to call themselves Russians and to speak of him outside only as the Prince Malinkoff. How he had sent for the four children and given her his orders concerning them. How Countess Destermere used to come here and bring the young lady to meet the Baron. And how the lovers had eloped to their bridal this very afternoon.

Half-mad with fear, Stephen shouted at her:

"Where? *Where?* Answer me, woman."

With the pistol at her bosom, Gretchen shrieked back:

"Little Hampton—to the church there, good sir."

"And afterwards, where?"

Gretchen knew. Gretchen had heard it all because Destiny in her happy, artless fashion earlier that day had told the four children that she was going to "The Mitre Inn" for her bridal night and Gretchen had been eavesdropping.

Stephen glared at her, his face livid, his whole body shivering. There were gaps in the story but the salient facts, the terrible implications, were enough to shake him to the foundations of his being. It had all been manœuvred—he could see—by that fiend in woman's clothing—Lady Destermere. He had often wondered what had happened to her brother Humbert. Well, *this* was it. The Baron had sneaked down here, a wolf dressed up as a lamb, calling himself a Prince; entertaining and beguiling the young ignorant girl.

Stephen beat one hand against his forehead.

"Why, why didn't you trust in me?" he cried to Destiny as though she were here in this room. "Why didn't you tell me about it?"

From what the children had said, he gathered that Destiny was much enamoured of the Prince. The thought of how she would feel when she learned who he really was, filled Stephen with horror. It would destroy her illusions, her faith in mankind, for ever.

I must save her, he thought, there is no time now for reflection or recrimination. I myself must go after this man and kill him.

He grew calm and resourceful again. He ordered Gretchen to put warm clothing on the children and then, afraid to leave them in this house took them outside and called to Thomas, his own trusted coachman.

"Take these children—guard them with your life," he said. "There will be horses and a vehicle in the stables belonging to the Lake House. Drive the children to your own home. I know your wife, Moll. She is a God-fearing woman and has children of her own. She can care for these three tonight."

The coachman, who was a good, honest fellow, touched his forehead to Stephen.

"Anything you say, sir. My Moll will look after the bairns."

"Listen carefully to what I say. Her ladyship, at Destermere House, is not to be told that you have the children with you. Do not let anybody see you but drive straight to your cottage and tell your good woman to put the children to bed after feeding them. In the morning I will collect them."

"Yes, sir."

"On your way back," continued Stephen tersely, "Rouse Mr. Jenkins, the undertaker in Richmondwyke. Ask him to come to the little Lake House at once—where lies the body of a small boy. He is to place him in the chapel with flowers and candles. He will receive a purse and further orders from me in due course. And put Ramilles—the blackamoor—where he will be safe until he is sold."

"Yes, sir," said the old coachman and hurried to obey for he was the type to do so without questioning his master's commands. He was also devoted to Mr. Godwin, and like the rest of the staff he had neither love nor respect for the late Earl's red-haired vixen of a widow.

When the three remaining children began to weep again thinking that Mr. Godwin was about to abandon them, Stephen was gentle with them and reassuring. He bade them be good and obedient and to trust in him. Tomorrow, he said, he would return them to their belovèd sister. They need not fear or cry any more.

Then, back to his own coach went Stephen, telling the driver to whip the horses up to a gallop. What a mercy that it was a fine night, and a good road to Little Hampton. It would not take them more than a half-hour to reach "The Mitre Inn." But as he sat back, letting the cool air fan his pale face, Stephen called on the Name of his Maker.

"God—God! Let me be in time to save her. She is

so young and ignorant of life. Save her, Oh, God, for Christ Jesus' sake."

It was his one thought. He had none other; even a sensation of his own pain or loss. It had always been at the back of his mind that one day he must lose Destiny when she was wedded to an approved young nobleman of her choosing. Then he would consider that he had carried out his obligations to her father. He would then feel justified in leaving her.

But not this way, he thought in great anguish. *Not this way.* Unless he could find her in time to open her eyes to the truth and rescue her, it would be the end of everything in life for *her.*

17

THE CHURCH BELL of Little Hampton was striking the hour of midnight when the silence of the village was broken by yet another and more startling noise—the clatter of horses galloping at a mad pace along the road; the "whooping" of men and the cracking of whips.

Then a coach turned into the courtyard, under an arch over which hung a sign "The Mitre Inn."

Stephen Godwin leapt out of the coach.

His face was deadly pale; his eyes red-rimmed with fatigue, but he was alert and full of nervous energy. One slender hand, shaking a little, rested against his hip, touching the butt of his pistol—a weapon he rarely fired, being man of peace and letters.

He pounded on the door of the inn. Within seconds came the flicker of lights, and a servant opened the door.

"Mercy on us—what is it?" the man began.

Stephen interrupted tersely:

"You have a guest here who calls himself Prince Malinkoff."

"Yes, surely, sir, but—"

"Where is he?" Stephen broke in again.

"I'll fetch me master, sir."

But at that moment Mr. Henessey, himself, appeared, yawning, running his fingers through a tousled head.

As he saw the soberly but well-attired figure of a young gentleman, he immediately bowed and began to apologize for his own appearance.

"I was asleep, Excellency. If you be seeking shelter. . . ."

"I am Mr. Godwin and I seek the gentleman who has come here under the name of Prince Malinkoff," cut in Stephen, breathing hard and fast.

The landlord glanced up at the ceiling, through which he had heard certain disconcerting cries and scuffling feet before he and his good wife betook themselves to their beds.

He coughed and nodded.

"The Prince, sir, ah yes, sir. Most certainly. He and his newly-married wife occupy the whole of the upstairs apartments."

The words "newly-married wife" pierced like dagger points into Stephen's breast. He winced. His pallor was replaced by a dark flush.

"Lead me to these rooms," he commanded.

Open-mouthed, the fat landlord gaped at the stranger.

"But, Excellency . . . at such an hour. . . ."

"The Prince's room, I say, or you will be the worse for your hesitance," thundered Stephen, who was in a ferment of anxiety and completely changed from his peaceable and tolerant self.

In his mind there was but one thought: to save *her*.

The landlord argued no further but carrying aloft a

pair of candles lit Mr. Godwin up the curved oak staircase which creaked as the two men mounted it.

A trifle fearfully, Mr. Henessey then paused and handed Stephen one of the candlesticks. He nodded at a door.

"In there, sir," he whispered, and wondered in amazement what was taking place in his respectable and usually quiet coffee-house.

Stephen tried the handle. The door did not yield. Without further ceremony he banged his clenched fist against it.

"Open up!" he commanded in a voice of furious urgency.

To his utter amazement, there came no protest in the Baron's voice, but a cry in that other one so well-beloved, so well-remembered. Destiny, herself, answered:

"Oh, Stephen, it is *you! Stephen!*"

The door was unlocked. He saw her. A sight which made his blood seem to turn to water in his veins. For instead of the dainty, charmingly-attired and well-groomed young lady to whom he had grown accustomed at Destermere House, here was a sorry spectacle. Her dress had been half-torn from her. She shivered, a quilt thrown around her bruised shoulders. Her face was livid under the tossed mane of black tangled hair, and her great eyes stricken like the eyes of a wounded fawn. She stumbled towards Stephen. He caught her by both arms and steadied her.

"In God's name, what has happened to you, my lady?"

She choked and began to sob hysterically, and pointed at the communicating door.

"He is in there, inebriated. He has been imbibing ever since we arrived here. He is a drunken beast and I loathe him. He is not the man I believed him to be. Everything has changed alarmingly. Oh, Stephen, *Stephen,* I can see that I have made a fearful mistake," added the girl, all pride eliminated by her extremity of terror.

"A fearful mistake, indeed," said Stephen in a low voice.

The tears began to run down Destiny's streaked, pitiful face. It bore little traces of beauty just now, and yet was still beautiful and appealing to Stephen. He put an arm around her, led her to the bed and made her sit down, gently holding one of her trembling, cold hands.

"What is he doing in there?"

"He is asleep. Listen—you will hear him."

Stephen lifted his head and listened. Yes, he could hear those loathesome snoring sounds, and was filled with disgust. This was typical of Mahla's brother whom he knew so well from the old days in Geneva; Humbert, the profligate and drunkard who had often offended Claud Destermere by his intemperate habits and who, when he was in the grip of alcohol, could become worse than an animal.

Stephen turned again to the stricken girl.

"Did he . . . did you—" he broke off, speechlessly, horribly embarrassed yet feeling that he must know the answer to the ghastly question which had been tormenting him ever since he learned of the elopement.

But now an emphatic shake of the head from Destiny and a cry of *"No!"* filled him with wild relief. He had not come too late. She had suffered cruelly at the Baron's hands but because of her own courage—that spirit that not even *he* had been able to break—she had safeguarded her honour this night.

"Twice I fought him like a mad thing," she declared. "Each time he took more drink to inflame him, swearing to come after me, then falling into a stupor. Just before you arrived, I was making up my mind to steal out of the inn and run away. But I have taken my vows to him in the church this day and I realized that I was his lawful wife. I did not know what to do," she ended piteously.

"Mad child. Why did you elope with him?"

"Do not reproach me, for I cannot endure any more," she said and put her face in her hands and sobbed as though her heart would break.

All his selfless adoration for her overflowed and drenched Stephen's heart. He could forgive her anything—even this mad folly. He took one of her hands, pressed it between his own and tried to comfort her.

"It is all right, it is all right now. I know that you were ill-advised. But your stepmother will be made to pay for this dastardly night's work. So also will her brother. I shall place this matter in the hands of those in higher places than myself and the marriage shall be annulled."

Now Destiny's head shot up and through the burning tears she stared at Stephen, wondering dazedly what he meant.

After the "Prince's" second attempt to subdue her completely to his will, she had felt almost at the end of her tether, half-crazy with regret for what she had done. To see Stephen again—to look on the nobility of his face and hear the quiet reassurance of his voice once more and know that he had saved her—filled her with the desire to fall on her knees and kiss his feet. But her bemused mind fastened now on to the thing that he had just said.

"What do you mean by those words *my stepmother's brother?*"

"You will learn in good time," said Stephen grimly. "First, let me look upon Prince Malinkoff, himself."

"I am here at your service, my dear Mr. Godwin," drawled a voice from the doorway, followed by a chilling laugh. Stephen and Destiny turned to see the Baron's tall, massive figure swaying before them. The candlelight threw his silhouette grotesquely upon the ceiling. Stephen sprang to his feet. He looked at Humbert with burning gaze.

"So! Prince Malinkoff indeed! You have found a new title, *Baron Faramund.*"

And he noted with anger and disgust the other man's disordered, wine-stained clothes, and the half-bald head (for the Baron had not troubled to put on his wig again). Once more he had come out of a stupor of alcohol determined to get the better of this "wild-cat" bride of his once and for all. He had awakened just now to hear Stephen's voice in the adjoining room and been filled with apprehension. But showing his teeth in that freezing smile, he regarded Stephen Godwin with his bloodshot, heavy eyes.

"May I ask what you are doing here, in this room— my bride's bedchamber?"

"You know well why I am come here, sir," snapped Stephen.

"Then you have come to your death, Mr. Godwin. For no self-respecting husband can allow such an intruder to live."

Destiny screamed.

"Stephen—beware!" She had seen the flash of a long pistol that the Baron had grabbed from the table behind him.

"Die, and be damn'd to you!" said Humbert Faramund through his teeth, and before Stephen had time to draw, released the trigger of the pistol.

Destiny's next cry was lost in a deafening report. The acrid tang of gunpowder filled the room. Stephen fell heavily across the bed.

"So much for your champion, my dear—" he began.

But now Destiny flung herself upon Stephen, shielding him with her arms as she had so often shielded the children from the blows that they used to receive from their father. And this time her desire to protect the helpless was mixed up with her true and impassioned desire to prove her gratitude to Stephen for coming here in spite of her conduct.

"Enough of this. Move away from Mr. Godwin—" began the Baron.

She broke in wildly:

"I will not. Shoot again and it will be my life that you take—mine and not his."

"His is already forfeited," said the Baron.

But at that moment Stephen stirred and, rolling over, flung Destiny's light weight away from him. The blood was pouring from a wound in his left shoulder. The Baron, who had been a fine enough shot in his day, had made a poor aim on this night of debauchery. Stephen's wound was far from fatal. And this time he knew no mercy. He waited for no further argument. If one of them must die this night, it must be Humbert Faramund before he could totally destroy Destiny.

Two more shots rang out, bringing the landlord and his wife and servants stumbling up the staircase, listening and staring in agitation.

The second bullet from the Baron's pistol had only touched the lobe of Stephen's right ear. But Stephen's aim had been more deadly. With a choking cry, the Baron tumbled forward on his face.

Destiny fainted.

Stephen turned the Baron's body over, and saw that he was dead. He had been shot through the heart. Then Stephen looked at the crowd huddled out in the corridor.

"Send for a physician," he said, "and bring me water and bandages. I must try to stop the bleeding."

The scared landlord nodded and rushed off. Mistress Henessey rushed down to find water and linen. Stephen addressed two of the gaping menservants.

"Carry the body of this—gentleman—down to the coach in which he came. Rouse his servants and bid them drive him immediately to the Lake House on the

Duke of Ancaster's estate, and then acquaint the Countess of Destermere of the shooting."

Glancing fearfully at the corpse, they nodded and began to stagger out with their heavy burden. Stephen, despite the pain in his shoulder lifted Destiny in his arms and carried her into the next room.

He was surprised at his own lack of concern at what he had done this night. True, in these times duelling was common enough and one dead man, or more was of little account. Besides which, he had shot the Baron in self-defence. He could not feel any guilt, but rather an ice-cold pleasure insomuch as he had killed the man who would have ruined Destiny's life. She had been hurt enough. The Baron could never now make another attempt to spoil her youth, and break that generous heart which, in her innocence, she had given him.

He laid Destiny on the couch upon which the Baron had so recently sprawled. Then he drew aside the curtain to let in some air. Through the open windows came the grey light of dawn. A cock was crowing from a nearby farm, followed by the first tremulous piping of newly-awakened birds.

It was another day. The fresh air came in through the casements and Stephen drew it into his lungs, trying to stave off the dizziness.

Destiny opened her eyes. As the heavy lashes lifted and she saw where she was, she gave a muffled cry.

"Oh, dear God . . . *Stephen*. . . ."

For him, faintness passed. Pressing a hand to his wounded shoulder, he advanced to the couch and looked down on the girl with a stiff little smile on his lips. His heart beat with fresh strong throbs of joy because she had called upon his name. She *needed* him.

"My lady," he said gently, "you are all right. Do not fear."

She sat up, pushing back her dark tangled hair.

"Where is *he*?"

"He is being taken away this moment. He will never trouble you again."

Her great eyes stared.

"You have—killed him?"

"Yes."

She drew a long shuddering breath.

"He deserved to die. First he shot at you. He would have murdered *you*. . . . Oh, Stephen, and all through my folly. . . ."

She got off the couch and came towards him, looking anxiously at the red stain that oozed steadily through the hole the bullet had torn in his coat.

"Oh, Stephen—your shoulder!"

"It is nothing," he said. "The surgeon will soon be here."

But now she saw that his face was waxen and perspiration beaded his forehead. She could think only of him, now. She did not want to remember that other man who was dead . . . that terrible man who had changed so appallingly from the prince of her dreams into a veritable monster.

With deft, gentle hands—hands that were used to taking care of little children—she drew off Stephen's coat and waistcoat and tore open the snowy linen of his sleeve, exposing the wound. In a remorseful voice she said:

"It is deep and you are suffering, and all for me. I do not deserve it. Oh, Stephen, I do not deserve it and will never forgive myself."

Before he could answer, the innkeeper's wife and a young maid entered the room bearing cans of water and linen towels. Now it was Destiny who grew calm and resourceful, and who attended the wounded man. In a few minutes, she had staunched the flow of blood with pads soaked in ice-cold wine. She tore the towels into strips and bound up the wound, giving Stephen some relief until the physician should arrive to extract the bullet.

He sat quiet, his eyes fixed on her, his senses hurt not by the wound but by the sight of her bruised and tragic face. If he lived to be one hundred years old, he would never forget this night, he thought grimly. What she had been through at the hands of that monster, he dared not think, neither did he wish to contemplate what he would like to do, in turn, to that woman in Destermere House who had delivered her into the hands of such a fiend.

The touch of Destiny's strong, capable little fingers was infinitely sweet to him, and more particularly so, her tenderness and solicitude. At length, alone with him again, she knelt beside him and began to question him.

"You said strange things about ... the Prince. I must ask you to explain."

Stephen sat back and shut his eyes, feeling a wave of deadly tiredness submerge him.

"Can it not wait?"

"No, I must know now."

He opened his eyes again and looked at her with a strange mixture of sternness and pity.

"You will be deeply shocked, my Lady Destiny."

"Do not call me that. After tonight and what you have done for my sake, I am Destiny, your friend."

He coloured.

"To me you must still be 'My lady'."

"As you wish," she said, with strange new meekness, "but tell me please why you called Alexis by another name?"

"Alexis was never his true name—nor Malinkoff. The man whom I have killed was the Baron Humbert Faramund. He was not a Russian but a German, and brother to the woman whom your father so unhappily married."

The girl sat back on her haunches, staring up at Stephen, twisting one of the towels between her hands. With every moment the room was growing lighter and the song of the birds, stronger and sweeter. But there was no sweetness in this hour for Destiny—only the odour of corruption . . . the stench of a crime that had been directed against her innocence, and for the sake of her estates. An intrigue so foul that it filled her with a sickness from which she felt she could never recover.

She whispered, unbelievingly:

"He . . . he was Mahla's *brother?"*

"Yes."

"I cannot credit such unspeakable villainy. She introduced me to him. She said he was her friend from Russia. She, my stepmother, whom I thought my guardian and my friend, encouraged the intrigue."

"She is a wicked woman, Destiny. . . ."

Unconsciously now he had dropped her title. He went on to explain further what had happened since the hour of Claud Destermere's passing. So at last Destiny learned what manner of woman Mahla was and how her father had learned the truth too late, and had besought Stephen with his final breath to find her, his child, and serve her. At last, Destiny knew the terrible difficulties under which Stephen had worked, and the immense folly that she, herself, had committed by allowing herself to be deceived by Mahla and the bogus prince. All his "romance," his songs, his poems, his wooing, had been part of a wicked plan to get hold of the Destermere fortune, and share it with his evil sister.

Slowly Destiny gained her feet. She walked to the casements and leaned out, shutting her eyes as the early morning breeze touched her hot, sore young face. She knew everything now. It was terrible—almost more than she could bear. Tonight, she thought, she had said good-bye for ever to Destiny, the child. There stood in her place, Destiny the woman who had reached maturity in exceeding bitterness, and with a remorse that would last to the end of her life.

She turned back at length to the young man who had rescued her.

"I owe you much, Stephen Godwin. So much more than I can ever repay," she said in a choked voice.

"I want no payment but only to see you happy and safe," he said.

"Safe I shall be, from now onwards, because you have opened my eyes to the truth. Happy—no, never."

But now he was able to smile at her childish exaggeration.

"Yes, you will get over it. You are but sixteen and you have your life and your children waiting for you."

She put the tips of her fingers against her lips.

"Dear God, my darlings, *are they safe?*"

He bowed his head. She had had enough to bear and yet the full story had yet to be told. He looked up at her, giving a deep sigh.

"It will grieve you, I know, but I must warn you all is not well with the youngest child."

"With little Matt? Why? What has happened?"

He told her, as gently as he could.

She stood like a frozen creature, her face the colour of marble. She was beyond tears. She stood like this for a long time without speaking, then looked with terrible eyes through the door that led into the other chamber.

"*He* did that; not the German woman, but that liar and traitor who called himself Prince Malinkoff. He sent for the children and used them as bait to trap me. I would that he were still alive so that I, myself, could kill him over again."

"A man can die but once," said Stephen. "Do not bruise your spirit with futile bitterness, or thoughts of further revenge. The little boy, Matt, lies at peace. As you know—he would never have grown to be a strong man. Try not to grieve for him too sorely. This morning, we will take the other three back to Destermere House and you shall never be separated from them again. Lady Destermere shall be confronted with this evil thing that she has done and Sir Edgar and your father's friends shall order her to leave the house, never to return. You alone will give orders in future in your home."

The girl flung herself on her knees at his feet, and laid her cheek against his knee, sobbing.

"My heart is broken, Stephen."

He looked down at the bent head. He dared suddenly to touch her hair and smooth it.

"Poor child. But I pray you be at peace," he said again. Then added:

"I, too, have my regrets. If I had let you bring the children with me when I first took you away from Bath, this might never have happened. It is your longing for the children that led you into this ... this marriage."

"I will not let you blame yourself. You have done all and more for me than my father asked of you," she sobbed.

"Oh, my dear!" whispered Stephen, in an agony of the love which he must not show her, and he was glad that the room filled suddenly with people. The surgeon had arrived. Mistress Henessey raised Destiny to her feet, looked at her with pity and said:

"Come with me, my lady, and let me bathe your face and brush your hair and give you some coffee."

With tears still streaming down her face, Destiny allowed herself to be led away.

18

THE DREADFUL NIGHT had passed into what seemed to Destiny an equally dreadful morning.

She lay on the humble but clean bed belonging to Mistress Henessey until the sun had risen and a new bright summer's day had begun. She lay sleepless, anguished, without speaking, letting the good woman lay cold compresses of vinegar and water on her bruised face, trying not to remember the terrible struggles she had had with the "Prince." Trying not to be sick ... physically sick at the thought that he had been Mahla's profligate brother, without a vestige of love in his heart for *her;* with nothing really in it but sadistic cruelty and the lust for power and money. *Her* money.

She went down into the very depths of shame and bitterness as she lay in the darkened chamber, raising a hand now and then to wipe away her scalding tears. It was a deep humiliation for one of her fine spirit and pride, to have to realize how completely she had been duped. A never-ending grief to remember how badly she had treated Stephen.

She spoke once to the innkeeper's wife who sat beside her raising her now and then to make her drink a cordial and that was to ask how Mr. Godwin fared. When the woman said that all was well with the young gentleman, and that the surgeon had found and extracted the bullet, and that the wound was clean, Destiny nodded and whispered: "God be praised," then closed her stricken eyes again.

Her one wish now was to rejoin Jem, Lucy and Luke; the three who were left to her. They must all follow poor little Matt's body to his grave. Stephen had promised that she might lay his casket in the Destermeres' vault in Richmondwyke Church.

It appalled Destiny to remember that she, herself, had been so far deceived as to hand the poor little things over to that German nurse who had ill-treated them, and thus hastened Matt's death. She tried not to imagine the horror and grief of the children when they learned how sorely they had been betrayed.

I will take them to my father's house and live with them there in peace for the rest of their days, and I will never believe in another man as long as I live, she

235

thought, shuddering away from the memory of the false, base Alexis.

Yet there *was* one in whom she could and would place her trust and to whom somehow she must show her remorse and her gratitude. Stephen. Stephen who had so nearly died last night because of her.

It was midday before the Desteremere coach left Little Hampton and bore the Lady Destiny Frane and her father's secretary over the dusty, sun-dappled road, along the river banks leading back to Richmondwyke.

When Destiny first saw Stephen again she was distressed to note how pale and tired he looked. Gently she touched his bandaged shoulder.

"Does it give you much pain?" she asked.

He looked into her beautiful eyes—so unlike the eyes of the girl he had first known. Then they had been brave, sparkling, eager for life. This morning they were dull, ashamed, full of pain. It was almost intolerable to him that she should have been so hurt. He answered, abruptly, out of his own misery:

"Thanks. I am well. My health is good and the wound will soon heal."

She kept silent then, believing that he was angry with her, humbly accepting his coldness as her just deserts.

As they passed it she did no more than glance with a thrill of horror at the little church in which she had been wed to "Prince Malinkoff," then shut those eyes tightly.

She had removed the marriage ring. She had torn up every poem or letter "Alexis" had written her, and which she had packed with her jewels. Now she was a widow, before ever she had really been a wife. For *that* mercy she must be thankful—grateful to Stephen who had killed the Baron Faramund.

There was still the Countess to face. Courageous though she had always been, Destiny shrank from the idea of coming in contact with the wicked wanton woman who had delivered her into the Baron's hands.

But when she had voiced this fear to Stephen as they breakfasted together he had said:

"Leave me to deal with her, my lady. You shall stay peacefully in your own rooms with—your children."

She was grateful and bowed her head. He stared stonily ahead at the familiar countryside; at the farm labourers already tilling the soil, and the cattle grazing under the shade of the tall elms in the lush green meadows, watching the coach roll by, with their large stupid eyes. A hot summer's morning, typically English and sweet. But Stephen was unappreciative of it. He could not bear to see Destiny's changed face. And he, himself, was changed, he thought grimly. He, who loved peace, beauty and things of the intellect, of the soul, had killed a man last night. Besides that, he loved Destiny Frane—loved her, better than life or death, itself, and without hope.

Soon he must leave her. He could not stay in her house, in her service, and continue to love her so desperately. It would be beyond his strength. Only for awhile he would remain to help straighten out her life a little; to help her to forget the stain of evil that had blotted some of her white innocence at the very start of her sweet womanhood; her new great position in life. Thank God, he kept thinking, it had been no worse.

They drove directly to the dwelling of Thomas, the good old coachman, where Destiny—her bruised face veiled from curious eyes—was reunited, touchingly, with the three children.

They went mad with joy to see their Dessie once more and realize that their troubles were over. Like small children, full of trust and simplicity, they accepted her word that they would never be left alone to suffer hardship or cruelty again, and were content.

For a few moments, also, they all knelt beside the bier of the tiny boy who had gone to his Maker. There in the candlelight of the quiet flower-filled chapel, Destiny wept and took fresh vows to put her little adopted family first and foremost in future—come what may. She was further beholden to Stephen when he led her from that Chapel vowing to support her wish to keep the three at Destermere House.

"I promise you, my dear lady, you shall be complete mistress of the house and Lady Destermere shall be forced to leave. She has so hideously dishonoured the name she bears."

Destiny found herself clinging to Stephen's good arm. The children followed. If he secretly dreaded the meeting with my Lady Destermere and the hysterics and explosions which he was sure would follow, he need not have troubled himself; neither need Destiny have feared coming to grips with her vile stepmother. For when the coach drove into the courtyard, Mrs. Perkins came running up to them, presented a ghastly countenance, and had a terrible story to tell; one which seemed to both Destiny and Stephen to be yet another sinister event which brought alteration to all their lives.

There would be no "scene" with Lady Destermere. *She was dead.*

"Lord have mercy on her soul, she was found lying across her bed with a knife wound in her throat," said Mrs. Perkins, and promptly had hysterics after delivering this news.

Stephen stood still a moment, supporting Destiny with his uninjured arm. He passed the back of his hand across his forehead and instinctively shivered.

"Dear heaven—what is this? Is there to be no end to fearful happenings?" he muttered.

Mrs. Perkins recovered herself sufficiently to go on with her grisly tale.

The perpetrator of the crime had been found and taken away into custody, she said. It was Adam, the new groom. It appeared that last night he must have climbed up the vine that grew outside her ladyship's balcony and after murdering her, started to climb down again. But the vine had broken and he had fallen to the ground, receiving a spinal injury which had prevented him from making his escape.

When my lady's French maid had taken the usual chocolate to her this morning, she had found the corpse—a fearful sight, indeed; great disorder in the room, blood spattered upon the silken sheets and golden spread, and every sign that a frightful struggle had taken place before the Countess died. Nobody had heard her utter a single sound. She must have been taken by surprise and immediately silenced, Mrs. Perkins declared.

Upon being questioned further by Stephen, the housekeeper said that the groom had been found lying semiparalysed beneath the balcony, with the blood-stained knife beside him. He had not been able to deny that he was the assassin. When asked to explain his actions, he had told everybody that it had been a deed of revenge. My lady had made certain promises to him which she had not kept. And then Mrs. Perkins, who had never approved of his lordship's wife, with a toss of the head, added:

"We all of us know why poor *William* threw himself into the river. We cannot help being sorry for poor misguided young Adam who must hang now for her ladyship's murder."

Destiny had listened to all this in frozen silence, her eyes hidden in her hands. Stephen heard her voice, a hoarse, hard little voice which he hardly recognized.

"She deserved her death. She was an unspeakable creature. She and her brother are well out of this world. If I have any power, I shall try to get a lighter sentence for poor Adam."

Stephen handed the trembling young girl over to Mrs. Perkins.

"Take her ladyship to her room and the three children, also. Look after them. I must see the people who will be dealing with her ladyship's body."

And to Destiny he said, gently:

"You must not dwell upon these horrors. They are but passing. I pray now we have heard and seen the end of death and disaster. Maybe now true peace will come to Destermere House."

Destiny nodded, unable to speak. As Mrs. Perkins walked away with her, the good housekeeper said: "Praise God you are safe at home again, my lady. . . ." then glanced at the three children and added: "May I ask, my lady, who these children might be?"

"They are my sisters, Jem and Lucy, and my little brother Luke," said Destiny, in a choked voice. "Pray be kind to them for my sake."

"I would be kind to all children for their own sakes, my lady," declared Mrs. Perkins, not quite understanding but she opened her motherly arms, and all three children ran to her, recognizing a friend.

For Stephen there was much unpleasantness to be faced before he could seek the rest he needed. His wound ached, and he craved for sleep. But first he had to steel himself to look upon what Mrs. Perkins had described all too vividly as a "fearful scene" in Lady Destermere's room. Yet he could find no pity in his heart when at last he looked upon the dead woman, sprawled there with her flame-red hair tossed across her staring eyes and that red gaping wound in her throat. He felt frozen and unmoved. She had dishonoured his belovèd master long before Destiny came into their lives. But that was the least of it. What she had almost succeeded in doing to the young girl who had been entrusted to her care, was beyond pardon.

As Destiny had said it was as well these two, brother and sister, were out of this world. They had died as they had lived, violently and shamefully. There would not be a single soul to shed a tear for either of them.

Shuddering, Stephen left the chamber of death and departed to the library to meet and talk to the officers from Richmondwyke who had taken the wretched Adam into custody.

After that he must arrange for a quiet and secret burial of Mahla and her brother. Best that they should be put quickly underground, he thought. Of course there would be a scandal. Tongues would wag and perhaps the truth would be unfolded, but he cared only for one thing—Destiny's fair name. If she were to make a brilliant marriage in the future, that name must remain unsullied. To achieve that would be one of his last gifts to her before he left her—his final service to the late Earl.

Stephen drove to the Lake House, paid off the German servants of the bogus prince, and bade them depart at once for the city of London, and their own homes.

Gretchen had already taken herself off, afraid of the punishment that might have been meted out to her by Lady Destiny Frane. It did not take long for Stephen to be rid of the unsavoury household and to close that house that wore the disguise of beauty and romance and was so inwardly corrupt.

Heavy-hearted, he then returned to Destermere, went into the library and divesting himself of his coat and wig, for the afternoon was hot and breathless, sat at his desk for a moment, brooding over the events of the last two days.

How did *she* fare upstairs, with her adored children? How was it possible that he had ever made her leave them in the first place? He kept thinking about that and blaming himself. And how come, he wondered, that he never so much as guessed that she was stealing out each day to clandestine meetings with that frightful Baron Faramund? How could he have been so blind; or ever imagined Mahla had really turned over a new leaf. He had feared her influence over Destiny right from the beginning.

He began to feel that he had failed Destermere's daughter ... yet what chance had he had up against

such a scheming abominable woman as the Jewess—
Mahalah?

Then Stephen remembered that Mahla was dead and
that he need never again dread her coming into this
room to disturb its quietude; that never again would he
hear her low, throaty laughter, mocking him, nor be
forced to reject her advances.

They had taken her away. Upstairs, the maids were
already busy scouring the death-chamber.

Already Destermere House felt cleaner and fresher,
thought Stephen; and Destiny was *safe*.

He dropped his head on his arms and suddenly overcome with exhaustion, fell asleep.

19

SEVEN MONTHS LATER.

It was winter again. In Switzerland the snow had
been falling for a week or more but today it was fine
and the high mountain peaks glittered magnificently in
the sun—diamond-bright against the cobalt blue of the
sky.

In one of the handsome *salons* of the *Château des
Cygnes* on Lac Leman, Monsieur Bertian sat drinking
a glass of excellent Swiss wine with his hostess.

Lady Destiny Frane sat opposite the notary, beside
a sweet-smelling pinewood fire. She was clad in dark
violet velvet edged with sable—and wore a little lace-
edged *fontange* on her smooth, dark hair. Two little
lappets hung down on either side a face that was still
essentially young and extremely beautiful. But the eyes,
Monsieur Bertian thought sadly, were the eyes of a
woman who had suffered despite the fact that the owner
was not yet seventeen. But this morning he believed

she looked more lively than he had seen her for some time.

She was saying:

"Mr. Godwin's coach should be here at any moment, should it not, Monsieur?"

"At any moment," nodded the Swiss. "And he should have had a good journey, milady. A mercy the weather is now so fine."

Destiny looked out at the limpid blue of the lake and at the glorious mountains beyond. She gave a little sigh.

"It is a year, is it not, Monsieur, since my father died here, with you beside him?"

"A little more, milady. He departed from us in the month of February. It is now the middle of March."

Destiny sighed.

"I wish I had known him."

"Yes, indeed. And you are like him in many of your ways, milady."

"So they tell me, both here and in England."

"You have not been too unhappy in your Swiss home, I trust, milady."

She looked with some affection at the old man who was a frequent visitor at the *Château* and had always shown her much kindness and so efficiently managed her affairs when Stephen was not here. *Ah, Stephen!* Her thoughts turned to him and the quick colour came into her face. Her large eyes, of a sudden, sparkled.

For nearly six weeks now, Stephen had been in England, controlling the Destermere estates. How she had missed him! Since the catastrophic events which had taken place over there last August, she had come more and more to lean upon him as a friend and brother.

What a lot had happened since that unforgettable August!

It had been Stephen's idea that she should leave Richmondwyke at once and escape from the scandal that was bound to break following the murder of her stepmother. She could well believe how they would gossip, all those frivolous titled people who had attended the ball at Destermere House.

Stephen, himself, had journeyed with her here. He had been certain that she would grow to love the lake and the pure mountain air would be good for the children. She would soon grow well and learn to hold her head up high again and to forget the dreadful past.

She had not protested. So long as Jem and little Lucy and Luke were with her, she was content. They had their own excellent Swiss nurse and the elder girl and boy had started to receive a little private tutoring. Destiny had bought them a boat to sail on the lake. They went up into the mountains for picnics while the weather was still warm. And in winter they found distraction in Geneva. They had all of them learned to be gay together here. She was not only "Sister Dessie" to them now but "little mother." The local peasants had grown used to seeing the beautiful richly-dressed young English milady walking with the *trois enfants* or driving with them in their special white-painted sledge, drawn by two white horses with silver bells on their blue harness.

Truly, Destiny reflected, she had learned to find peace and a simple happiness in the *Château des Cygnes*. She had quite fallen in love with Switzerland, too. At the same time she missed her native country and after a lapse of time hoped that she would be able to return to Richmondwyke and reopen Destermere House. But she had made many friends here. Several of the big Swiss families who had known her father had called and she had returned the call.

She had also, at the suggestion of her father's good friend, Sir Roger, engaged the services of a certain widow, the Comtesse de Valpaise (a Swiss lady of mature years and some elegance), who had been only too willing to come and live in the *Château* as Lady Destiny's companion and counsellor.

When Stephen on one occasion warned Destiny that

out here she would be considered just as in England—
a great matrimonial "catch," and that she must be careful, she had changed colour and quickly said:

"Have no fear. Any attention that any man may pay
to me from now on will be unacceptable. I only want
the children—and you, Stephen—my friend."

He had said nothing but turned away.

But now there were things on Destiny's mind beside
friendship, or even the idolized children. *Stephen was
on her mind*. And when she thought about him, which
was often, it was no longer only as a friend, or secretary.

It had all begun to change, she mused—on that
Christmas Day, here in the *Château*. She had been holding a party for Jem, Lucy and Luke. Casting off the
terrible memories of the past, living only in the present,
she had returned for a while to her old light-hearted,
spirited self. Gay and glowing, she danced with the children while the Comtesse busied herself entertaining the
parents of the other small guests who had come to play
with the Barleys.

Then they started a game in which Dessie had been
blindfolded and set to catch the children who hopped
around her on their dancing feet. Somehow or other
she had groped her way out of the *salon* and into the
marble-floored hall. Somehow, she had bumped into
someone and felt herself caught and steadied by a pair
of strong arms. Then Stephen's laughing voice had said:

"Careful, lest you slip on this polished floor, my
lady."

For a moment she had gripped his shoulders, laughing back at him.

"Dear Stephen! Are you too playing our childish
game?"

"No, I was passing through—" he began awkwardly.

"Dear Stephen," she said again, "You are always
very serious. Can you not cast off your cares and secretarial duties this Christmas Day and laugh a little with
the rest of us?"

She could not see what lay in his eyes but she had felt a sudden shudder go through his body and heard his quickened breathing. Then in a stifled voice he muttered:

"My lady. . . ."

"Am I not yet to be 'Destiny' to you who have done so much for me?"

"Let me go, I pray," he had broken in.

"No, I will not," she had laughed, meaning to tease him. "You are far too much of a sober-sides."

"Oh, God!" he had said, "I cannot stand this. I must go away from here. For a long time I have wanted to go but you would not let me."

She had experienced a sense of shock. There was silence. Then she had pulled the silken scarf from her eyes and stared up at him.

He was dressed in his finery, wearing his best wig, and looked very handsome; but far too harassed and pale. And far too often she found him looking thus; and when he cut short his talks with her she had begun to fret over it and presume that he had still not forgiven her for her past duplicity.

But in this hour, she would not have been a woman if she had not known what ailed him. He trembled and in those grey honest eyes of his there lay such an agony of repressed longing that it stirred her to the very foundations of her being.

She had put the tips of her fingers against her lips and whispered:

"*Stephen*. . . ."

Then he had seized both her hands, kissing them passionately as he had done once, and once only, in his life before, and cried out to her:

"Let me go in peace, I pray you."

The scales fell completely from Destiny's eyes and the frozen wall that she had built up around her own heart and emotions since she had thought herself enamoured of the *soi-distant* prince, melted. And she knew that she had been starved of love and all its meaning, and that it need not be a terrible lustful thing, but beautiful and noble and self-effacing. Like Stephen Godwin's love for *her*.

He had turned to go but she held him back.

"Stephen—" she said again.

"Go back to your party," he said hoarsely.

She persisted.

"No, I will not let you go until you have told me *why* you want to leave me."

He had tried not to look at her. The muscles of his cheeks worked and his face was on fire. He stammered:

"I have served my appointed time. There is no more to do for you—your father would not wish me to spend the rest of my life managing your affairs. I wish to proceed with the writing of my book. I beg for my release."

She knew then what it would mean to her—if he left her—if there were to be no more Stephen in this house—in her life. Suddenly she touched the shoulder that had long since healed but which had once received the impact of that bullet from the Baron's pistol.

"You really wish to leave me?" she asked, in a smothered voice.

"Yes," he said between his teeth.

"But you do not," she protested, all afire now with her new-found feeling for him, and with her feminine coquetry a-sparkle.

"Destiny . . . for God's sake—" he began.

"You shall not go," she interrupted and flung her arms around his neck. Then the poor man resisted her no further but caught her against his heart and she had felt his firm, boyish lips against hers, moving, deeper and yet deeper, into a kiss which wiped out the memory of all those other base kisses and all base love.

"I worship you," he said in a wild voice, "and because of that I must go."

"But I love you, too, Stephen," she said slowly and wonderingly, "I know it now. What I felt for . . . for that other man ... was the stupid passion of an inexperienced girl. And I thought never to love again but I *do,* I know what I am doing now and I have grown to love *you.*"

He had looked as though through the gates of heaven. He had kissed her hands again, then her hair and her cheeks, coming to rest upon her mouth. Then like a man in a delirium he thrust her away from him.

"For God's sake, Destiny, this is not possible."

"Why not?"

"Because you are the Lady Destiny Frane, and I—your penniless secretary."

"Pennies, pennies!" she scoffed. "Haven't I enough for both of us? Isn't my fortune so considerable that every eligible man in England or Switzerland has an eye to it?"

"All the more reason why I cannot ask what I should like, which is your hand in marriage, my most belovèd."

She sighed and leaned her cheek against his breast. Such peace, such joy, filled that young heart of hers that she had not known possible. She whispered:

"If indeed I am your most belovèd, then I can also be your wife."

But nothing that she could say altered his decision. It was not possible, he said, and he could not marry her for he had nothing to offer her of his own, neither titles, income nor land. She had honoured him more than he had ever dared hope by her friendship. She dazzled him by her words of love today, but he could not take advantage of her.

"You must understand," he had finished painfully, "you must realize what it means to me to decline your offer, my dearest lady. But you must see that I would despise myself if I took advantage of your generosity."

Then Destiny had stamped her foot and, fiery-tempered, demanded why he did not stop thinking of himself and his attitude and consider *hers.* If she wanted him for a husband, why should he not take her? Did he wish her to be miserable?

"Oh, my dearest, and most dear," he had groaned, "You will not be miserable because of me—I pray you let me go."

"Very well," she had said, in a choked voice, and picking up the scarf which had fallen to the floor, turned and ran back to the children. She let them bind it over her eyes again so that they should not see her tears.

The next few weeks had been difficult and unhappy. Stephen avoided seeing her alone, and never once betrayed by word or sign what had passed between them on Christmas Day. But he suffered, too, she was sure, for he went about the *Château* and his duties, looking strained and white. And she suffered knowing with each new day that dawned that Stephen Godwin was her true love and that because he loved her something must be done to break down those barriers which his pride had erected between them.

Then various business matters of urgency recalled Stephen to London, to meet her father's bankers. He had to help straighten out certain legal matters connected with the Destermere estate.

Just before he left Geneva he had said good-bye to Destiny alone. Then she had broken the ice between them. She said:

"You mean to come back, do you not?"

He had lowered his gaze. She could see him biting his lips.

"Yes, my lady. But for now—farewell."

Fearing that she might humiliate herself by breaking down and making a fresh appeal to him, she had turned speechlessly and run away. When she came downstairs again he had gone.

There had followed a week alone with the Comtesse de Valpaise and the three children. They were snowed up and unable to get out and time had never dragged more cruelly for Destiny. She could settle to nothing, neither her needlework, her music nor her reading. She thought continually about Stephen. She dreamed of his passionate kisses and of his tender boyish love which differed so completely from that *other* one. She nearly went mad, wondering what to do for the best and how to put this matter aright.

It was then that she decided to consult Monsieur Bertian. She told him the whole story. It seemed at first to shock him beyond measure. Then after he had considered the matter, he said:

"Milady, you have been through a fearful time and suffered much. But you are young and I feel that you should be given now, the chance of true happiness. If that happiness lies with Stephen Godwin—I cannot see why you should not take it, seeing that he is of the same mind."

"But he will not. He feels inferior to me because of his position in my house. But lord knows I am at heart still the simple drudge that ran the Barley household and really not a great lady," cried the girl through her tears.

"*Mon Dieu,* no, you have become a great lady," protested Bertian.

Until late that day, the two discussed the situation. Then of a sudden Destiny said to the old notary:

"Am I indeed controller of my fortune, Monsieur? Can I do with it what I wish?"

"Up to a point, yes, milady. Not that we who served your father would allow you to dissipate the fortune."

"Would it be called dissipation if I signed away this *Château* which belongs to me now and all its lands and the monies which my father banked in Geneva to him? Whilst I keep Destermere and my hotel in Paris."

M. Bertian looked startled. He hummed and hawed and considered this thing. It would be taking a grave step, he said, and unfortunately now that the late Lady Destermere had come to an untimely end, Mr. Godwin was her sole guardian.

"No—Sir Edgar took my stepmother's place and the other bankers agreed and so did you, Monsieur," said Destiny triumphantly.

He nodded. Yes, yes, she was right. But if Mr. Godwin still disapproved. . . .

Then Destiny interrupted. Passionately she said that he could not disapprove if all the gentlemen handling the estate should give their consent. It remained only for him, M. Bertian, to write to Sir Edgar and send an immediate despatch to London, asking for their approving signatures and acceptance of Mr. Godwin as her husband. They liked and trusted him. They had said so in her presence. M. Bertian must ask, too, that they should keep the matter sacred and say nothing of it to him. They must be made to realize that he loved her truly and had saved her from the Baron, and that as far as she was concerned, her whole life's joy depended on this marriage.

The old Swiss, growing sentimental as he looked into the young girl's soft, love-filled, swimming eyes, agreed. So the letter to the gentlemen in London was written. The document prepared by the notary signing away Lady Destiny's estates in Switzerland to Stephen Godwin, was despatched. Now there remained only for Mr. Godwin's own name to be affixed to the new Deeds.

"To be sure, the youth is valiant and steadfast and will make milady a good husband," the old man told himself after the papers had been sent off.

Today they waited for the coach which was bringing Stephen back . . . and in the drawer of the buhl desk in the *salon,* lay the exciting document—the Deed and the letters. Every one of the gentlemen had signed, including Sir Edgar. They extolled Mr. Godwin's virtue and complimented my lady on her final choice.

But every time Destiny thought of Stephen and what his reactions might be to those documents, her courage failed and she almost swooned. If she should be stubborn and still refuse . . . dear heaven! . . .

He cannot, she kept telling herself. *He cannot wish to cause me so much pain.*

The coach was late. Destiny grew anxious. Left alone with Monsieur and the Comtesse, she felt nervous and impatient and worked herself into a fever of anxiety. Finally as the violet dusk fell upon the snow-covered *Château,* Stephen returned.

The Comtesse drew M. Bertian out of the *salon.* She had been let into the secret and she approved, personally, because she was both sentimental and fond of the two young people. The two old ones greeted the secretary in the hall and told him that milady awaited him.

Stephen walked quickly into the warm, firelit salon. By the light of the tall wax candles, burning so brightly in their sconces, the white and gold room looked delightful and welcoming after his long hard journey. And the sight of the girl standing by the fireplace was more than delightful. He thought he had not seen that violet velvet robe with the sable trimming before, and that the *fontange* suited her. Her grace and beauty of her eyes when she greeted him, silenced the formal words he had prepared. He unbuttoned his coat and threw it with his cocked hat on to a chair. Then he advanced, took her hand and raised it to his lips.

"My lady. . .," he said in a low tone.

"Still the same awkward stand-offish Stephen!" she exclaimed, laughing a little, although her cheeks were rosy and her eyes brilliant with feeling.

He drew away.

"You know . . . I have explained—" he began.

She broke in.

"Say you have missed me."

He swallowed, trying to maintain his attitude and be what she termed, "formidable." But all his body trembled at the sight of her and the sound of her voice.

"You know that I have. . . ." he muttered.

"Very much?"

"Yes," he said unwillingly.

"As much as I have missed you?"

"How can I gauge how much that is?" he asked in an agony.

She came closer and clasped her hands about one of his arms.

"Stephen, Stephen, have done with dissembling. Be true to yourself and fair to me."

"Am I not trying to be fair to you?"

"Stephen, I cannot continue thus—nor can you. We love each other. Life is short. True love comes not easily. How can we throw it away so recklessly, you and I?"

Heavens, he thought, *how she has grown up ... my wild, childish, impetuous lady. How gravely and with what passion she speaks of her love and mine. I cannot bear it. She tries me beyond my strength.*

He said hoarsely:

"I have come from London with kind messages from your bankers, my lady. I have carried out all necessary business. I ask now as I asked at Christmas, that you should release me."

Her heart pounding, she looked up at him.

"Release you so that you might start to run your own house and estates?"

"Do not mock me. I have nothing of my own. You know that," he said.

She caught her lip excitedly between her small teeth and walked to the bureau and unlocked it. She took out a portfolio and thrust it into his hands.

"Read what lies in here, Stephen," she said.

"What—?" he began.

But she had gone. Startled and wondering, he sat down by the leaping fire, warmed his hands, and then opened the portfolio. When he had read every word— the Deed of Exchange on the estates appertaining to the *Château des Cygnes,* and certain monies that went with it, he gave a low protesting cry. Then he opened Sir Edgar's personal letter to himself. Brief but warmly expressed, begging him to accept what my lady offered, and to accept, too, the approval and good wishes of them all, on his marriage to her ladyship. It ended:

> *"Somehow, dear boy, we feel that Claud Destermere would have approved this union, for he looked upon you as a son. We are convinced that Lady Destiny's happiness lies in your hands. Take it, and prosper, and God be with you both."*

Stephen was so overcome by this that he could not for a moment believe what he saw written. His hands trembled. His cheeks burned, and his heart was full to the brim. Then the door of the *salon* opened. A sweet, shy voice from the doorway, said:

"Stephen—the children are a-bed but they heard the horses and they ask that you should go up and bid them good night."

He looked up from Sir Edgar's letter. As Destiny came slowly towards him, he was unable to speak, or tear his gaze from her beloved face. She went on:

"They have grown to love you greatly and you love them now, I know. Would it displease you if they continued to live under our roof—I mean *your* roof, here, in Geneva, or my roof at Richmondwyke once we return there?"

The full meaning of what she said—of what he was being offered—broke over him. He went down on one knee before her, bending his head over her hand, as once before.

"My lady . . . oh, dear God, my Lady Destiny," he said brokenly.

"Will you take what I so gladly offer—and marry me, Stephen?" she whispered.

He looked up at her.

"Destiny . . . my dearest . . . if you are sure."

"I am very sure this time," she said.

And this time he did not refuse, but rose and gathered her hungrily into his arms.

The glittering
romantic epic—
spanning oceans,
continents, and
the infinite
reaches of love!

FAUNA

DENISE ROBINS

*Sweeping from Jamaican slaver's coves
to dazzling London ballrooms and private
royal chambers, FAUNA is the enthralling
story of an unmatched beauty,
the men who craved to posses
her, and the searing
pain in her heart
nothing could ease—nothing but vengeance
on the only man
she had ever loved!*